Maaya

A tryst with self

Love so deep in my heart
The pain hurts my very soul
Every breath touches the core
Beneath which lies the hope
The hope of being held again
Of being caressed and cared for
The purity of that transparent light
That bonds us and our very beings
Whispers in my ears each day
We shall be together again
When there will only be the love
The pain will go away forever!

Maaya

A tryst with self

Minal Arora

Ocean Paperbacks

A Division of Ocean Books Pvt. Ltd.

ISO 9001:2008 Publishers

Published by
Ocean Paperbacks
A Division of Ocean Books Pvt. Ltd.
4/19 Asaf Ali Road,
New Delhi-110 002 (INDIA)
e-mail: info@oceanbooks.in

ISBN 978-81-8430-276-9
Maaya: A tryst with self
by Minal Arora

Edition
First, 2014

Price
Rs. 175.00 (Rs. One Hundred Seventy Five only)

Printed at
Bhanu Printers, Delhi

This story is dedicated to
my papa, S.P.Arora
who's always supported me unconditionally,
my mumma, Sunita Arora
who's nurtured me unconditionally and
my son, Sanat who's loved me unconditionally

Acknowledgements

First and foremost, I would like to acknowledge by mom and dad who have stood by me through my joy and grief, who have supported me unreasonably. When I went through the deepest pain of my life, it was my dad who said to me, 'My child, I will support you through everything. Just make sure you never cry. I can never see you cry. Rest I will handle for I chose to, by giving birth to you. You are precious to me'. It touched me. My mom does everything to allow me the freedom to work, heal people and travel. She takes care of my child as a mother would. I couldn't have asked for more on the name of parents.

Secondly, I would like to mention Sanat, my sunny as I lovingly call him. He's not only my son but also my angel and guide. Ever since he was little, I have learnt through and grown him. He strengthens my belief that our children are probably more evolved souls than us who have come to us most of all to teach us how to adapt to change and become new!

Gratitude to Akshay Dwivedi for helping me express the character of 'Maaya' the way I could. His critical review of the script helped me tremendously in framing it such that it touched each soul who read it henceforth.

I can't thank Cynthia Roli Gupta enough for her love and support in editing and proof reading my book. She's read the script several times in the process of helping me improvise the expression and create a balance in every way. Each time when she read it and said 'It's one hell of a love story and I think it should be made into a freaking movie!', it inspired me and instilled confidence in me that I have been able to touch at least one soul through my work. Many hugs to her for all the hard work she did and at her young age, she's one bright author herself I see in the making!

The book's cover design is inspired by a painting I once saw and couldn't remember the painter or the exact details. Sonia Singh with the help of Shilpi Singh had to make it some 20-22 times to get it look exactly the way I wanted it to be. She's done a beautiful job and to top it she added the background which represents the universe and brought a sense of completion to the work. Much gratitude to Sonia for her spirit and grace for she worked on it limitlessly and soulfully. Thanks to Shilpi for having provided the much desired support to conclude the cover. I owe the beauty of this cover to both these amazing souls.

I am grateful to my mentor and friend Shivi Dua who helps me at each stage of life to see myself from a higher perspective. She ensures I always choose self-love and compassion as a way of life and spread it too through the Serenity Surrender (SS) workshops. As I walk on this path of awareness, through which I gain deeper acceptance of self in each moment, I find her at each step, as if lighting it for me and yet, allowing me to make my own mistakes and learn from what I experience.

I can't forget to mention Harish Baweja and Kirti Dixit Narang for allowing me to be myself at each moment and for accepting me for who I am with my strengths and weaknesses. Whenever I was weak, they were by my side, just to be there, without expecting me to even acknowledge their presence. Whenever I judged myself, they reminded me that I am special. Such friends are a blessing that each one of us aspire to have and I am blessed beyond words.

I would also like to thank Suman Nalwa, who's my dearest friend and a loving soul. She's always encouraged me to follow my heart, come what may! Her belief in me allows me to trust myself even more. She has watched my journey closely and we have together learnt to appreciate and celebrate our existence with each moment.

Finally, I would like to thank Arch Angel Michael, the Creator and my Spirit Guide to always be there invisibly yet surely by my side to show me my path and give me the resilience to walk through to each next step.

Author's Note

Maaya – A tryst with self, is the story of a woman, Maaya, who, through her love for a man, Rahul, took on an incredible journey within, where she understood and experienced love in its purest, truest form. When Maaya first met Rahul, he touched a part of her soul that she had suppressed long ago in order to become the perfect girl for the love of her life, Kunal, whom she was engaged to. As Rahul and Maaya realised their feelings for each other, they also realised the futility of it all. A few days of togetherness was all they enjoyed before they accepted that they weren't meant to be. Maaya gracefully let go of him to marry Kunal and have her happily ever after. Little did she expect that he would show up again in her life, at a point where she had separated from Kunal after six years of marriage, and her pursuit for his love would lead her to see love in a light she had never seen it in before. She never knew her inner journey was awaiting to be unleashed. She goes through ecstasy, joy, grief, failure, misery and sadness due to the love she longs to have in her life. On the road she travels to re-unite with her twin-soul, unexpectedly leads her to becoming a spiritual healer, the experience of which, opened her up to an infinite horizon where she not only found love, but found herself.

Maaya is the essence of human experience through a woman, beyond time, which began with her loving someone so intensely that she dissolved in whom she loved and then finding herself through what followed. The book carries deep revelations about soul mate and twin-soul relationships including how they have been a source to spiritual upliftment for both the twins and how they can prove instrumental in transcending the limitations of each other. Time and again these lovers meet and part, giving each other an experience so intense that it leaves each in a state where they have no choice but to look within for the void they experience while the other isn't around. The book carries deeper experiential understanding of what the need for love might bring one to experience. It is a tryst with self-facilitated through the twin.

Maaya is a journey deep within, all the way to the sub-conscious and exploring long lost memories from past lives and beyond. In her desperation to be loved by Rahul, Maaya travels into her several past lives, encounters herself as love, as sadness, as betrayal, as grief, as loss, as failure and yet realizes that all these were mere experiences transient in nature and they only led her to loving herself and believing in herself even more in this moment.

I, as a past life therapist and mentor have held the hand of many, to allow their journey within, to explore the explored dimensions of their being, to understand how the soul operates out of human consciousness and how relationships, both good and bad, play a vital role in learning our lessons. All relationships are important but this book is focused on how the relationship with a twin-soul can allow us to reveal deep secrets or mysteries of the universe to live a more powerful or rather magical existence.

Love is the one pursuit that each soul carries knowingly or unknowingly and it's one experience that can stretch to the depth of one's awareness and yet seem to bring a longing for more or a need to hold-on to the experience. Whenever love knocks the door of the soul, it is welcome with all the warmth and yet, what it brings along and how it shows us our fears and our inability to be unconditional about it decides how long it stays and how long it gives us joy. Love is the one emotion that has the ability to take us to the highs of ecstasy and the lows of grief in a few moments and many times through the same people. When it stays, it gives is peace, joy and stability and when it leaves, we experience grief, blame, anger and resentment or loss. We want to hold-on to every moment of love because we do not trust it to stay forever, because we fear losing it. This book is a deep understanding of the cycle of love, of how it can impact one's life and how one can transform their experiences of loss and failure in love to what empowers them with love itself.

I invite you to travel with path of eternal love with Maaya. I would say it's a story each should read: thou who loves and wants to be loved.

Foreword

As we go through life's journey, we come across many ups and downs, all supposedly to teach us some lessons and to help us grow in some manner. In this journey of learning, I guess the biggest lessons are taught to us in a conjugal relationship. This is the relationship, which brings out the best and the worst in us. As it blossoms its pure divine but as it turns sour it has the potential to bring out a lifetime of misery. During the course of my professional life, I have come across many such people who deal with love and the pain it brings about in varied ways. Many turn hostile, cynical and weary and then there are a few who see the light. They learn their lessons and move on, turning to spirituality, faith in destiny with greater maturity and able mindedness.

However, going beyond the soulmates concept or rather even among the soulmates, at the end of the day one of the most important keys to any relationship is communication. While it is very important to keep the communication lines open in any relationship, it is equally important to keep the ego out. One has to be truly transparent with each other without worrying about a perceived self-image, with a faith and confidence that the other will cherish this openness and respond in a similar manner. As we walk through our life, we start collecting hurts; small hurts, big hurts and they end up being a huge mountain of hurts in no time at all. For a relationship to grow, to sustain and to flourish both partners in a relationship have to talk their inner most fears or hurts with their counter parts. This creates a level of mutual trust and faith in each other, which brings about a lifetime of bonding. It is not easy to finds such a transparency in relationship in today's time, because we are too stuck in instant gratification and do not want to invest time from our busy schedule to have an open communication line. Also, we are very prone to getting hurt with other person's ridicule, as it invalidates our very existence of being right. We are so caught up in ourselves, and it really hurts our pride when someone points out our fallacies. We really find it beneath ourselves to admit that we do get hurt by silliest of things.

Here is a story of Maaya and her journey through love and loss, a woman who had the courage to move on, to have faith and not be sucked up in the acrimony of betrayal but to keep searching for her destiny and learning many life lessons in the process. Many of us can associate with her dreams and aspirations of finding that true love but few have the courage to take chances and not be complacent in the security and mediocrity life offers. Here is wishing all the readers courage to follow their dreams and convictions and lives lived to the fullest.

–Suman Nalwa
A Celebrated Author and Deputy
Commissioner of Police (DCP)
Special Branch,
Delhi Police

Contents

Letting Go

My dearest Rahul,

We have come a long way, having started years ago with our souls recognising each other in the midst of the most inappropriate circumstances and yet accepting the recognition.

The longing of our energies for each other, that hunger for finding our other halves drew us again at a point in life where we were shown the path to become one. We magnetically fell into embracing what was ours and loved each other like nothing else was of significance.

You became my definition of love, every bit of it. You became my reason to love myself for I belonged to you. You were embedded in my heart. Each time you hugged me, I sensed your breath as mine. Each time you held me, something secretly connected from inside me to the heavens to thank the one up there for that divine moment. It was perfect.

We have experienced the soul of love itself, between us. Today, I wonder if we are being tested for trusting ourselves, trusting our love, trusting our togetherness! The bliss between us seems to be slipping away Rahul. There is a shadow setting in. I don't see my soul in your eyes anymore.

Lately, you have avoided taking my calls, responding to my messages or even meeting me. Something between us has changed.

I have waited patiently to see that craving, that innocence, that child in you that I resonated with all this while. I have prayed, asked God, asked the universe to show me the glimpse of that love again but it is lost in some sadness you seem to carry.

Maybe it's the guilt of not being able to preserve that love anymore is making you sad, and is tearing you apart. I feel saddened and responsible for it. It is becoming about 'I' and 'You' rather than 'Us'. 'We' are getting dissolved. I can see it's slowly breaking you and that misery you feel is making me miserable too.

I am slowly becoming this person who cries and pities herself all the time. I can't seem to forget all those moments of compassion, of togetherness we shared. I can't help missing the sheer bliss of my existence I felt in the presence of your love. I can't help feeling this way, Rahul.

I cannot bear myself anymore. I cannot relate to my own weakness. I cannot survive with this person I am becoming.

I find it difficult to love myself anymore for it was only through your love for me that I could love myself. The mirror questions me. I don't have an answer.

You will be much bigger than a fond memory for me. You are a part of me – probably the best one – but in the endeavour of preserving you as the best part, I must let you go. I request you for your permission to walk away from you.

Love

Maaya

PS: I will always love u and cherish u along with the memories of our togetherness.

I took a print of the letter from Deeksha's printer, shut the screen and just whiffed off. I couldn't look at the letter on the screen any longer. I had poured my heart in it. I had to give it to Rahul before I changed my mind. I immediately left her place.

A few hours later, while I was lost in my emptiness, I heard my phone beep. It was Deeksha. She had already called several times it seems but, somehow, I didn't notice.

'Maaya, where are you?' she asked in a worried tone.

'I am ok, Deeksha. I just want to be by myself for some time.'

'I read your letter, Maaya. I am very concerned about you right now. You didn't pick my calls earlier in the day too. Please tell me where are you? You can share your pain with me, sweetheart.'

I could imagine Deeksha taking short walks in her lobby with her hair neatly tied in a French plat swinging from left to right. She always did that when she was anxious.

'I am fine, Deeksha. I really am. Please don't worry. I am just allowing myself to experience a few moments of the past that I wish to leave behind. I am sorry. I left your lunch get-together all of a sudden. I am sure your friends must be feeling odd but I couldn't help it. I hope you understand.'

'I can understand Maaya. You don't need to be sorry. I know it hurts,' she said.

I didn't feel the need to respond. I was lost in my thoughts. Sensing this, she again made an effort to break the silence.

'Love has its own ways, Maaya. It will all fall into place when it's the right time. Give him some space while you take care of Aryan and yourself. Have faith in your love, sweetheart. Surrender!'

'Yes, I know what you mean, Deeksha. Just want to reflect a bit. I will be home in an hour, I promise,' and I just put the phone down.

After hanging the phone, I found myself wondering about myself. I wondered what Rahul thought about me. Was I not good enough for him? Deeksha always admired me for being who I was. I had many friends who adored me, yet there was so much unworthiness I was experiencing in that moment. I still carried the few lines Deeksha wrote about me in a game where we were to describe our partner as we see them from our hearts. What she wrote touched me so much that I saved that little piece of paper. It was precious. I finally managed to locate it in my bag and read it to myself one more time. Maybe I wanted reassurance for being good enough.

'Maaya has eyes full of mischief, a kind heart and an intriguing aura. Her smile conveys the beauty of innocence.

She is discreet, humble and obliging; every word she says conveys the touch of a higher wisdom. She is a blessing to her friends for her benevolence is commendable. Yet, at times, she's lost in a world of her own, the doors of which are closed for all!

Her beauty comes from the grace in her heart; her soul carries gratitude towards its creator. When misery and suffering knock her door, she invites them in. Then quietly but firmly she prays to the universe to teach her the lessons upon which they shall gracefully depart. She trusts the lord, she trusts her destiny, she trusts all that there is. She is unpredictable at times, very sure at others. She knows what to say to bring peace within, while she's where I draw courage when I must stand-up for what I truly believe in.

Her eyes seem to glow when she sheds tears. Her heart forgives; she allows herself to trust yet again. She restores her faith in the ultimate good almost as quickly as she reflects on it.

She shall rejoice the world to come. Maaya is a mystery to all that know her and yet sometimes it feels she is just another ordinary woman whose heart could be broken.'

The note reminded me of the time when I met Deeksha for the first time. We were doing a self-help workshop together.

During lunch-time, we hung out together. She was in pain. There was something she was holding back. While waiting for our food to arrive, I bent forward a little and held her hand. She broke down. She still loved Maanav but wasn't sure whether it was her chase or the relationship still had something that was serving them. They had stopped having sex for two years now. He was busy working or socialising most of the times. She always found herself waiting for him to be at home, spend time with her, acknowledge her presence, which rarely happened. Slowly, she had started asking herself: 'Is this what I deserve? Am I only worth being a trophy wife?' and loads of more questions, which she didn't have answers to.

She was a graduate from Delhi College of Fine Arts. She married Maanav and decided to let go of her ambitions and career to serve his expectations of having an ideal Indian wife. It had been five years since they were together. She was a very talented woman. Her spirit needed more than what she settled for.

I let her vent, let her speak, let her be. It seemed like that was the first time she let her guard down. In those moments, I became the channel for her to be able to acknowledge the pain, the hurt and her own internal conflict.

'I haven't cried in front of anyone ever. I don't know why I broke down in front of you. I am so sorry,' she said, looking at me with the kind of guilt one could see on a child's face after breaking a neighbour's window pane with his cricket ball.

'It's ok to be weak, Deeksha. It's ok to cry. It's ok to acknowledge your weakness. It's ok to accept we can't deal with everything in our own strength. This is when we allow the universe to take over and our life flows in divine strength.'

As I put the little piece of paper back, my thoughts rushed back to Rahul.

I took a deep breath and looked at the scene in front of me. It was almost sunset time and the view of the little water body ahead of me looked breathtakingly beautiful. There were small children playing all around and people from various walks of life admiring the sunset.

I couldn't help missing Rahul. I was reminded of the first time I broke down in front of Rahul at this very place.

'What happened baby?' he asked as he got into my car. 'He called. He says he wants to get back with me. I don't want to see him, Rahul. I am so scared. What do I do?' I found myself sobbing like a child and hugging him tight. 'Don't worry Maaya. You are not alone. I am with you. He has no right to march in or out of your life whenever he chooses to. Don't worry and please don't cry. I can't see you cry,' and saying this, he held my face in his hands and slowly bent forward to kiss me. 'Oh Rahul. I love you so much. I don't know what I would have done if you weren't there with me.'

'I will always be there with you, my sweetheart. Never worry and never think you are alone. Trust me.'

My heart was breaking. Those words were echoing in my mind. I wondered what happened to that Rahul. I wondered if Rahul could understand whatever I was going through. I wondered if he could feel my hurt, my misery, my suffering. My thoughts were confused. In one part of my heart, I felt he still loved me and that he wouldn't let me go. It was all a bad dream that would get over once he realised he could lose me otherwise. Another part of me knew it was not so simple. He needed time. A string of memories and thoughts were waiting to be acknowledged and each one of them brought with them more pain, more hurt and more grief.

My thoughts were broken when a small child's balloon came and hit me and the child came running to get it. I held the balloon and passed it back to the kid, who kept smiling looking at me. The kid reminded me of Aryan. I recalled when Aryan met Rahul. It was Aryan's seventh birthday a few months back when I invited Rahul over for his birthday party. He gave Aryan an awesome set of Ben-10 toys. Aryan was so happy. Rahul was really nice to him and they both loved each other.

Just then, my attention went to my watch. It was 7:00 p.m. and time to go pick up Aryan from mom's place. I rushed to my mom's place to pick my son and we finally landed at our apartment which we shared with Pooja.

'Hey Maaya! Hey buddy! How was your day today?' Pooja asked Aryan, rubbing her fingers in his hair as they entered the living room. 'I had loads of fun, aunty. Nani made me pizza today and I watched Nemo too. You know when Nemo goes missing, his dad goes all over the ocean to look for him. It's so amazing, aunty. You must see it,' said Aryan excitedly to Pooja.

'Sure baby, I will watch it with you one day. You go and change and be off to bed. The weekend is now over. It's Monday tomorrow and you have school,' she said, pushing Aryan to his room.

'Aunty, does my dad love me as much?' he asked Pooja.

'Sure he does, Aryan. You are his sweetheart. Both your mom and dad love you baby. They might have their own differences, but for you, they will always stand together,' she told Aryan, putting him to bed. She smiled and he smiled back at her as she put off the light of the room.

I watched them from the door of his room, still lost in my own thoughts. Aryan's concern over his father's love pushed me further into the grave. I felt numb. I could hear, understand, think and yet didn't know if I could feel more dead inside. To distract myself from these thoughts, I diverted my attention to Pooja's perfect figure in her pink night gown. Her black hair was flowing, like always, in a smooth motion, like one of those shampoo advertisements.

Pooja belonged to Chandigarh and was working as a professional model for a few advertisers in Delhi and Mumbai.

Her dad owned the house that we lived in. She and I had been college mates. When I separated from Kunal, I didn't want to stay with my parents. She convinced her parents to allow me to stay with her. She travelled a lot for her work, so was hardly at home. Most of the time, I and Aryan had the house all to us. While she was around, she and Aryan bonded well, so we all enjoyed even more.

She belonged to an extremely rich Punjabi family, where modelling was not really a preferred profession. Her dad wasn't too happy with the whole thing, yet because she was their only child, he allowed her to be. They did visit the apartment once in a while to check-up on us.

Pooja didn't agree initially but I got her to sign up for a rent agreement between us. I didn't want money to come between our friendship. It was far more precious.

'Deeksha called me. How are you feeling now?' she asked me, moving closer to me.

'I am ok. I will be ok. It will just take some time to sink in but I'll be fine,' I told her in a reassuring tone.

Pooja bid good night to me. I was now left lying on my bed, looking out of the window. Each sweet little memory of my moments with Rahul came flashing back to me.

For some strange reason, Pooja stepped back into my room after a few minutes and sat by my bed. 'You sure you're okay,' she inquired. All it took for her was to hold my hands gently and I couldn't hold my tears for any longer. I hugged Pooja on her waist with my head on her lap and cried.

'I am not ok, Pooja. How can I be? I love him, I love him so much. It may never be the same again and that makes me sad,' I said while my tears couldn't stop rolling.

She patted my back as she said, 'I can understand dear. Maybe Rahul has thoughts, fears or whatever that he can't share with you now, but are weighing him down. Maybe he still loves you the same way but something is holding him back. In such matters, it's best to just stay away for a while. It will all resolve on its own. Just trust Maaya.'

'Have you given the letter to him yet?' she asked.

'No. Will do it tomorrow at lunch time. I just wanted to spend a little more time, thinking if it was the right thing to do.'

'You are a very strong woman, Maaya and love has its own ways. Just follow your heart, as you have always done.'

'I guess.'

Pooja resisted a bit before saying, 'This is where I am forced to think in terms of how men and women behave in relationships. They truly belong to Mars and Venus. It's not that one's way is right and the other's is wrong but given a situation in a relationship, women are the ones who can either give up everything and merge their identity in the other person, or if they want to move away, they can completely stand firm and have individualism like no other. Men usually find it more difficult to resolve emotions. They have compartmentalised thinking where if one area of life isn't working well, it's not very hard to keep focusing on other areas. Women, on the other hand, tend to get stuck in what isn't working.

One can't generalise but this is my understanding and till now, I have rarely met men who don't behave that way. Maybe it's because, genetically, their existence is aimed at survival and taking responsibility while the women are focused on nurturing. Generally, men have an issue with commitment, Maaya. It might be that way with Rahul too. They are scared of commitment. They love their freedom more than anything else.

It takes a while for a guy to take responsibility and sometimes it takes too much time. He isn't even divorced as yet. Who knows what's going on in his head? Maybe he is not sure he wants to commit to you at this point in time. He did after all allow his wife and child to come and stay with him. Even though you believe that is temporary, I am sure it's making an impact on your relationship with him. He is not sure of what he wants. Give him some time.'

'Hmmmmm'....is all I could say. Maybe she was right.

'I am not sure I really asked him for commitment as yet, but yes, I can feel it. As they say, a woman always knows. I know there is something that isn't right with him. I want nothing more from this relationship but the ability to be myself. I can't be the way I am becoming. I can't allow myself to fall into self-pity. I have made a long journey to realise that true happiness comes from within. It can't be created. I want to walk this path with him only if it's a journey for growth, for love, for sharing to the core. It can't be from the head, it can only be unreasonable and from the heart.'

'Yes, I agree. If one wants something, they must be unreasonable about it.'

I was slowly realising that there was no point denying to myself that my perfect love story was nearing an end or at least a pause. I wondered, at that point, if it was the perfection only, which I wasn't willing to compromise but quickly realised it was only about feeling right. It didn't feel right anymore.

'You will be ok, Maaya. I know you too well. It will disturb you more if you have to live with this state of his. You are not the kind of person who can live life 50% or even 80%. You know how to live it a 100% and that is the right way. You are not alone. Just relax now and get some sleep. It's going to be a long day for you tomorrow.' And she walked out of my room, switching off the lights.

I had a weird night. It seemed like all the moments I had shared with Rahul were crossing my thoughts one by one. Each one of them becoming alive, sometimes more than once. I allowed myself to delve to the rock bottom in my pain.

In the morning, I woke up early. I was to hand over the letter to Rahul before going to work. After getting ready, I took a quick glance at myself in the mirror. My eyes were swollen and my face was red. My slender figure looked perfect in the tight black skirt of my business suit. I quickly applied a bit of makeup and I was ready. It was time to end the misery. The least I could care about, at the time, was my looks. I wondered if Rahul had any clue about whatever I was going to do. I shoved the thought aside and moved out of my house. There was no point. Maybe he didn't but that also didn't matter. Some day he would know why it happened.

'I am sorry I am late,' said Rahul as he stepped into my car. 'Just got caught up with some concalls with US Office. Sorry.'

'Close your eyes for me,' I said looking at him with a deep thoughtful expression.

He closed his eyes and I moved slightly towards him to hold his face in my hands. How I wanted that moment to freeze! I found myself giving him one soft kiss on his left cheek, one on his forehead, one on the right cheek, then one on the chin and somehow my pace increased and I randomly started kissing him all over his face and lastly on his lips. He kissed back furiously, as if he knew that could be the last time. Both of us held each other for a while till I forced myself to withdraw.

It was intense—the pain of allowing myself to let him go. For a split second, I almost reconsidered my decision of giving him the letter. Maybe it was all in my mind. Maybe he loved me just as much. Maybe I was getting extra-sensitive. Maybe he won't agree to it. All sorts of thoughts crossed my mind in a few seconds while my hands were still cupping his face. He was gazing at me intensely. I then firmed up and straightened myself. 'I must do it now,' I told myself.

'What is the matter, Maaya? Is something wrong? What is bothering you?' said Rahul, looking at me intently.

I pulled out the letter from my purse and gave it to him. 'Read this when you get off the car. It's important for us but I want you to read it when you have some time on your hands. Please,' I said to him. As I saw him open the letter there, I immediately snatched it from his hands. 'Please Rahul. Please read it when you have time and you are alone. It's important. We will talk after you have done so. I have some articles to get published tomorrow, so I have to rush to office now. Will catch you later! Bye,' saying which I handed over the letter back to him. He then got off the car with a slightly quizzical look on his face.

I drove off out of sight in a jiffy and, for the next few minutes, I didn't dare look at him in the rear view. His thoughts never ceased clouding my mind. I had always admired Rahul for being tall and handsome. He looked classy when he was in his formals. He had lately taken up gymming and it was doing his appearance a lot of good. His curly black short hair and fair complexion gave him the cuteness in his looks while his glasses gave him the style. I was always so proud of his looks and never kept it a secret from him.

All of the reasons why I loved him came rushing to me. He was innocent, yet smart. He could be clever when required but he was childlike to me. I had access to that side of him that needed compassion, tenderness, care and appreciation. He yearned to be loved. Once he made this huge business deal on his trip to New York, he called me and said he felt sad because he couldn't kiss me and celebrate. He desperately waited to get back to Delhi till he could hold me and acknowledge his success. He was crazy and his craziness was what made me feel so blessed to have him. He followed his heart and his heart was full of love for me.

I then focused on my driving since each of these passing memories made me sad.

I stopped my car in the parking lot of the building and handed over the keys to the guard to park it while I rushed towards the lift. The lift seemed to be crowded since it was 10:30 a.m. and people were still coming to work. I got off the elevator on the 26th floor and swiftly moved towards my desk.

I wondered if Rahul had already read the letter. A sudden gush of emotions made me panic inside. 'I couldn't afford to think about him then,' I told myself. I was at work and was already late. I immediately pulled my attention back to tidying my office desk and getting ready for work.

'Did Hitler arrive?' I asked Dev, lifting a cup of coffee from the tray a peon was probably carrying to the conference room.

Dev was my colleague. He worked on the same magazine pages as I did. Both of us were handling creative and media planning for a leading lifestyle magazine.

'Nopes. He hasn't as yet, darling, but he can be here any minute,' replied Dev as he moved towards my table to help me settle in with the coffee, a stack of pictures and some papers in my hands.

Dev was a phenomenal guy. There was more to him apart from just the fact that he was gay. I loved the way we both got along with each other. It was always fun. He had a fantastic sense of humour and most of all, he cared for me. He was about 5′10″, very fair and quite attractive. His ability to convert a concept into design was amazing. At times, I thought, the way Dev cared for me, Rahul could never come close.

'So, you got the pictures from Wednesday's party at Ruby's mansion?' said Dev excitedly looking at the pictures.

'Yeah, I got them. Used my womanly charm and drew them out faster than anyone could ever do. They have to go in tomorrow's cover story, so you better get working. I am a little low today, so you have to help me get this off my table,' as I handed over a few sheets of printed paper to him.

'Yeah, I know. You are a sensitive girl. You need someone who understands you and appreciates your feelings. It's sad, but if only I had the slightest of interests in women, you would have been my girlfriend,' whispered Dev bending towards my desk. I was still lost in my own thoughts.

Gagan walked in. He gave a slight gesture of 'hello' when he walked past everyone's desks, but without a smile. He then marched into the biggest cabin in that hall. His cabin was almost next to my desk. 'Think of the devil and the devil is here,' said Dev in a very low pitch, looking towards me.

'These pictures are good. I think it will make a good story. Since you have already written up most of the stuff, I am just going to compile the whole thing and set it up before you show it to him. I am sure he will like it. They include a few celebrities who have been missing from the radar for some time now,' said Dev, while typing on his PC.

I was still sipping my coffee and thinking about how Rahul would react to the letter. I couldn't help but constantly look at my mobile in anticipation. 'What happened? You seem far away. Is everything ok?' inquired Dev when he couldn't help noticing that worried look on my face.

'I am fine, Dev. Just thinking about something. Will you please compile these? I, meanwhile, will tell Gagan about all the stuff planned to be pushed into tomorrow's edition from our side?' I said moving towards the cabin next to mine.

'Yes, do that,' replied Dev. I pushed the empty coffee cup into the bin below my desk. Straightening my posture, I knocked on my boss's cabin door.

Gagan was an MBA from IIM, Ahmedabad. He was the creative director of the company. He was a little more serious and sincere than most people at work. He was also a perfectionist. Behind his back, he was addressed as 'Hitler'. He wasn't so bad when it came to team management though. Only when anyone made the slightest mistake, he took it very seriously. He smiled occasionally, usually only with his clients.

Gagan and I hardly exchanged more than a few words with each other ever. It worked well for both of us. He was courteous, professional and we kept it strictly to work. At times, he allowed the more humane side of him to reveal but only very briefly.

I walked into his cabin to stand opposite him while he was about to finish a call. He signalled me to take a seat, while he finished the call. I showed that I was busy looking out of the window but I noticed his gaze.

'So, Maaya! Tell me. What do we have on board for the next edition?' he asked in a slightly cheeky tone.

'Well, I managed to get the pictures from Ruby's party, so that will be the highlight for this issue. The pictures are good and they include Amit Sethi and Poonam Keshav. Both of them have not been in the scene for a few months. I think it will make an interesting compilation.'

'Sounds good! Get going on it and show me the final version when it's ready,' he said, while turning his attention back to his laptop.

I hadn't expected it to be so short and sweet, but realizing this, I quickly got up and left the cabin.

When I reached my desk, I saw my phone blinking with a green light. I rushed to pick it up, hoping to see a missed call from Rahul, but it was Deeksha instead. I ignored it.

After a few minutes, my mobile beeped. 'Let's meet in the evening at 6:00. Cafe Coffee Day next to Taj. Does that work for you?' said the SMS from Rahul. 'Yeah. See you,' I replied back.

I reached the coffee shop a bit early. I had already ordered a coffee and was reading a magazine when Rahul came right at 6:00 and quietly sat down opposite me. 'Have you ordered already?' he inquired. 'Yes, I came in a bit early. What do you want me to order for you?'

'It's ok. I'll go place my order. I'll be back in two minutes,' he said. He went to the counter, ordered a café latte and settled next to me in less than two minutes.

There was an odd silence between us. The best relationship is when two people can be comfortable with each other in silence, but this was different. This silence was uncomfortable. It was as if we were holding back.

Just as I was lost in these thoughts, he slowly bent forward and held my hand.

'Why are you doing this, Maaya? You know I love you, don't you?' he said, looking into my eyes.

This was the moment I was dreading because I knew he loved me. Although I was not sure he knew it well enough, he needed to be more trusting of his love for me. Unfortunately, this was the only way I could let him make that journey, by setting him free.

'I don't know Rahul. It's not the same between us anymore. I don't know if you see it but the magic is dying. By evading anything between us, we will end up spoiling the beautiful moments we have shared. I can't see my soul in your eyes anymore.'

He was quiet, so I went on. 'Your eyes have some fear, some feeling of being at a distance. I don't know what to make of it. We both had one thing in common. We only loved with our hearts. I feel the presence of the mind between us now.

Rahul, you are in some conflict, which you are not ready to share with me. I don't feel the same when you put your hand around my shoulder. That warmth, that bonding is missing. It hurts me to see us this way, Rahul. It's only getting worse each day. I wouldn't want that to happen. It's been a lovely one year Rahul. I want these memories to remain with me forever.

I am not going anywhere. I am just stepping back for a while. I will be waiting for you, Rahul. Take your time,' I said, as I wiped the tears that fell off my eyes.

Rahul kept looking all around the cafe as if in search for a reply with all the blankness. He had always known me to be the stronger one. He always said that I did the right thing. I knew it was him who needed time. I was doing it for him. I was making it easier for him, yet he didn't feel happy about it. He was afraid; afraid of losing me forever. I was also afraid and yet, I strongly felt Rahul needed to be away from me to get a sense of whatever conflict he was in.

He didn't say a word, which to me was more hurting because it meant he was in acceptance of all I had said. On one hand, I was feeling shattered, but on another, it was a sort of validation for me that whatever I was experiencing was not baseless. I was angry at him and angry at myself too. He didn't try to stop me. He just lowered his head. He didn't have anything to say. It hurt. Something inside me broke that moment. I surprised myself with the accuracy of my reading of Rahul's state of mind. I got this feeling as if I hated myself for holding on to him when he really didn't want to stay with me. I hated myself for not seeing it coming. I held all that pain within for I didn't want to be weak in front of him.

'Let's just do this, Rahul. If God has a plan, it will be revealed. Let's just stay away for a while. Yesterday, Gagan made me an offer to move to Singapore for six months since we will be starting a new magazine for Asia Pacific, based out of there. I have accepted the offer. Dev and I will both be based out of Singapore and the company will be giving us apartments to live in as well,' I said in one breath, without looking at Rahul.

'So, you have all of it already planned. Is that boss of yours also going to Singapore? Who will take care of Aryan?' inquired Rahul. He seemed upset and possibly angry.

'Yes he is. He will be travelling in and out since he will be handling some stuff here as well. Aryan will stay back with Mom but will visit me during vacations. I don't want to interrupt his studies,' I said, aware of what Rahul must be thinking. To say the least, he was jealous. He never liked the idea of Gagan and me interacting too often.

'Cool. Have a great time in Singapore. Take care!' he said, while giving me a peck on my cheeks. He rose up quickly and walked away, towards the parking.

I sat there looking at the sunset for another 5-10 minutes, thinking if what just happened was for the good or bad. By letting Neha in his life again, he had proved it that there was something that was not clear in his mind yet. I wanted him to be absolutely sure. I wanted him to know he loved me. Really know and believe.

I didn't want myself to be the reason he walked out on his marriage. He needed to take a stand for himself. I didn't want him to regret his decision for the rest of his life. He had to know that he was not happy in his relationship with his wife and he needed to move away for 'his' own happiness. He had to resolve his conflict, his guilt, his confusion. I couldn't help him with that and it didn't seem like he was seeking my help either. He had somewhere decided to take it all onto himself. I had no choice but to accept and respect his stand. I had to give him that time, I told myself.

Yet again, I thought, if God has a plan, it will be revealed.

□

Across Borders

'What an amazing place! Wow!' exclaimed Dev, looking out of the window while he and I were on our way to our new apartments from Changi Airport.

'We love it here, Maaya. What do you think? Aren't you happy to be here?' he said, looking at me with a curious look.

'I am, Dev. I am happy to be here and I have to make the most of these six months. I want to do a lot that I have been pushing around for a while.'

A sort of sadness gripped me, realising that I was finally away from Rahul.

'Everything will be alright,' Dev patted his hand over mine. He knew about me and Rahul falling apart. I had shared all the details with him over the flight.

'I have heard it's an amazing place. I am especially excited about all the sea-food that we can have here. You love sea-food, don't you?' he tried to divert my attention.

'Yes, I love sea-food. I want to try Japanese, Korean, Indonesian, Malaysian and so many other cuisines here. I want to read loads of books. I have been missing reading. Gagan mentioned our apartments are quite nice and in the Central Business District.' I found myself a bit more relaxed, thinking about all the catching-up on life that I could do while in Singapore. The place seemed to have some strange, positive impact on me. I was sensing an acceptance of something within myself.

Soon the car stopped in the lobby of a huge building.

'Madam, this is where your apartments are. I will take both of you upstairs la...ok?' said the guy, who was sitting on the front seat. Our Singapore office had sent him to pick us from the airport.

'Yes, thank you,' I said, getting off the cab. The guy paid off the cabbie and got the suitcases offloaded to the bay. He took out a round plastic thing and pressed it right in the middle and the door flung open to a very plush-looking reception. He then directed us towards it while he carried the two suitcases in his hands.

We both were quite pleased to see the apartments on the 40th floor.

'Thanks for bringing us here. May I know your name please?' I asked him.

'Jim Soon, ma'am. I work in the same office as you. I will show you around this apartment la. It's very good la. The best in Singapore ma'am. You will love it la. It has a swimming pool on the seventh floor, barbeque pits next to it, Jacuzzis on the 31st floor, steam, sauna, theatre...everything la. The Tanjong Pagar MRT is just next door and the market is also closeby. You both will like it la,' he replied looking excited himself.

'Mr. Soon, what's with the la?' asked Dev.

'Sir, I am sorry la. This is how we Singaporeans speak la. That is why Singapore is also called the "la la city",' he replied and all of us started laughing.

We took a quick view at the facilities and called it a day. Before sleeping, I decided to call home. I had not bought a local number yet so I used my cell instead, which was on roaming.

'Hello mummy. How are you guys doing? How is Aryan?'

'We are all fine dear. Hope you had a great flight. Aryan is here. He has been waiting for your call,' and, as expected, Aryan had grabbed the phone.

'Mumma...how are you? How is Singapore? I am already missing you. I want to come there to stay with you. Nani didn't let me have another ice-cream today. I don't like it here,' he said in a soft-cute voice, all in one breath.

'I am good my baby. I am also missing you so much. You are a sweetheart, aren't you and you know mummy has come here only for work. Don't behave like a bad baby. Listen to your grandmother and I am arranging for you to come and stay here for your summer vacations with me. The apartments are amazing. The building has a children's play area and a swimming pool too, so I am sure you will love it here. When you pack your stuff, pack your costume and swimming glasses too.'

'Ok mumma. I will be a good boy. Good Night.'

'Bye baby,' reluctantly I cut the call. I realised I was missing him a lot.

The next day morning, Dev woke me up by ringing my bell and then tapping on the door at 7:30 a.m. We were late to get ready and leave for office.

Somehow, we managed to move out of the building by 8:30 a.m. We picked up some coffee from Starbucks on the way. The office was at Raffle's place, which wasn't too far. We decided to take a cab in the morning and explore the MRT later in the evening when there was extra time at hand.

Upon reaching office, we were guided to our cabins, which were overlooking the Clarke Quay. Gagan was to join us the next morning, while we got some work done before he arrived.

The office had very few Indians and mostly Singaporeans, Chinese and a few Americans. It was a good cultural mix and people usually started office early, around 8:00 a.m. and finished by 5:00 p.m.

'I like the office, Maaya and I absolutely love the view from my window. These guys are quite nice, aren't they?'

I was busy checking my e-mails and taking some printouts, so I merely nodded at Dev's comment.

'Maaya, we will need to shop for some cooking utensils and crockery, etc. You can do most of the cooking for us. I will just buy a few basic things for my apartment,' he said with a naughty smile.

'Hmmmm...,' I was engrossed in my work, so I didn't bother to look up.

'We could actually go to Little India. I've heard they have a mall that has practically everything we will need. It's open 24 hours and since tomorrow is a Saturday, we could do some late night shopping and then settle in. What say?' he said, trying to get my attention.

'Yeah, sounds good, Dev. For now we have a few things to sort out since Gagan is arriving tomorrow. He will want to see us tomorrow. Can you please get me the scripts for these articles mentioned here and also a printout of that mail that Gagan sent to you yesterday?'

I wondered how he had the capability to think about all the unimportant things on earth. After all, we had to prepare for Gagan's arrival.

We worked all day. In the evening, we got our monthly passes made and explored the MRT.

Upon stopping by a hawker's stall for some food, Dev said, 'I love the food, Maaya. Awesome food for three dollars, what more can you expect? This is an amazing country, man! Starbucks sells coffee for 5.30 dollars and there is the local authentic yummy food for three dollars!'

'Hmmmmm.'

'I am sorry, you'll have to cook for me too. Maybe I'll find someone here who can love me and cook for me. Till then, eggs are all I can cook, so I will make you breakfast and you make us dinner. Lunch we will manage at office. How does that sound?' Dev extended his hands for a shake.

'Sure Dev. That's a deal. You do the dishes too sometimes,' I gave him a nudge with my elbow.

'Yeah sure,' he said with a long face.

We did some shopping at Mustafa Centre in the evening and made it home by 10:00 p.m. It was a tiring trip. Dev left for his apartment straightaway.

As I entered my apartment, my phone beeped. Deeksha was waiting for me on skype. We connected for a good two hours over skype, catching up on all the latest happenings in our lives. Thankfully, Deeksha had decided to act on my suggestion and get trained for a corporate job. She was tired of waiting for Maanav to love her for being unemployed. I was glad to hear that.

We ended the conversation with a little more chatter about how we allow ourselves to be moulded just the way another person wants. When the 'honeymoon' period of a relationship is over, it gets tougher and tougher to hold on to what we aren't. Most relationships suffer when one partner tries to change the other. In my belief, change doesn't last. Transformation does.

I was quite sleepy by the time we hung up. Unsurprisingly, I found myself thinking about Deeksha and Maanav before falling asleep.

Maanav was a dentist and a very busy one at that. Deeksha went to him for a check-up and, during the course of her treatment, they fell in love. His parents were dead set against the marriage and so were hers. His parents wanted him to marry a doctor just like they had and her parents wanted an artist in the family. After they were unsuccessful in convincing their parents, they had actually eloped and married each other in a temple. Ever since, they lived in an independent house. Deeksha was never accepted by his family. His parents made-up with him after a while but they hardly liked her till date. Her parents sort of accepted them but since they live in Mumbai, she really couldn't count on them for emotional support when she needed it.

As time passed, Maanav got busier and busier. Slowly, Deeksha found herself getting lonely and frustrated. She gave up her career for love and the love didn't last as long. Sometimes, Maanav surprised her by being very kind and warm but it was occasional. I wouldn't say he didn't love her but he had very little expression. The race he was running had become so involving that he had forgotten why he was running. It is so ironical, I wondered. Some people don't seem to get the relationships they would like to be in and those who do, don't value them. Life is funny. When Rahul and I met, both of us felt this connect, which was so special. It was as if it was an angel set out to make us meet. Whenever I looked in his eyes, I could see my soul in them. They were deep and full of love for me. I didn't know what went wrong but once both of us had believed it was a connection from many lives.

I recalled a weird dream I once had. I found myself standing in a big white hall. Right in the middle of the hall, I saw a white figure. I couldn't make out whether it was a man or a woman until it spoke to me. The room was white and this figure was blissfully white. I felt extremely calm and at peace in his presence. I found myself asking, 'Who are you?'

'I have come here to deliver a message to you.'

'How do you know me?'

'I know all about you. I watch over you. You are about to enter a very important phase of your life. I will be there to help you. Just trust and hold on.'

'How do I know you are real?'

'You must check your mobile phone right now. You have an important message from someone you love. He is guided too.'

I woke up in amazement. My mobile was lying right beside me on my bedside table and it was blinking with a red light. I checked it and just about ten seconds ago, Rahul had sent me a message saying 'I love you Maaya. I don't know what got me to write to you at this hour but I love you very much. Never leave me.'

I had goose bumps all over my hands. It was so surreal. I didn't know how to react. It was the most amazing experience. I wanted to share it with Rahul but I couldn't. I didn't think he would understand.

The next afternoon, Rahul was on his weekly off. I had a busy day at work. He was getting bored, so he decided to take a nap. He had a similar dream in which he was told to check his mobile. He checked and I had sent him a message just then, saying, 'Just realised how special you are to me. I wouldn't want to live a moment without you.'

Unlike me, Rahul couldn't hold his excitement. He called me to share his dream and the follow-on experience. This was when I told him about my dream too. Our belief became even stronger that we had a deep connection. It wasn't a coincidence that we had met again.

I was sitting by my window, looking out at the pool. As my thoughts raced to Rahul, the familiar pain in my heart was back.

My inability to give up on Rahul amazed me. Every single day I told myself that it was over. Every single day I went through the misery of allowing myself to look through his Facebook profile at least once, of allowing myself to believe he really did love me and finally the sadness of realising that in spite of all that love, he was now the reason for my tears.

The next morning was a bit of a mess.

'Why do you take so long to open the door, Dev? I got a call from Gagan and he wants us to report at office sharp at 10:00. Please get up and get ready. I am trying to make something for us to bite before leaving. See you in fifteen minutes at my place,' I said while shutting the door of Dev's apartment to rush back to mine. I am sure he took a while to grasp what I had said but it didn't matter. We were late!

Both of us quickly got ready. We were about ten minutes late by the time we reached the lift in the office building. I guess I was visibly stressed.

'Relax Maaya. It's a Saturday and, without any prior notice, he can't really blame us for not being available ten minutes early. It's ok. Just take a deep breath and relax.' Dev tried to calm me down.

This was one of the rare days when he looked more calm and composed than me. We were soon outside Gagan's cabin while he was inside talking to some people. We waited till he was done with his meeting. Soon three-four men walked out of his room and we were called in.

'Hello guys! Well, we have a magazine to launch in a new country in exactly thirty days and there is just so much to do. There should be fire under your feet, Maaya!' he said.

'Yes Gagan. I will arrange for all the stuff you might require right away. In case you need me, give me a shout,' I replied. His aggression gave me jitters. Dev moved out of the cabin. Just before I could step out, 'Where are you having your lunch?' he inquired. I was a little taken aback by this sudden inquisitiveness of my boss about my whereabouts.

'Well, nothing planned. Maybe just go down and grab something,' I answered, keeping my posture composed and not giving away my emotions.

'I want you to accompany me to lunch today. There is a nice Singaporean restaurant here. We have a few things to talk about work too. Do you like Singaporean or do you have any other preferences?' he retorted in a swift reply.

'No, Singaporean is fine. See you at lunch then. Will be mailing you all the stuff just now along with the new cover designs Dev did. Do let me know if you need anything else,' I said as I turned to look towards the door and then out.

Dev was already sitting in my cabin waiting for me to return. I felt a bit lost.

'Gagan invited me to lunch. I really don't feel like going but I think he didn't really give me a choice.'

I was already looking at my computer screen and sending e-mails from my laptop.

'Take care and don't let him bother you. Let's see what he has to discuss with you. I think I will just have a muffin and coffee from Starbucks for lunch and finish off the cover story designs for him to see and approve. You enjoy your lunch. Call me if you need anything from me,' saying which Dev disappeared into his cabin.

'Sure. Thanks Dev.'

Gagan walked to my cabin and pushed the door to open gently. I was busy working and didn't notice him. He probably stood there for a few seconds before he said, 'Ready to go?'

I almost jumped from my chair as I hadn't expected him to come but only call.

I lowered the screen of my laptop, picked my sling and moved along with him through the door. We walked together to a restaurant just one block left to our office building. As always, we hardly exchanged any words while walking.

'This is a very old restaurant and it is very famous for its authentic Singaporean food. What do you prefer, sea-food or meat?' he said while he took his seat right across me. I was still looking at our surroundings in the restaurant and seemingly appreciating the plush interiors.

'I would like sea-food. Thank you. This place looks awesome,' I said looking at Gagan. I liked the place and it helped in making me comfortable in his company.

'Well, that's good then. They serve great chilly crab. Would you like to try it?' he inquired.

'Yeah sure. I haven't had a chilly crab as yet but I sure would like to try,' I replied with a slight smile. Gagan took up most of the ordering and ordered two-three varieties of snacks including the crab. He looked quite used to doing that. It seemed like he knew his way around the menu quite well.

'So, do you like Singapore?' asked Gagan, looking at me casually.

'I think it's a nice place. Easy to settle in.'

'Can I ask you a personal question?' he inquired, looking at me. I felt a pit in my stomach. I wondered what was he about to ask me.

I immediately changed my posture on the sofa, feeling a bit uncomfortable. Not being rude and in anticipation of what was to come, I replied, 'Yeah, sure. I will try and answer it, if I can.'

'Do you believe in the existence of souls?'

I was a bit surprised at the nature of the question but I replied almost instantly, saying, 'Yes. I do.'

'Hmmmmm. I have seen something in your eyes that tells me you are at an important transition in your life. Do you want to share it with me?' This statement of his drew my attention to his eyes. He had this intense gaze in his eyes. They seemed deep.

'How can you read my eyes and how can you be so sure?' I was curious.

'Trust me I can. I am good at reading people's moods and energies and something tells me your energies are a little distorted right now. I am sorry if I am interfering but if you ever want to share, let me know.'

'Thanks Gagan and I will keep that in mind.' Both of us had some general conversation all through the meal. He ensured he briefed me about the cover design of the new magazine and a few details of the vendors I had to deal with.

Gagan had a cab for him all through his stay. He dropped me to the apartment after the meal.

Next morning, Dev asked me, 'So, how was it then? I hope he didn't talk about work all the time!' with a wink.

'Well, not really. It was not quite what I had expected. He seemed a little more sensitive than I had assumed him to be.'

His gesture about me sharing my concerns with him was a little overwhelming.

'Hmmmm. Someone seems impressed and in deep thought. Is everything ok, Maaya?'

'Yes Dev. Everything is ok.'

I was lost trying to link a few things. I could clearly recall having a strange dream the night before I had dinner with Gagan. It made more sense that morning. I saw the same being of light again in my dream. This time though, he made his presence felt more vividly. He was dressed in a white dress. His eyes were compassionate and his dressing was warrior like. He was serene and composed. This time we were in some open place. I could see the sea at a distance and it seemed like day time.

'Who are you, dear being of light?'

'I am your spirit guide, child. I am here to guide you. You are going through a "transition" period. All that is going on around you will not make much sense, and yet, you must trust.'

'I don't understand what you say dear being of light. Why is Rahul not with me?'

'Don't be sad, sweet one. Look at this,' he said while opening both his hands towards the sky.

I suddenly found myself trapped in a maze. I tried running around and finding a way but every way I went, I ended up getting even more lost. I went around and tried various ways to get out of the trap. Eventually, I said, 'Dear Lord. Help me. I am stuck.'

Immediately, the maze disappeared and I found myself face to face with the light being again.

'What did you experience?'

'Confusion, anxiety, stress!'

'And now I shall show you where you were,' saying which he waved his hands in the air again and a very clear picture appeared in the sky. It looked like a puzzle with many criss-cross lines, geometrically crossing each other.

'What does it look like now?'

'A plan.'

I realised – A divine plan!

'Trust dear one. Perseverance and courage are the key. You are being guided. Just follow the signs. I am with you,' saying which he disappeared.

When Gagan said I seemed to be in a 'transition' period, it was an exact match. An instant recognition of a validation for my guidance. I was indeed guided. I felt deep gratitude towards the universe. It was amazing synchronicity.

I then realised how amazingly I was being guided. I had started experiencing a sense of awareness of the presence of a higher power.

That night I found myself acknowledging the presence of Dev in my life. I didn't know how Dev became an important part of my life. He was the only reason I smiled during those days and somehow his mere presence made me feel warm and cared for. I was thankful for having him with me in Singapore.

Mostly, we fail to acknowledge the small mercies of the universe. When we are given a difficult life experience, we are also given the strength to deal with it and a support system to be able to survive it. All we need to do is to be aware and trust.

□

Back in Time

'Aryan...' is all that I could say before he jumped on me pulling himself away from the air hostess who was accompanying him out of the green channel.

'Oh my baby! How much I have missed you!' I said hugging him and feeling his body curled up into mine. I had never been away from him for that long and I could see he so needed the warmth of my presence before he could utter a word.

'I missed you too, mummy. Nani doesn't let me do anything. She keeps saying, "All the stupid stunts you want to do, do them when your mummy is back. I am old, so don't make me run around the house." It's not fair mumma!' he said in a sad voice.

For the first time, I realised how simple my problems were when I was little. They were anything from which colour do I use to paint my drawing to how can I trick my grandmother or do some mischief. I was beginning to realise that we ourselves make complications and worries bigger and bigger as we grow. Ironically, choosing the right colour for the drawing was of equal significance to me as a child.

'Ok Aryan. We will talk to her about giving you some space, but for now, you must be tired and we should go home and rest.'

He clung to me as we walked towards the air hostess who accompanied him.

'Thanks darling. I am really grateful to you for taking care of him during the flight. I hope he wasn't a handful,' I politely said to her.

'No ma'am. He was quite well behaved and nice during the flight. He kept entertaining another child on the next seat who was younger to him and we all enjoyed his company. He is a sweet boy,' she said smiling and ruffling Aryan's hair.

'I will take your leave, mam. Have a great time in Singapore. Aryan, it was great flying with you. See you again soon,' she said while she handed over a small Air India airplane memento in Aryan's hand.

He smiled, looking at me for consent. I nodded, and in a jiffy, he was out of sight with his airplane. It was now my turn to run after him. He was a handful, at least when it came to being with family.

I finally caught hold of him. He was asked to sit quietly till we reached the apartment. He seemed to be tired and, hence, he obeyed.

'I want to see the swimming pool and the barbeque pits and the children's play area. I want to see the whole building that you live in mumma,' he said excitedly looking at me.

'Yes, you will baby. I will show you everything. Now since you are here for almost two months, you have plenty of time to explore. Right now, I want you to first come with me to the apartment and rest for a while. Then when you wake up, I will take you to the pool,' I said in a slightly firm tone.

He slumped a bit. One could see the tiredness on his face. The poor baby could sure use some sleep. I felt happy to have Aryan in my arms again. He had been my anchor, ever since he was very little. He gave meaning to my life, like no other. I hugged him tight. Soon, we made it to our apartment.

'Wow...! This is cool. This is so nice, mumma! I love this...! It feels like I am in a five-star hotel,' said Aryan as I took him through the reception of the apartments towards the lift.

Aryan seemed to be quite tired in the cab but suddenly he became alert again, noticing every small thing about the building and the apartment. It's tough to understand how kids have so much energy for things that interest them. They never seem to get tired.

He kept looking out of the window of the living room to get a good glimpse of anyone near the swimming pool. There was no one at that hour since it was a working day and the weather was not that great for poolside outings. Somehow he was still enjoying the view.

Soon Aryan changed his clothes, jumped on the bed two-three times and was asleep within a few minutes.

I had missed seeing him sleep. It's such an amazing feeling to see someone you love, sleeping. They look so vulnerable and innocent. The scene traced me back to when I saw Rahul sleeping in the car. I had picked him up from the airport on his last trip to his parents in the US. It must have been a long tiring journey. He fell asleep almost immediately when I started driving the car. I didn't realise it until I noticed there was no response from him to anything I said. I turned to look at him. He was fast asleep. When I saw him that way, I had a strange feeling that we had been there before...that it wasn't the first time I was seeing the child in him. He looked so adorable.

There was something about him that drew me to love him as much. The bond was special. I got goose bumps whenever any of his memories came back.

I didn't even realise how days passed with Aryan around. He enjoyed swimming in the pool, reading Tin-Tin comics, going up and down in the lift and playing with Dev. He was learning abacus and a lot of creative stuff at the day-care too.

'Hey Deeksha. How are you?' I said to Deeksha, trying to fix the headphone onto my ears.

'I am good. You tell me. What's up with you? How is Aryan finding it in Singapore?' she replied.

'Aryan is very happy here. He can be as naughty as he wants. He is enjoying the premises and facilities too. It's great to have him here. It's rejuvenating for me and a reminder that my life has more than I need for survival a reminder of my blessings. He is an angel.'

'I can understand what you mean, Maaya. I am glad that Aryan is there with you. He's an innocent distraction. I wish I had one like him,' she replied in a slight sad tone.

'You tell me. How is your course coming along?' I said attempting to change the topic.

'My course is coming along great. I am enjoying it. Surprisingly, I never knew I had so much creativity stocked inside me. I am quite good at the designs. We will be having companies coming in for placements next week. My trainer thinks I will be the first one to get picked, so I am keeping my fingers crossed. It's keeping me occupied. Creating something gives me this sense of satisfaction which I never had before. It's fun, Maaya and I have to thank you for pushing me to do it all the way through,' she replied.

'I am really happy to hear that Deeksha. You are doing a great job. What does Maanav think about your work? Is he happy for you?'

'Well Maanav is too busy to notice what I am up to. He spends most of his time in office and when he is around, he is either busy watching TV or socializing on the phone. Whenever I seek his attention, he indirectly blames me for not being able to give him children. Slowly, I have started keeping myself busy in my designs and it is giving me an outlet.'

Deeksha's voice became heavier. She was unable to get pregnant. She had got herself treated for a long time but in vain. Initially, I used to wonder why God would deny the happiness of a child to someone as affectionate as her. Slowly, I realised the way their relationship with each other was, it was likely that the child would suffer. Maybe it was not the right time. On the other hand, when I saw Aryan, I was most grateful to God. Even though Kunal and I were not together anymore, Aryan continued to be my source of happiness.

'Continue to do that Deeksha. You are able to contain your emotions and manifest them through your creativity and designs and that is what is required for now. Have faith in the ultimate good and do whatever it takes to be happy. If you can, start meditating for a few minutes everyday. It will help in settling in your energies.'

'How will meditation help Maaya? I am bad at concentrating on nothingness for a long while.'

'Ok. Let me teach you the simplest way to meditate. I have done a lot of experimentation when I started and struggled with exactly this problem. Just sit in a quiet place, and if you can't sit, then lie down. Close your eyes and just focus on your breathing. If any thoughts come up, watch them from the outside but don't entertain them. Slowly, when the focus increases on the breath, automatically thoughts will stop coming up. It takes a while so allow yourself that time. It's the simplest technique. Slowly, in a few days, you will notice how you will start getting guidance from the inside. You will just know the direction you are expected to follow. Trust it. It will also provide you with the inner strength to face life.'

'How did it help you?'

'In the days that I was confused about ending my relationship with Kunal, I was guided by Pooja to meditate. She had learnt it in a retreat she once went to and it had benefitted her. I just thought it couldn't do any harm. I expected it to help me to take a decision with a relatively calmer mind. Pooja helped me by sharing this simple technique to meditate after I shared with her my plight about the various techniques of meditation that I had tried and how they didn't work for me.'

She first assessed my expectations from a meditative experience and set them right. I thought some people felt a high, some saw blue or yellow lights, some felt their body floating while some saw divine beings, so I was expected to have some of those, to the least. I didn't get any of that from my attempts till then. The more I told my mind to shut-up, the more it chattered. I wanted to experience the nothingness.

Upon her guidance, I realised it was my own expectation which was blocking my experience. It was like I told my mind not to think of the elephant and all it did was think of the elephant. The mind does not know how to shut-up. Its identity is to talk.

Pooja made a very interesting point to me, which clicked. She showed me that all the above experiences I mentioned seemed 'something' and, hence, they couldn't possibly be equivalent to 'nothing'. I understood that when I will feel or experience 'nothingness', it will not be equivalent, similar or explainable to 'something'. I had to drop my expectations. Be open to the universe. Let my own experience come to me.

I realised that it may or may not be anything like what I had read or heard but it will sure be what I would 'need'.

I learnt that unlike prayer, meditation was the art of 'listening' or being open to receive from the universe. One will get what they 'need' and it may not be what they 'want'. Want always comes from our mind, our ego but our needs are what come from our sub-conscious and hence help us resolve inner conflicts in our energy system. At the right time, the right knowledge will flow to those who surrender.

This knowledge helped me a lot. The burden of performing, achieving a particular state went off me. I felt more at ease. In just a few days, my meditative experience became deeper and more profound.

Initially, I did it barely for twenty minutes and later extended it up to about an hour. More and more clarity appeared inside me about the direction I was to choose in my life.

'Ok Maaya. Let me try this. I am sure it would help. Thanks. In case I do chase my thoughts and entertain them, what do I do to get back to my meditative state?'

'Then be aware that you are chasing and then stop the chase. Start observing them all over again and let them be.'

'Ok.'

Soon, we ended the conversation and hung up. It was late and I had work the next morning.

It was a tough week ahead for me. Aryan demanded a lot of attention and work was also hectic. Soon it was time for Aryan to go back since his vacations were getting over.

Aryan was sure to miss his day care and his new friends. He was particularly fond of a girl named 'Masooma' in his day care. The previous morning, when I went to drop him, Masooma's mom said she wanted to share something with me. She was an Indonesian lady and her hubby was a Pakistani. She was quite friendly and many times we stood catch-up for a few minutes, if our drop and pickup timings coincided.

I asked her what the matter was and she said she told Masooma to wear jeans in the morning and she refused saying she wanted to wear a dress. She said the girl didn't budge even upon her insisting and finally wore a dress. Then she went in front of the mirror and, admiring her dress, she said, 'Aryan will be happy to see me today'. Her mom was so surprised at this conversation of hers with herself. After all, she was just six. Both she and I were amused and found it quite cute. Just then I saw Masooma come to Aryan and she bowed and flaunted her dress to him. Aryan smiled and gave her a thumbs-up. Both her mother and I were observing them from a distance. It was so amazing but love had no language. Their family had recently shifted to Singapore from London. Aryan didn't quite catch the British accent in her English yet, but that didn't stop them from communicating at every level.

That evening, Aryan quietly came to me in the kitchen while I was working. He pulled a stool and sat on the slab next to me. Very politely he asked me, 'Mumma, can't I stay here with you in Singapore?'

'No, my baby. You have school in India. I will be back soon. We are not here forever.'

'But mumma, I will also miss Masooma.'

I saw his naughty smile and decided to play on. 'But you have so many Masoomas' in your class, Aryan.'

Upon this remark, he suddenly sat up erect and said, 'But mumma, you know na, I love only Masooma...' with a sulk on his face!

I laughed at his expression and yet felt bad for him for I knew he had to leave. I hugged him and kissed him on his forehead. With a slight sadness, he slipped off from the slab and went into his room. I didn't know what to make of this episode. It was amazingly cute and yet I felt helpless for him. I mentally made a note to take Masooma's mom's e-mail address before I left the country so that Aryan could stay in touch with her.

As soon as I dropped him at the airport, I noticed the emptiness in my life without him. It gave me a weird sensation in my stomach. I was quick to ignore it. There wasn't too much time to lose, since there was a lot to be achieved over the next few weeks.

The new magazine launch was not too far. Not knowing Mandarin was becoming a major hassle for us, it took a lot more time to communicate things at times. Many people, especially vendors and junior staff, couldn't understand English so well. We took it as another challenge. They had to manage the situation and the limitations on time.

I was lost in thought while relaxing on my sofa at home on a Thursday evening. We had a long weekend ahead. I was sure we would still end up working for a while over that weekend too. Nonetheless, it was to be more relaxed than the usual ones because of the lesser staff at office.

'Maaya, let's go shopping and clubbing tomorrow. It's been a while we haven't done anything like that. Ever since Aryan has gone, it's been only work and it's getting boring. Another two weeks and Gagan will be back and while he is here, I feel he will want your time and attention, too, for obvious reasons. Let's make the most of this time now,' Dev said while muttering something under his tongue.

'Come on Dev. He isn't such a bad guy and he is not interested in me, trust me. I saw some depth in that person that day when we met over lunch. Not that I am really keen to be friends with him, but I guess it's not fair to judge him. Let him be and we will handle him when he gets here. Don't get upset.'

'Hmmmm.'

The next day, as per Dev's insistence, we decided to go shopping to Orchard Road. It is the most happening place in Singapore. One could just forget themself in the big malls and huge signature showrooms of the world's leading brands.

We accidentally came across a bookshop called Kinokuniya. It turned out that it was one of the most celebrated book stores in Asia. You name it and they had it. I could lose myself in it. Strangely, ever since we entered that place, I felt there was something that drew me there. We spent close to two hours browsing through the huge collection of books they had. When I was in the queue to pay for the books I chose, my eyes fell on this book whose title really attracted me. I just had a flashing thought from somewhere in my mind, which said 'Buy this'. I didn't think twice and picked it up.

That night, before going to sleep, I decided to read that last book I had picked off the counter. It intrigued me. Once started, it took me on an unbelievable journey. I didn't realise it was morning already. I couldn't believe what I had read. It was about Reincarnation, Rebirth or the idea that people live many times and what we are today is a consequence of what we were in our past lives. It was with amazing detail and conviction. Somewhere I had an implicit belief in reincarnation. Having read this book, I remained in awe of it for a few days. It had planted a new belief somewhere in my mind that life has explanations for the way it is, other than the ones we are already aware of or can conclude on.

Next day, while at work, Dev dropped into my cabin. 'You know Maaya, I have something to share with you. I had a word with Rosy. You remember she vaguely knew Rahul too,' he said with a slight seriousness in his eyes.

'What about her, Dev?'

'Well, I didn't want to share this with you but I guess I should. She said she saw Rahul with his wife yesterday in a restaurant having dinner. They looked happy and it seems like they have made up. She thinks their marriage is working at last.'

I didn't know how to react to this. There was this sudden sadness and disappointment that moved from the top of my head to my heart. It was a deep sinking feeling.

I had once asked Rahul about his relationship with Neha. He said initially, their relationship had been good. He cared for her, pampered her, really loved her till slowly she started taking him for granted to the point he felt hurt and abused. He said immediately after their baby was born, she decided to go for further studies to London, which is where her parents lived. He expressed his concern about his job and inability to move to London out of the blue but she was adamant. She even managed to get a scholarship in one of the universities and decided to go for two years, leaving him behind. He said he was miserable because he didn't want to stay without his baby and her but she refused to listen. He tried changing jobs and getting a break there but those days the financial market was down and there were no chances of getting a new job in a new city. He became very sad and couldn't stop thinking about them. I recalled when once he got very emotional and said, 'I begged her to come back, I pleaded, I told her how lonely and miserable I was feeling but she said it was all in my head. It was only a matter of a year and a half left.'

He took leave to go and live with them for one month. He then realised she was too obsessed with her freedom and lifestyle in that city. His existence didn't matter to her that much. She had the opportunity to do the last six months of her internship in Mumbai, which is where Rahul lived at that time. He had expected her to take it up but she said she didn't want to stay in Mumbai. She would rather stay in London and do it. That was the last straw. It was evident in his eyes that he was heartbroken.

He shared with me that slowly in those last six-eight months, his emotions for her nearly died or froze. He never felt the same for her again. Slowly, their differences started showing and when the fights got intense, he decided to move out.

With all of this about Rahul coming flashing back to me, came the fear that maybe he had finally forgiven her now. I then had someone speak to me in my head saying, 'Is that all it takes, Maaya?' I couldn't afford Rahul and his thoughts to mess me up all over again. I didn't know the whole picture and I had decided to trust the universe to guide me. I immediately brought myself into awareness of the moment and brushed aside all the sadness. I just wanted to focus on my own journey in that moment.

'Thanks Dev. I can understand your concern, but it's ok. If it's meant to be, it will be. I did set him free. I don't want to interfere in my own faith.'

'Whatever you wish!' said Dev and started looking at his PC. He wasn't convinced. I didn't want to discuss it any further. We subsequently worked pretty much in silence that day.

At night, when I was alone, I realised what Dev had said had not completely gone off my mind. Tears started dropping off my eyes. It was after so many weeks that all those memories of the days I spent with Rahul came flashing back to my memory.

He was such a crazy lover. I couldn't accept that he could ever be the same way with anyone else as he was with me. It was so deep. He didn't even go home after a haircut if he didn't show it to me. One night when he and I were driving back from a club, it was 2:00 a.m. and our car met with an accident.

Rahul was always very protective about this car and would never let anyone drive his CRV. The car was hit while both of us were in it and the impact was huge. The guy who bumped into us managed to vanish in the darkness. We could hardly recognize what hit our vehicle. Rahul's car looked like a real mess. It was smashed badly from the front and one side.

Both of us got really scared and especially me because I hadn't told my mom anything about my whereabouts. I had just said I was with Deeksha. We had then barely escaped landing up in a hospital. Rahul was shit scared and very blank. Surprisingly, he didn't lose his patience or temper, though I was convinced it was entirely my fault.

I had just had a fight with Deeksha over the phone. While I was upset and crying, he just tried to hug me. Just then this other vehicle crossed over and bumped into us.

The car was making noises and we didn't want a Delhi police cop to stop us and enquire about wherever we were coming from since it could get really odd. Rahul decided that he would drop me home and drive the car to his place and manage something the next day.

He was very tensed and yet he was the one calming me down. I couldn't believe that he would be driving in that half broken, noisy car all the way to his place. I decided to call him and stay on call with him while he drove so that he at least wouldn't feel lonely or scared. Simply ignoring the instructions about no talking on the mobile while driving, I called him up after reaching home. He was happy and relieved to take my call. I talked to him and relaxed him while he pulled that jammed car to his parking lot.

It was a crazy night. I couldn't sleep at all. I kept thinking about all that had happened and waited for the morning before I could call Rahul and ask how he was feeling. I was so scared that he might be angry with me in the morning. After all, the entire fault was mine and the accident happened because of me. I couldn't stop blaming myself and hoping Rahul would still talk to me and love me just as much.

The next morning he called me instead. Before I could say anything, he said, 'I love you sweety…it's only your love that we survived this smash. It's because of you I remained sane in a situation like that, otherwise, I could have gotten really angry and messed up. You bring out the best in me. Thank you for being a part of me.'

I put off the lights and went to bed with Rahul held close to my heart, without worrying about our future and with just the pure emotion of love and compassion. He was always there with me in spirit.

□

The Small Mercies

Gagan arrived the following week. He was in his usual high energies and with a long list of tasks that he wanted me and Dev to finish within the next few days. One of those days, Gagan landed up at my table for a CD that he needed. He picked up a book that I was reading from my table.

'I didn't know you had any interest or inclination to read these kind of books,' he said casually.

'Well, I have recently developed an interest in them, while in Singapore. I find myself drawn to them. Have you read this book?'

'Yeah, I have. It's a good one. If you want, I can lend you a few books from my personal collection on this topic. I am sure you will find some of them very fascinating,' Gagan offered me.

'That will be great. Thanks.'

The next day, Gagan was getting ready to leave in the evening when a woman came looking for him. She met me at the reception while she was waiting for Gagan. Gagan walked upto us and introduced her to me. Her name was Shirley and she seemed to be a good friend of his.

'We are going for drinks and dinner, Maaya. Why don't you join us?' Gagan asked me suddenly.

'No, thanks Gagan. It's sweet of you to ask, but you guys go ahead. I have some more work left.'

'You don't want to miss this chance, Maaya. Shirley is a past life regression therapist too. After all of the stuff you have been reading these days, I am sure there is a lot Shirley and you might have in common,' Gagan winked.

Past Life Regression! That certainly rang a few bells in me. I quickly decided to join them. I sure wanted to spend some time with Shirley and understand more about how past lives affect our current lives. Shirley looked like a very warm person and there was something about her that also attracted me towards her. Dev also joined us.

It was a fun evening and a very interesting one too. This was when I discovered that Past Life Regression is not limited only to books. There are real therapists who practise it as well. It was possible for them to take us to our past lives and reveal a few secrets.

'Have you seen any past lives of yours?' I asked Gagan. To my surprise, he said, 'Yes. Five of them.' My disbelief was quite evident with my eyes wide open and my jaw dropping slightly, too. He wouldn't say any more.

'Shirley, what if we see past lives and they tell us things that would disturb us in our current lives?'

'Maaya, as a rule, past life information is revealed at a time and in the intensity that is the most appropriate for one in that moment. Past life memories are neither meant to entertain us, nor to disturb us. These are unresolved past lives where our soul fragments are still stuck. This is "past" that hasn't "passed" as yet. A lot of these are responsible for our behaviours in relationships, life situations, etc. where there is almost no explanation of why we behave opposite to what we know ourselves as. When we therapeutically deal with these memories, we are able to help our souls learn the respective lesson due to which it was still holding on to a negative past. Once done, the negative emotions or thought patterns created due to this past dissolve, hence bringing a resolution or relief in our current life situation or relationship. Each past life information is revealed only when you are ready to deal with it and learn the unlearnt lesson,' Shirley explained.

'All this sounds too absurd to me. I don't know if I believe in past lives and their existence, Shirley,' Dev said.

'Well, you are on your own journey. When the time is right, you will start believing and, till then, stay happy with whatever you believe in. That's what is best for you in this moment,' she said with a smile.

I had to admire the patience and maturity with which she responded to the hundreds of questions Dev and I asked her that evening. She didn't seem to believe in convincing either of us about the existence or significance of past lives. She truly believed that when we are ready, if our past journey is meant to help us, we shall be guided.

Gagan looked a bit lost that evening, as if in some deep thought. Ever since I had asked him about his own past lives, he seemed to be a bit turned off. The three of us were busy enjoying ourselves, especially with the new, fascinating topic of reincarnation. Gagan chose to observe us, not saying much.

I had a good night's sleep after dinner. I had taken a few drinks. I also felt a little high otherwise, for I now had something interesting to explore in life. I was all geared up to do some research on Past Life Regression and understand more about the purpose of my own life. Before that day, I had never thought about why I existed. Slowly, my life had moved into a vacuum and blankness. I was being drawn to questions like 'who am I?', 'why am I here?', 'why do we suffer in relationships?', 'why is it that many times love does not get back love?' and so many more. I had to find my answers.

Dev had started with not believing Shirley but, by the end of the day, he carried a certain curiosity and understanding about the topic. It certainly was new and offbeat. The idea that we have lived before and every challenging moment in our current lives is built on some unresolved experience in our past, seemed fascinating. We as souls plan our current lives, including our life situations, relationships, relationship break-ups and many other things, just to learn some lessons and get wiser. There was more to this 'planning' that I was to discover much later in my journey.

I could resonate with it. I could feel more love for Rahul, even though I had not been in touch with him for weeks. I always knew it had something to do with some connection that I felt but was not aware of. I started reading and researching on the net about souls, reincarnation and the cycle of evolution of the soul.

Suddenly, my life's context had changed. I had started looking at my life as an experience. I realised everything that happened to me may not have a logical answer in the context of this life but I could look beyond. The connection I felt with Rahul intrigued me. I wanted to know more.

The next few days at work were busy. Gagan was in Singapore till the launch of the campaign. He was making sure we worked hard.

One evening, Dev fell sick and he decided to go home at 5. I was feeling exceptionally low that day. Rahul had posted some latest snaps of him and his wife together, on a social networking site. He looked happy. I wanted to be happy for him but I couldn't feel the happiness. I felt disturbed. Something inside kept telling me, 'Something will happen if I am not with him. I am responsible for him. He can't do without me.' I felt as if I had to save him from some danger.

I struggled with these weird thoughts for two-three days. They were weird, since he was doing pretty well on his own. Yet, they got overwhelming.

I always knew it that was my own decision to come to Singapore. If I had stayed, probably things would have been different. Something told me that if he wasn't mine, the heart break was inevitable, sooner or later. I kept telling myself to calm down and stay in the now. I listened to the audio tapes of Eckhart Tolle which I borrowed from the city library. He was an author and a motivational speaker. He talked about the power of now and to me, it made a lot of sense too. The tapes helped me ground my energies and stay in the moment, though I must admit, it was tough.

Gagan and I were the only ones left in office till about 8. Gagan came to my cabin and said, 'Up for a good Thai dinner?' I was not sure, since that wasn't the best day to socialise.

I looked at him and he probably read it in my eyes that I was having second thoughts. He came closer and held me by the shoulder. 'It's ok. You will be alright. Let's go.' I nodded.

The ambience in the Suntec city centre was fantastic. Singapore looked so beautiful in the evening. The beauty of the place made me feel even sadder. As I looked out of the window of the car, I felt lonelier than before. I wanted to be happy. I wanted to enjoy the beauty and serenity of this city. Yet, I wasn't able to. I was low on energies.

Gagan looked at me.

'Tell me Maaya. What is bothering you?'

I was a little taken aback. I didn't know that my attempt at smiling and looking normal wasn't working. Just then, something happened. I just looked at him and broke down. I sobbed and sobbed. I didn't know why I was crying in front of my boss. The pain was intense. I allowed it to flow.

Gagan didn't say a word but just let me be. I could feel his hand press my hand in reassurance. He then left me alone to let out all that sadness.

When I was a little calmer, he handed me a tissue and gently asked, 'Do you want to tell me what it is that is bothering you so much? Maybe I can help'.

'I don't know if anyone can help, but me. It's just this relationship I was in which is shattering me. I seem to be unable to handle the pain.'

'It's alright Maaya. You are lucky that you can feel such intense emotions. I am sure there is some sort of learning that is coming your way by means of this relationship. Allow yourself to experience it.'

'I don't understand. How can the breaking of a relationship teach me something? I loved him, I loved him so much. He was like a part of me and now it seems like he has completely forgotten the times that we spent together. He is happy and busy in his own life and here I am, shedding tears for him.'

'It's alright dear. Life is only an experience. He will have his role to play in your life and I am sure you have played some role in his. Did he tell you that he doesn't love you anymore?'

'I don't know. We haven't spoken in four months but it doesn't seem like he cares.'

'Stop making assumptions, Maaya. If it's bothering you so much, drop your ego and call him. Maybe he doesn't feel the way you think he does. Maybe he still cares.'

We had a quiet dinner. When I got back, I kept thinking whether I should call Rahul or not. The thoughts of us together and all those beautiful times we had were haunting me. I felt cheated. Finally, I decided to call him.

The bell rang and Rahul picked up. 'Hey,' I said. He seemed a bit confused about who was on the line. I sensed his confusion and said, 'Maaya.'

'Hey,' he replied. 'How are you?' I asked him. 'I am great. What about you?'

'Did you miss me?' I couldn't help asking him straightaway.

'I guess I did but I don't think I feel the same emotions anymore, Maaya. I have been thinking about this for a few days. I don't think I have the kind of intensity anymore that I once carried for you. I am sorry Maaya, please give me some time. I so badly want to be the same person and feel that connection just as I used to but it seems it's not in my hands. I am trying Maaya, just give me some time,' he said.

It hit me so hard in my heart that I couldn't hold the phone any longer. He sounded like a stranger to me. I disconnected the call and sat next to my window, blankly looking outside at the city.

That night was tough for me. I don't know whether I slept or got lost. There was so much anger, so much resentment. I couldn't think of one thing I had done to Rahul to deserve all that was happening to me. I was always there for him, all the way. How could he just have lost emotions for me? We made promises, to be there for each other. After all, he also turned out to be one of those men for whom their fears, the society and being right were more important than their happiness. It was okay for him to hurt me than hurt his wife. I found myself sitting on the living room sofa early morning. The plate I had dinner on was lying on the floor, broken. I was so blank. I didn't know if I could see anything in my future. It was so easy for him to say he didn't feel that intensity anymore but for me—those words tore me apart. In those past few months, I had assumed that Rahul didn't love me the same but hearing it from him was different. It just tore me apart.

Dev knocked on my door around 8:30 a.m. I composed myself and opened the door. He stretched and said, 'Wow, I feel so fresh. I guess I just needed a good night's sleep,' as he entered.

'What happened to you? Why do you look like a zombie?'

'Nothing Dev. I am fine. Let me go freshen up and come,' and I moved towards the washroom. He caught me by my arm on the way and said, 'Sweetheart, what's wrong?' and that was enough for my tears to flow again.

'Rahul doesn't love me anymore. He told me so. Dev, can you believe it? You saw him in those days. I so hate him for doing this to me. Why did he give me so much pain? I can't accept this Dev. I feel so lost,' I said, hugging him.

'It's ok, Maaya. I could see it coming. I know it's hard but time will heal this, sweetheart. You deserve a lot more than him. Let him go. He isn't worth it.'

After a while, we got ready for work and ate breakfast silently. While I was getting ready, thankfully, Dev made eggs and toast for breakfast in my kitchen. It was a long day and I pretty much went through it mechanically.

It was time to heal, I told myself. I had a life, a son to take care of and loads of other things that mattered. I couldn't slip into depression. I couldn't behave like a teenager. I had responsibilities. I just couldn't. Also, Rahul wasn't worth it. He couldn't make me so helpless and miserable. For the next few days, I gathered myself. I didn't give myself the permission to cry at all. I had to get out of my mess.

One night while I was trying to sleep, for a change, I found myself thinking about Kunal. Kunal was my ex-husband. We had taken a mutual divorce two years back. I hadn't thought of him in a very long time.

I didn't know why he was haunting me then. I felt as if he was saying whatever goes around comes around. The thought disturbed me.

I kept slipping from one side to the other in restlessness. Kunal's thoughts didn't leave me. As if Kunal was happy somewhere for I was lonely. As if I was being punished for leaving him lonely. I hadn't known until then that I carried so much from Kunal I hadn't dealt with as yet.

Kunal and I had a love marriage. I was pretty crazy about him while we were together. We shared everything with each other and cared for each other. I always felt I cared more for him than he did for me but that didn't bother me at all. Sometimes, he even took me for granted. At times, it affected me but I let it go thinking that just because I love him, I will stay unconditional and absolutely unreasonable.

We spent four years together before deciding to marry. We didn't meet everyday, since he had a tough job and I was studying and working part time as well. Yet, we shared the kind of bond where meeting or talking all the time wasn't necessary.

Slowly, Kunal's work started getting tougher. He was a doctor and he had to take care of emergency surgeries, OPDs and so much stuff that he was pretty much working round the clock. I was proud of him for being what he was. Sometimes, I did feel the strong need to be with him, to hold him, to talk to him for long hours, to just be, without having a reason to justify it. But it was rarely that it happened in our lives because of the routines we were living.

Kunal was a nice guy and he did try his best to keep me happy. At times I felt he was a little too self-obsessed but at others, he would just surprise me with little gestures. Occasionally, he would bring flowers for me out of the blue or just send me a nice little present or even take me out for a nice dinner at a cool place.

He wasn't the best at dealing with women or when it came to my sensitivity as a woman. Yet, he had his own way of keeping me happy and making me feel loved.

When his job started getting tougher, I started feeling the need for more communication but sadly that couldn't happen. I accepted it as a part and parcel of life, since he was doing that job for our future together. He got busier and busier. I didn't realise it, but it had become habitual for me to not expect too much time from him. I knew he couldn't handle that request. I wanted to be his strength and not his weakness.

It was a perfect relationship and perfect understanding. I was proud of myself for being able to pull it off gracefully, until I went to Kolkata.

My best friend, Sonali was a Bengali and she was getting married in Kolkata. I decided to attend her wedding. She wouldn't let me skip it by any means. My dad was quite reluctant to send me all the way to Kolkata alone but I managed to convince him nevertheless. This was about a year before Kunal and I got married.

Sonali and my friendship dated back to our school years. She was a brilliant singer. She was famous in our school for both, her singing skills and her good looks. She was so beautiful that whenever I looked at her, I wondered how someone could have been created so 'perfect'. We got along well. As we grew closer, I realised, unlike her image at school, she was a sweet, genuine and sensitive person.

After we finished school, she joined an engineering college in Pune and we had no choice but to keep in touch through letters and postcards.

I reached Kolkata for her wedding. I was so excited, since I had not met her fiancé Prathik yet. I was looking forward to meeting him at a ceremony that evening. Barely two days were left for the wedding. He had been Sonali's boyfriend for ages but since he never travelled to Delhi with her, I had not met him until that day.

That evening, I wore a light blue-colored salwar-kameez with a few shiny sequins on it's dupatta.

Soon the guests arrived. Prathik was a tall and good looking guy. I liked him instantly. He was one of those no fuss and simple kind of guys whom you could talk to without the fear of being judged. He was accompanied by his cousins and his mother. His father had expired long ago. They were a small and sweet family.

Prathik had a younger brother who was away to the US for higher studies and unfortunately wasn't present at the wedding. Instead, his best friend, Rahul was there to take care of the wedding arrangements on his behalf. He was to make sure Prathik wouldn't miss his kiddo brother so much.

The dinner was arranged on the rooftop, next to the fireplace. There was music arranged for a cosy evening. Kolkata doesn't have the ideal temperature to hold a fireplace but since it was slightly chilly those days, it didn't seem like such a bad idea. We talked, danced, ate and enjoyed ourselves.

As it was past midnight, Prathik's mom announced that they would like to leave. Only two days were left for the wedding and a few ceremonies were to start the next day. Both families had to get busy. In a few minutes, the house was empty. Sonali and I moved up to her room.

The next day, as I was leaving for shopping, Sonali requested me to get her a matching scarf for one of her dresses. She said someone from Prathik's house would hand the dress over to me in the market. Since she was to wear it next day for the ceremony, I was a little sceptical about whether she would like what I got.

'Oh I always like what you get sweetheart. Thank you,' she said and hugged me. It was nice to be around someone who is so lovely. I was very happy for her.

She immediately called Prathik and the arrangement was made for the dress to be handed over to me at Shopper's Stop near the market I was being taken to.

While sitting in the car, as I was looking for my lip guard in my bag, a small paper came in my hand where Kunal has scribbled something when we last had lunch together. It reminded me of him. It was already two days that I was in Kolkata and I hadn't felt the need to call him yet. Anyway, he had told me he would call me whenever he found time. I had given him Sonali's landline number and even Prathik's mobile number for emergency use.

I soon reached Shopper's Stop. The driver dropped me at the entry while he looked for a parking spot. As I entered, I saw Rahul standing there, waiting for me.

'Here you go,' he said, handing over a packet with Sonali's dress to me.

'Thanks Rahul. I didn't know you were coming to give me this. I hope you didn't have to wait too long,' I said to him.

'Nopes ma'am. At your service! I am here to help with whatever is needed at Prathik's wedding and nothing bothers me with regards to that,' he answered.

'Hmmmm. So, do you work nearby?'

'No. I work for the Taj in Mumbai. I have taken a week off for the wedding so that I can do whatever Romil would have done if he was here. I am very close to him, so...' he said trailing off.

'That is quite nice. So you are all in service. Sounds good,' I replied.

We didn't realise that while talking, we had already climbed up the stairs and gotton onto the women's floor.

'Can I just choose my shoes and earrings in a few minutes?' I looked at him for approval.

'Oh yeah sure. Actually, you carry on, I'll wait downstairs,' he said.

'No no, Rahul, come-on. You can help me choose. I always want second opinion on my stuff.'

He reluctantly followed. I heard him murmur, 'If mom ever comes to know that I actually entered and stayed on the women's floor for over five minutes, she will freak-out. Never done this dear.'

I smiled. He was cute.

We had coffee at Barista before we moved to our respective chores. I liked him almost instantly.

Sonali absolutely loved the scarf I got for her. It was such a relief. I also picked a pair of nice earrings for her, matching that dress.

Finally, the day of the wedding came. I had to accompany her to the place of wedding and reception, both, on the same day and night respectively. Her wedding was in traditional Bengali style. She was looking very sweet with the white and red saree and so was Prathik in his traditional outfit. The ceremony was simple. I had a lot of fun with Sonali's cousins, Rahul and Prathik.

At the wedding, I noticed a certain fondness in Rahul for me. This was the first time I noticed he was quite handsome, with his tall, well-built body.

As I was still lost in my thoughts, Prathik's phone rang. It was Kunal. I was slightly taken aback and quickly moved out of the hall to talk to him.

'How are you doing?'

'Yes yes, I am good. What about you? How are you doing?' I replied.

'I am missing you terribly. I want you back here as soon as possible. I didn't realise I would miss you so much but I do sweety. Please come back soon,' he said and hung up the phone.

I stood there thinking what was all of this that was happening. This was a sign for me to remember I was committed. I had no right to give myself the opportunity to enjoy the feeling of Rahul getting attracted to me.

I composed myself and went into the hall and did all the rituals without giving anything else much thought. I was glad Kunal called and I was also missing him, I realised. He loved me and he trusted me. I reminded myself.

In the evening, it was time for the reception. The reception was an elaborate event. Sonali was so excited. She was wearing a beautiful dress and so was I. I had chosen a fawn-coloured organdi-based evening dress for myself. I knew I looked reasonably good in it. It showed off my curves quite nicely.

Rahul picked us up from the beauty salon. He looked very handsome but there was a slight sadness in his eyes.

I saw him noticing me while we were entering the car but decided to not give it further thought. He complimented me. I just said thanks and let it be. I was in a firm, determined mood to not let anything affect me and my love for Kunal.

We soon reached the hall. Prathik was already there. There were loads of people waiting to give gifts and blessings to the bride and groom. I was to stand on the left side of Sonali and Rahul was on the right side of Prathik. We were meant to collect their gifts and keep them in a safe place. The people wouldn't stop coming. Constantly, though I made no attempt to look towards Rahul, I was sort of conscious that he was looking at me.

Once, I happened to look at him and found him looking straight into my eyes as if trying to say something. Just then, I overheard Prathik mentioning to Sonali that he was thinking that if I wasn't engaged already, then Rahul and I would have made a very graceful couple. He thought it was a bit unfortunate. Rahul heard it too and immediately turned his head to the other side as I looked at him.

I just told myself that this wasn't happening and I was not affected. I focused back on the gifts and guests and just stood there like I didn't know anyone else except Sonali.

I soon took a break to go and eat something with one of Sonali's cousins.

I could sense Rahul's eyes following me.

I ignored my own confusion about my feelings for him and decided to enjoy the wedding. When I returned after a few minutes, Rahul wasn't next to Prathik. I sighed and I went up to the dias to stand near Sonali. In a few minutes, Rahul walked up to the dias from my side, without me noticing him. 'Hey. Why are you avoiding me? Did I do something?' he whispered.

I didn't know what to say. I just lowered my eyes and said I was missing my family.

'Hmmmm. Are you sure you were missing only family?' he said immediately. I looked at him and it was evident from that look that he badly wanted me to say 'Yes' but I said, 'No. I was also missing Kunal.'

He smiled to hide away his disappointment. I turned my attention to the guests who were waiting to handover a gift to me.

Soon, the time came when Sonali was meant to leave her home and move to Prathik's home. She kept sobbing for at least an hour. I could sense how tough it must be to leave one's own home and family and live with another family. I stood there patiently, waiting for her to be ready. Out of the blue, she asked Prathik, 'Can we please take Maaya with us? Please?'

Prathik's mom was a very sweet and gentle lady. She sensed Sonali's unsettledness and she immediately said, 'Well yes, let's take Maaya with us. She is anyway a guest and she came all the way for your wedding. It's our responsibility to make her feel comfortable. You will also find it easy to settle down while she is around. Come Maaya, you come with us,' she said looking at me.

I looked at Sonali's mom and the reluctance on her face. Sonali had already made-up her mind, so I just followed. Anyway I didn't want to get stuck with her relatives while she was gone. I took a few minutes to pack my bags and left with them to Prathik's place.

Prathik had a nice house and I somehow found his family much more warm and welcoming than Sonali's. Just as we entered, Rahul followed me with my bags and showed me my room. This is when I discovered that he was also living in the same house.

I was terribly confused about my feelings for him. Something about Rahul drew me to him. I couldn't understand. As I sat to watch a movie in the living room, Rahul decided to stick around too. We casually started talking.

He told me that guys in Mumbai are always very weary of Delhi girls since they seem to be fast and a handful to handle. It made me laugh. For a while I just let my guilt rest and talked to him. We talked for another two-three hours. As I said something and he didn't respond, I looked at him. He was leaning on the sofa and fast asleep.

Somehow, my eyes got stuck too that innocent look of his while he was sleeping. I took the time to look at him closely since now no one was watching or judging me. Something about that look was very attractive. He looked like an angel and I couldn't stop looking. Soon I realised I needed some rest too. I switched off the light and went off to my room.

We all spent the whole of the following day resting. In the evening, Prathik said to me, 'Maaya, didn't you want to go to Digha beach?'

'Yes and you promised you would take me there,' I replied excitedly.

'Then let's go now. It's a two-three hour drive from here. We shall reach by late evening and can drive back at night, whenever we want to. How's that?' he said, looking at Sonali.

'Yeah. That sounds fun,' she joined in. 'Well, I wouldn't go. You guys have fun. I am planning to do some stuff I have been postponing for a few days. I also have to prepare to get back to work the day after,' said Rahul.

When he said that, it did make me a little sad. On second thoughts, I told myself that it was better that way. By then, I was feeling this intense guilt cropping in me whenever he was around.

'Come-on dude! You will come with us. I can't drive back at night since I plan to booze. You don't drink so you will be our driver back. Maaya is here only for two more days and so are you, so don't be a fuss,' he said in a little commanding voice.

He nodded, stealing a glance at me.

'Get some stuff to eat and one extra pair of clothes, just in case. We are ready to go. My car needs a long drive anyway,' said Prathik excitedly.

Prathik had one of the old Fiat cars which he had saved till then. It was in a pretty decent shape. It was a fun journey. We ate so much on the way. Almost as we were about to reach, Sonali and Prathik had a fight over something Prathik's mom had said to Sonali that she didn't like. Sonali could be very childish at times. She didn't mean to, but managed to hurt people or herself unnecessarily.

The argument flared up and she was so angry that as soon as Rahul stopped the car near the beach, she opened the door and stormed out, slamming the door almost on Prathik's face. Prathik followed her. Rahul parked the car and we were then left to ourselves to spend some time while the love birds patched up.

It was late evening. The sun had almost set and the tides were getting higher. There were a few coconut water stalls nearby and there was a beer garden very close. A chilly breeze was blowing all through and it felt as if I wanted to stay in that place forever.

Rahul and I decided to remove our shoes and walk closer to the water and get the feel of it. I loved beaches and more so, since Delhi didn't have one.

We talked almost about everything under the sun. There was not much sense of time. Neither Rahul nor I was wearing a watch and we decided that we might as well just wait for Sonali and Prathik to patch up and get back to us in a good mood. We couldn't see them anymore. Maybe they were somewhere trying to resolve their fight with a bit of love. I talked and talked and I was enjoying myself.

I didn't have a mobile phone with a roaming till then. None of us had a phone on us at that time, except Prathik. These were the days when mobile phones were not so common. I had one but it was at home. I couldn't afford the roaming charges so I didn't carry it with me.

The tides at the beach were rising and we had to be louder in our conversation. While we were talking, all the time, I was conscious of the fact that Rahul was walking very close to me. Sometimes, his hands would brush against mine and there was sort of a chill that went through me when that happened. I had not felt those kinds of sensations in my body for a very long time. Probably, never!

Slowly, I started getting anxious as to where Sonali and Prathik were. It was getting late and there were no signs of them nearby.

I was a bit lost while walking and one big tide came. As I was about to slip, Rahul instantly held my hand and drew me closer to him from the side, saving me from the slip. We shared a moment then, in each other's eyes.

It was a magical moment. There was surely something I saw in his eyes that I recognised from somewhere. It was so surreal. Suddenly, something came to Rahul's mind and he suddenly let go of me and broke the spell. I also realised the awkwardness of the whole situation. I must admit, that sense of magic was heavy on my head for a very long time.

I recalled that I had to make a call to my family that day, to tell them my plans about coming back and the rest of the details. We decided to walk-up to the phone booth nearby. We had to call Prathik too.

I first called Prathik and he said they were nearby, sitting and talking and they would meet us near the booth in another 15-20 minutes. I then called home and talked to my sister. She said Kunal was missing me badly and suggested that I call him too. I felt a pit in my stomach and my throat went dry. I suddenly felt so guilty especially since all this while, Rahul was standing next to me.

I called Kunal, without warning Rahul. He picked the phone instantly and he seemed to be really sad over something. Rahul was lost in some thought so he didn't notice when I dialled another number.

'Hey,' I said.

'Maaya is that you?' I heard him say.

'Come back Maaya. I am missing you badly. I want you here. There is so much shit going on in office and I can't even share it with you. Anyway, it's been so many days. Don't you miss me at all?'

'Yes, I miss you Kunal. Will be back soon.'

Rahul heard this and he walked out of the booth. He waited for me outside.

'What are you going through at office, tell me,' I asked Kunal.

'Nothing! That same shitty politics and you know I can't handle it. Had a row with a few people on Saturday. Just wanted to tell you about it all. I would have felt lighter. Lately, I have been feeling I never acknowledged you were such a big part of my life, till you went on this trip. It's like you were always there so I never bothered to pay attention. This trip of yours has made me realise it's tough for me to live without your love and support,' he said with a voice that sounded so honest and genuine. I wasn't sure I was happy or sad to hear his confession.

I finished the conversation in a total of five minutes and came out of the booth. There was this terrible chaos going on in my head where I didn't know what I was doing.

I had this very sweet man I loved and who loved me back and I was committed to him for years. I had another sweet man who ever since I had met, I was feeling there was something that was to unfold through this connection. I felt split between the two. I didn't want to hurt either. I didn't know for whom I felt stronger. I hardly knew Rahul till then but the attraction towards him was unimaginable. His likes, dislikes, mannerisms and way of looking at life seemed to be exactly like mine.

Whenever I was with him, I felt a strong sense of divinity between us for some reason. As if someone was pushing me towards him. Kunal, on the other hand, had spent so many years with me. I knew him well. I did love him, but the kind of feelings I was experiencing for Rahul, were unexplored for me too. I didn't know this part of me that Rahul was able to touch. I was becoming more and more aware of how spellbound I felt in his presence. It was a tug of war that was going on in my heart and I didn't even know till then, if Rahul felt anything close to what I did. It didn't seem like a connection of five days, it seemed deeper, much deeper!

I felt very burdened all of a sudden. I was feeling ungrateful, for all the love and blessings that God had showered on me. I felt as if I was getting greedy, I wanted too much and that didn't resonate too well, since I always wanted little but real.

As soon as I came out of the booth, Rahul had this slight sadness on his face and yet he smiled and said, 'You ok?'

I looked at him and said, 'Rahul, I am so confused. What is all this happening to me?'

'It's ok sweety. You love him and for me, you just came at the right time. It's fine. Just give it time. You will sort yourself out,' he said and it seemed as if he knew exactly what was going on.

Meanwhile, we were still looking for words to begin a conversation again, when Prathik and Sonali stepped in and both of them looked visible happy.

'I am sorry for the fuss I created in the car,' she said to both me and Rahul.

'No Sonali, it happens. Sometimes we all get angry or upset. It's a part of being human so you don't have to be sorry at all,' I said and hugged her.

I was happy that Prathik and Sonali had patched up. I was confused and worried about myself though. I couldn't understand why all what happened, did happen and what was meant to happen in the future. We decided to drive back. I had a very disturbed sleep that night.

I was meant to fly back to Delhi the very next day. I said my goodbyes to everyone and at the last minute, Prathik came and announced that since he and Sonali had to go somewhere for some work, Rahul would be dropping me to the airport.

I felt this mix of emotions come back to me all over again. I sat in the car next to him and we didn't speak anything all the way to the airport. As we neared the airport, I felt this twitch in my stomach, as if there was this intense sense of loss. I was cursing myself to have not spoken the whole way and having wasted the time. Nothing could be done then.

When he stopped the car, I just said 'Rahul'and he just put his hand on my mouth and said 'Don't! Don't think so much and don't worry so much. Give yourself time.'

I went quiet.

He bent a little towards me and kissed me very lightly on my lips...almost just touched.

'You will sort it out. Be easy on yourself. I am not running away anywhere. Before you reach Delhi, you will have an e-mail in your mailbox from me. Just take it one day at a time, that's all you can do. Life will unfold. Give yourself three months. I don't want to know anything right now, just give yourself time,' he said.

I sort of felt relieved because I knew this man understood all that was going on with me. He was willing to give me time and the biggest thing was, he promised to keep in touch with me.

The stomach ache eased off a bit and I felt consoled. It was a reassurance that I would be able to resolve my life situation. I had to go slow and give it time. It seemed like the right thing to do. He got out and I realised he had this red rose tucked in his seat pocket. He handed it over to me and kissed me on the forehead. Take care, be safe and don't worry, everything will be ok.

I felt overwhelmed with the whole gesture and was at a loss of words. Just as I quickly took a trolley, he helped me load my baggage on it. I left. When I looked back from the door, he was still there looking at me from the car, as if waiting for me to go in. I went in.

Kunal used to give me red roses when we had begun seeing each other. He knew how much I loved them. Slowly, as our lives got busy, we stopped doing those small little things we used to do for each other. Especially what he did for me.

I missed those moments. They made me feel loved and special. On another hand, I was always conscious of the fact that Kunal was working hard for our future. I couldn't let him be bothered with my small little fantasies.

I was quite confused and stressed all through the flight because there was a continuous flow of negative thoughts going around my head. Finally, I decided to just close my eyes and sleep for a while. The last few days had been hectic and without much sleep, so it wasn't tough to take a nap and forget the whole mess in my head for a while.

Soon I was back to my city. Delhi seemed different suddenly. It was rainy season and I felt that there was some sort of change in my energies from the time I had left this city. Some change within me was evident. All these thoughts were making me nervous. I tried to distract myself by looking and smiling at a cute little child standing near me while I was waiting for my baggage to arrive at the airport.

My parents and my sister were waiting for me anxiously. I couldn't let them notice any of my stress. I straightened up, told my mind to shut up and be normal and walked up to the exit to greet my family after ten days.

Tina was my little sister. She was tall and slender and she was missing me the most, I knew. She hugged me and so did my mom, the moment they saw me. My dad placed a kiss on my cheeks as always. I was happy to see them.

Everything started feeling nice again and whatever was bothering me, didn't seem to last anymore, while I was back with my family.

We were home. Upon sharing my whole experience, I went off to sleep. I hadn't sleep too much in Kolkata anyway so I took a long nap.

When I woke up in the evening, Tina asked me, 'Don't you want to call-up Kunal and tell him you have arrived. He has been missing you. I haven't seen him so sad in years. He really missed you. He called me twice to find out if you were ok and if you were coming today. He called again while you were sleeping.'

All of what had gone, started coming back all over again. Shit, how will I ever face Kunal. I didn't know what to say. I started getting pale and nervous and Tina noticed my nervousness.

'My darling big sister, is everything ok?'

'Yes, Tina. I am just a little tired,' I replied and moved up to the washroom.

As I sat next to the phone to call him, it rang. It was him, I knew.

'Hello,' I said in a little nervous voice.

'Where have you been, Maaya? I have been calling ever since you would have landed. Are you ok?' Kunal said in a little upset tone.

'Yes, I am ok, Kunal. I am sorry but I was very exhausted and just fell asleep after I got home. I should have called,' I replied.

'Yes you should have, but never mind. I am coming near your house in One hour. Say something to your mom and let's meet. It's been so many days,' he said.

It was quite surprising that Kunal wanted to meet me at 6:00 on a weekday evening. He usually worked very hard and till late at night so we didn't get much of an opportunity to meet except on weekends, that too not on all. Whenever he said anything about meeting up, it got me excited but this time, it was different.

I was guilty. I was burdened. I was confused. We fixed up a meeting at 6:00 at the Nirulas near my house.

Kunal got me a rose. As saw it, I couldn't help wondering at the irony that when I wanted a rose, no one gave me one and now it was two in a day.

He hugged me tight and then started asking me about my trip. I requested him to go for a drive. He agreed. While he was driving, he said, 'Are you ok, Maaya? I sense something's wrong with you. Did anything happen in Kolkata?' he said.

I couldn't hold it any further. I had never ever lied to Kunal or hidden anything from him. I was myself confused about what was going on with me. I started sobbing. He parked the car on one side of the road and asked me, 'What happened Maaya? Why are you crying?'

I didn't say a word. I didn't know what to say so I kept quiet. He obviously started asking me again and again and then I finally said, 'I don't know what's going on with me. I met someone in Kolkata Kunal and I sort of got attracted to him,' while I lowered my glance. I didn't want to see his hurt face.

He didn't say a word and just started looking out of the window on the other side.

'Did you sleep with him?' he said suddenly. I sort of froze. I didn't know where that came from. I wondered how that could be the most important question in that moment.

'Of course not!' I said. I felt disgusted even answering that one. It wasn't about the body, it was about the heart. He missed it completely.

This is when I realised how important it was for him to find out if I had a physical relationship with the guy. For me, I always thought emotions matter more but certainly that wasn't the way Kunal thought. I almost felt as if I was a private property of his that had just been encroached. It hurt. From a practical standpoint, I was the one at fault, so I decided to just let it be.

He asked me, 'You still want to marry me?' I didn't know what to say.

He then took us to a coffee bar and we sat there trying to avoid each other's glance. I know I had broken his heart and, more than that, his ego; I was guilty. I just kept quiet as I didn't know what to say or do, since I didn't want to lie any further.

In my heart of hearts, it was less troubling that I fell for Rahul, but what was more disturbing was that my pride broke—the pride I carried for the perfect relationship I had managed to create with Kunal.

Somewhere we were perfect since we didn't fight, we didn't stop each other from doing anything, we didn't need to meet too often for reassurance of our love and we were both mature and sensible. I was happy to become the very woman Kunal wanted.

Rahul was a sign for me that something between me and Kunal was over. In all the years of building the perfect relationship with him, I had lost myself. I had lost my own identity. Rahul introduced me to it after so long. I realised I had forgotten to be myself. I had forgotten my needs, my desires, and my small little wishes. I had become a trophy girlfriend. In my need to be accepted and loved by Kunal, I had left myself behind. The little time I spent with Rahul made me feel myself. There were no dos and don'ts. There was no judgement. There were no restrictions. I could be happy just being myself.

I was not the kind of person Kunal wanted. When we started dating, he made it pretty evident to me that I was not the perfect woman for him but instead I had to work hard to become one. I was overweight, I had a silly sense of dressing and I didn't know when to talk and when to leave him alone. I was so much in love with him that being myself was unacceptable for me.

I reduced a good 30 kgs, I improved my dressing style, I learnt to judge his moods and talk accordingly. I even learnt when I was allowed to call him and when I wasn't. I learnt not to expect anything from him. I learnt that he will shower me with love and affection only when I behave and be what he prefers me to be. I became the ideal woman for him. I was not allowed to crib for his time like other girls did with their boyfriends. I was not allowed to call him whenever I felt like. I was to wait for him to tell me when it's convenient for him to meet me, talk to me, etc. The biggest of all, I was not allowed to say 'NO' to anything.

I managed to do all of the above and more. Till I met Rahul, that seemed like the perfect way to be. I was proud of myself. It was like for love, one has to be unconditional and so was I being unconditional.

Those ten days that I was in Kolkata, I was what I really was, I wasn't trying to expect less, be mature, be unconditional, be understanding but was just being me.

Rahul managed to tap into that space within me which was hidden from Kunal because of what he expected from me. I couldn't understand all of this back then. I was neck deep in guilt and it was all my fault, so I just went with it.

Kunal was making rolls of tissue paper and then putting them on the table and then making holes in the roles using a fork. He was upset. I was not in the state of mind to say or explain anything, since I was also taken aback by what had happened. It sure was not intentional.

I played this big moralistic role in my family and now I was not sure if I could face myself anymore but something inside me said, don't judge, everything happens for a reason.

Kunal looked at me and asked me weird questions about Rahul like what did he look like, what did I like about him, what exactly attracted me to him, was it emotional or physical attraction, did we touch each other, how did it feel when he looked at me and after a point I felt well, I didn't want to answer all of that.

Somehow, I was feeling bad for Kunal and for our relationship but I still felt I didn't deserve to be interrogated like a criminal and neither did I have to feel like one. I said it was an attraction and I couldn't define it in any other terms. It was as much as a shock to me as it was to him because I wasn't really the kind of girl who kept falling for men as and when it suited her.

'So, will you still marry me?' he asked me.

'Do you want to still marry me?' I asked him back.

He went quiet for a moment.

'Yes. Let's put it behind us.' And he came and hugged me. I felt so relieved to know he had forgiven me. When I went back home that day, I was still not sure of what had happened. I didn't know if Kunal and I still had that same relationship that we once had. I felt the crack and it didn't seem like he would let go of it so easily.

I sensed there was more to it but I couldn't be bothered. At that moment, there was one big burden off my chest.

In a few days, a common friend that Kunal and I had and who was very close to Kunal, told me that he had shared with her, what I had done and was asking her for a woman's perspective on the whole thing, I knew Kunal wouldn't let go of it so easily, since he was a logic driven guy with a big ego. It had hurt his ego more than anything else but I decided to give him time, since he wasn't entirely wrong anyway.

In the next few days, no matter how much I tried to avoid it, Rahul kept coming into my thoughts. More and more realisation was strengthening that there was something special with him that I would never be able to experience. The e-mail he promised me wasn't there in my mailbox yet.

I would start crying anywhere, anytime and I didn't know why he was so heavy on my mind. I finally decided to give him a call and see if he had a solution for me.

He picked my call and I said, 'Rahul, how are you?'

'Who's this?'

'Maaya.'

'Oh yes Maaya. I am fine. Hope you are fine too. I am just slightly busy. Can we talk another time please?' he said.

'Yes sure Rahul. It's just that I was getting these thoughts about us and I didn't know how to handle them,' I replied not knowing whatever I was saying.

Suddenly, he said, Us? There is no 'us', Maaya. There never was. You just happened to come at the right time when I had some time to spare and it was all just about a bit of fun. Don't be foolish. You have a planned life ahead of you. Don't ruin it for any silly fantasies Maaya. I am very busy now. Give yourself 90 days, that's the magic number and after that time, you wouldn't have any thoughts about 'us'. Take care!' he said and slammed the phone.

I felt like the biggest fool on earth. It was a miserable situation to be in. The least I could expect from Rahul was to understand. He said it was all fun because he had spare time. Well, that pinched!

The next few weeks, it took me a lot of self-control and will-power to stay sane and focus on my studies, family and Kunal. Kunal was a changed person since the episode. At times when he was angry, he did taunt me about what I had done to him. I thought well, I deserved that so I didn't say anything back. His anger had increased significantly and he tried to control me more than before. His trust was broken and it didn't seem like there was going to be any mending soon.

Many times, when Kunal got upset, he said nasty stuff to me or raised his pitch. I used to cry a lot. We were engaged and my mom once said to me, 'If he makes you cry so much now, I wonder what he will do after you guys get married. Be sure of what you are getting into Maaya. We are with you.'

I took it all on me. That emotion that 'I deserve to be punished' was so strong that it didn't matter. Kunal was always right.

Slowly, as time passed, my determination to do something in my life and keep my relationship with Kunal strengthened. I owed it to him and our years of togetherness. Something inside told me we weren't so much in love anymore. As if all was broken. Yet, I used my willpower to overcome every single thought that bothered me. Kunal and a future with him, however bleak it felt, seemed to promise sanity to me. I couldn't allow myself to drown in my misery. I had to fight. I had to live. I had to love him. It was my destiny.

Every time on yahoo messenger, I found myself wondering if Rahul would ever show up online but I sort of knew he wouldn't.

One day when I just logged into yahoo, I saw Rahul online. Before I could make up my mind about anything, he pinged me. I was quite surprised. I said 'Hey'.

He wrote: 'So, how's it been? ninety days over today'.

I was sort of taken aback. I had forgotten the whole thing about ninety days. It seemed to me as if he was counting days. I couldn't afford to get into the misery again. I had made up my mind. I had a life ahead of me and I was not going to ruin it.

'Yes. I know. It's been good. You were right. Ninety days is all it takes,' and left him thinking I had got over him.

I could sense he was disappointed. I couldn't forget how he had treated me on the call. I couldn't forgive him for the suffering I went through. I couldn't allow myself to crave for him again. I know I wasn't completely successful in winning that war within myself but I was determined.

'Well...I always knew it. Take care and I am glad you are happy,' he said and he logged off and so did I.

I never heard from Rahul again for a while. About five days after I got married to Kunal, I went to the cafe to check my e-mails. I was off from office for a few days while Kunal was busy working. My mailbox blinked with a mail from Rahul. It read:

'Hey Maaya.

Prathik told me that he was in Delhi for your wedding. I am glad you and Kunal finally decided to tie the knot. I would have come to your wedding if you had invited me. Wanted to see you dressed as a bride. I know you must be looking beautiful. My blessings are with you for the rest of your life.

I will pray you have an amazing life Maaya. You deserve it.

Love

Rahul

PS: Kunal is a lucky bastard and I always knew you loved him. Didn't mean to hurt you ever Maaya but I said all of that because I knew in ninety days, you would get over me. You did well. It was not meant to be. God Bless.'

I went numb. Something happened to me. I completely lost track of where I was and what I was doing for a few moments. It was as if time stopped.

This was when it dawned on me. He said all of that on purpose. Rahul wanted me to take the call of staying with Kunal or leaving him on my own free will. He loved me too. He just wanted me to reclaim my life on my own strength and decisions. He just wanted me to make a place for him in my life.

What had I done!

I had failed. I didn't get it all the way. I felt so small in front of him. So silly! It was true, I didn't trust him, and I didn't trust myself.

That day, that moment, I felt like some part of my heart broke forever. It wasn't about Kunal and neither was it about Rahul, it was about me and my relationship with myself that was scared.

I had lost the biggest happiness in my life. Not because I was guilty for Kunal or my commitment to him but because I was guilty for being happy, for deserving my own happiness. It took me a long journey to realise that there is no real need to punish ourselves for being wrong, immoral or sinful.

Most of us will stand against our own happiness in the name of 'sacrifice'. It took me a lot of wisdom to understand what I thought was my 'sacrifice' was only a choice I couldn't make. Even though in that moment I thought it will save Kunal from hurt, it inevitably created more hurt for both of us in the long run.

I so worried about creating bad *karma* against Kunal by hurting him. Only in that moment after reading that letter did I realise I had instead chosen to hurt myself. I did meet my true soulmate but I lost him. I lost him because the opportunity to be with him came with a challenge to stand-up for myself, to trust myself, to trust my feelings. I couldn't do it. I failed.

It's not that hurting Kunal would have been right but it was only a few years later that I realise that by not choosing Rahul, I only postponed the suffering for Kunal and me by a few years. When we got divorced, I knew Rahul had a role to play. He came to show me how I didn't love Kunal anymore, but I didn't get it then. I often told myself maybe Aryan was to come to me that way. He was also my soulmate. He came to help and support me in my journey. Maybe that is why Kunal and I went along the journey together. But when we separated, we had valid reasons by then to walk out on each other because enough effort, time and work had gone into trying to make our relationship work. It just seemed more justified, though we both lost a few years in the process and maybe gained some wisdom, if not anything more.

I also know it didn't happen in that moment because Kunal and I had to experience strong *karma* together. That explanation only seemed lame compared to the pain I felt in the instance.

□

What Never Was

It had been so long since Sonali's wedding but those days remained vivid in my memory till now. It was strange but I understood it much later that God gave me a sign to understand I was not meant to be with Kunal but I chose on my own free will to ignore it.

Years later, Rahul and I recognised each other instantly when we met at a café which was in his office building. I was waiting for Pooja there.

He came up to me and said, 'Hey Sweets! Remember me?' while I was busy searching for something in my sling. I couldn't believe it when I saw him that close.

'Hi.....' My mouth fell open.

'Good! So you do remember me Ms. Maaya,' he said smiling and pushed his hand forward to close my mouth. I was thinking well, I couldn't have forgotten you Rahul. Never ever!

I straightened up quickly realising what a fool I must be looking like completely zapped.

'So, how have you been? What are you doing here?' I asked him sounding as if it was absolutely normal that I met this man, who had turned my life upside down once.

'I am good. I must be asking you that one though. I work here, with an American bank right on the 7th floor. Came down to have a coffee,' he replied.

'What about you? How have you been, Maaya? We never kept in touch, it's a shame. How is Kunal doing?' he said. Was I glad to know he had moved to Delhi, I wondered.

'I am good and getting better. Kunal and I are not together anymore. We got divorced a year back. I have a 7-year-old son. I now live here and am working for an ad agency, my office is in CP.' I said all of that in one long breath in order to avoid a series of questions he was about to ask me.

He looked visibly sad hearing about me and Kunal splitting up. Before he could express himself, I saw my friend Pooja coming from behind, so I said, 'No need to be sorry, Rahul. I am happy. I really am. Everything happens for a reason and my Aryan was the reason we married. He was to come to me. I am really sorry but I have to go as my friend is here. I handed over my business card to him and said, 'Call me when you have time, we'll catch-up. Bye'.

Somehow being in the presence of Rahul after so many years was making me feel weird vibrations in my stomach. I needed time to digest it.

Before Pooja could realise I was standing with Rahul, I told him we'll catch-up later, gave him my business card and moved towards her. I wanted to let the feeling sink in first.

In my big fuss, I absolutely forgot to ask Rahul about his family. Pooja and I moved out of that building soon after and that night, all those memories from Sonali's wedding came rushing back. I told my mind to give it a rest, since I assumed he must be a happily married man. He knew what he wanted in life. There was no reason for me to get affected by whatever happened ages ago.

The very next day, Rahul called me. I was almost waiting for that call.

'Hey sweetie', is what he said as he always did.

'Hey Rahul. How are you?' I replied. He had messaged me his number the previous evening.

'Hmmmm. To be honest. I am a bit lost. I don't know what to say but I believed you and Kunal were meant for each other,' he said.

'I don't want to discuss this, Rahul. Let's please talk about something else,' I said.

'Ok, tell me about your family. How are you doing?' I said, trying to change the topic.

'I have a beautiful wife and a 3-year-old daughter,' he said. I had a sort of sinking feeling in my body but I quickly regained my balance and said, 'Congratulations Rahul. I am happy for you'.

'I am sure you are Maaya. I am currently separated from my wife due to some issues between us. I am not exactly sure where my life is heading, so not really at a stage where I can congratulate myself,' he replied.

I felt a sort of sadness in my heart for this was one man I had always seen and imagined to be happy and high on spirits.

'I don't know what to say, Rahul,' I said.

'Nothing Maaya. It's all a part of life. Let's celebrate for old time sakes because I am living alone here in Delhi. I am sick of the food my cook makes.'

'Can I take you out for dinner?' he said.

I was excited at the prospect of spending time with him. I had always wanted to meet him sometime again in life and maybe just talk.

'Can we go tomorrow Rahul? I will leave Aryan at my mom's place since tomorrow is Friday. I will then be free. On other days, I need to send him to school in the morning and hence dinner is not an option,' I replied.

'Sounds like a plan. Shall pick you up at 8:00 tomorrow. Send me your address over a message,' he said and put the phone down.

Next evening, sharp at 8:00, Rahul was right outside my apartment gate to pick me up. As I rushed to the gate and hopped into his long car, he said, 'Hey sweetie. Looking sexy!', I think I blushed.

I had not heard anyone call me 'sexy' in a while. I knew I was pretty and good looking but 'sexy' was a word not many people dared to use with me. Rahul was different.

'Same old Sufi music?' I asked Rahul.

'Wow, you still remember! I love this music and as far as I remember you liked it too,' he said.

'I had never heard Sufi before I met you but I must admit I have been a fan ever since. It has helped me in tough times. Love it too.'

He smiled and it showed on his face how proud he was to introduce me to one of the most amazing forms of music. I was thankful to him for that. Over the years, I had developed a taste for it and couldn't have imagined spending time with myself, without Sufi. It was nice to sit with him in his car and listen to our favourite music. It reminded me of old days.

For me, music, and especially Sufi music, had the ability to calm my energies and make me comfortable even in pain. Each song's lyrics came from the writer's heart, sung by the singer's soul. I wondered how they managed to project such deep insights about life and love in such rhythm. It touched me deep. With Rahul next to me, it seemed like I needed nothing more. I was in bliss. I wonder if I was pushing myself back into the old misery but I seem to have lost the power to think back then.

We decided to go and eat Thai because that was one cuisine both of us loved and agreed on. We talked about our lives ever since we met and all about what worked and what didn't work.

Not once did we touch upon the subject of 'US' in the whole conversation. It was nice to be with Rahul again and now those days and those memories looked silly somehow.

He dropped me at my place and just when I was about to get out of the car, he flipped me back in by pulling my hand and we shared a moment, just like the one ages ago.

All my blood came rushing to my heart. I almost skipped a beat. It felt as if we were transported back in time. Suddenly, he cupped my face in his hands and kissed me on my forehead. My breath was so heavy and for a few moments it seemed like I'd lost sense of everything. He then quickly pulled himself back, giving me this teary, emotional look in his eyes and resorted to putting on his seatbelt.

I was still awestruck when I reached my apartment and unlocked it. 'What was that meant to be?' – was the question doing its rounds in my head.

I was quite tired, so I didn't think about all of it too much and just went to sleep. I was actually scared of giving too much attention to Rahul all over again. I was scared of getting myself into a state of mind where I once used to be. I didn't want any of that. I was happy with my life and was not really looking for too much except giving all I could to my Aryan.

Kunal and I had separated after six years of staying together and trying to make it work. We really didn't have too much in common. I had changed and transformed myself to what he wanted me to be. Slowly as I started to be what I really was, he didn't like the 'me' that I was.

Basically, a lot of our love was probably over much before we started realising it and we drifted apart quickly in our ambitious careers and zero sex life.

We were good friends and we shared a lot of stuff but somewhere Kunal couldn't become what I always wanted him to be...a lover.

Slowly, we started arguing, fighting, disagreeing and it became evident that it was getting tougher to stay under the same roof. The love between us, whatever left, was over. It made more sense to separate and still share an amicable relationship than fight and abuse each other and end up as enemies.

Obviously, my parents didn't want us to separate. They had their own insecurities. Kunal's parents had passed away, so it was up to him to take all decisions of his life, unlike me. Sometimes, even in the midst of all of the turbulence, Kunal mentioned that he loved me but I guess the gap between us was too much to be mended. The love, whatever little was left, had lost its authenticity in the fights and arguments. He had stopped touching my heart. We had gone too far in hurting and disrespecting each other that loving each other again seemed to be too much of an effort. I didn't like who I became when I was with him. It was too suffocating and it didn't seem like 'me' anymore. We did realise in our own ways that by staying in the marriage, we were only increasing our misery.

I felt guilty at times because I blamed myself for being responsible for this relationship dying. At other times, I knew we were not made for each other.

We finally decided to call it off. I found it easier to deal with the vacuum the relationship left in my life than with misery of being in it and I knew it was nothing to do with Kunal. It was mostly to do with this journey I was being prepared for, which I found out later.

While living in the Indian culture, breaking a marriage is a very big thing. Even in modern times, our society expects people to have 'big' or 'tragic' reasons to walk out on each other. The ability to love each other and live by it, mostly comes after the ability to compromise and just stay in the marriage. It's more about the family, the elders, and the children. It's hardly about the love and happiness of the two individuals involved. In each marriage, there are a set of relationships that are formed and good or bad, each of them contribute to each other's *karmic* journey. There is no 'right' time to walk out of a marriage and there isn't any judgement about it too. The soul has lived so many times, been married so many times, so as much as the sanctity of a marriage needs to be preserved, so does the love.

In the absence of love and compassion, even if the two individuals decide to stay with each other, they only create more misery for each other and lead incomplete lives. Each soul involved in such a situation has chosen the situation to be able to face it and learn something from it. It is wiser to take the route of lesser hurt for both involved and end it gracefully than suffocating in the relationship and then ending up blaming and torturing each other for life.

When a marriage breaks for no apparent tragic reason, it is overwhelming for all. It gives an opportunity to all your neighbours, friends and relatives to give you advice or seek more insight into the whole situation.

There were very few people who were genuinely concerned for me or Kunal while for all others, either it was just a sad thing or they were just excited about the prospect of something unusual happening.

Thankfully, my parents were very supportive of me. I didn't have to really go through the process of unnecessary advice, which was a relief.

I immediately shifted to Pooja's place near my parent's place. Aryan was happy to have a stable life, a good school and no fights between his parents. I had to recreate a life for myself. My parents didn't interfere at all but their love and concern for me was understandable and yet it was overwhelming at times.

I was so proud of my father who just told me one thing before my divorce. He said, 'My child, I just want a promise from you and you are free to do whatever you want. You will have all my support.' 'What is it papa?' I asked nervously. He said, 'You will never cry. I can't see you cry. If you are not happy, move out. Till I am alive, you will never feel you are alone. Just don't ever make yourself miserable. Make this an opportunity to recreate life. You can. You must.'

I hugged him and the blessing I felt at that moment is tough to define in words.

I wonder why I was recalling all that went wrong between me and Kunal upon meeting Rahul again. The time that Rahul and I spent together over dinner was refreshing. I was just escaping the thought of us getting together again. Those were dangerous thoughts. I tried ignoring them completely for a few days at least.

The next few days, Rahul and I didn't interact. I got busy with my work and he probably got busy with his. Suddenly, about two weeks later, I received an SMS from him saying, 'Hey Sweetie. Up for a coffee in the evening?'

I was relatively free that evening and Aryan was at his friend's place for a sleep-over, so I said 'yes'.

Rahul looked really low that day.

'What's wrong, Rahul? Is everything ok with you?' I asked.

'Well, yes. Did you miss me ever since the last time we met?'

I was not prepared for this question, but I replied, 'Not really. I did think of you once or twice but I got busy with my work. Why do you ask me that, Rahul?'

'Nothing. I have been thinking of you ever since that day. I have been wondering what was the reason we met when we did and what is the reason that we met again at this stage in life? It's like a puzzle I have been trying to solve,' he said, looking at me with tenderness in his eyes.

I didn't know what to say. I had a lot of anxiousness with regards to getting personal with Rahul. I dreaded a situation where I could be miserable all over again. I had been through enough in life and I really didn't want surprises anymore.

I adjusted my posture in my seat and said, 'I don't know, Rahul. Maybe it's not worth analysing too much,' as I picked my cup of hot cappuccino and sipped it, looking at him in the eye.

'Maybe. I must admit I didn't feel as if so much time has passed between our last meeting and this one. I don't feel like a stranger to you even after so many years,' he said, looking down and trying to avoid my gaze.

I just told myself to stop thinking in the direction I was getting inclined to. I had to stop looking at his face. Rahul was quite good-looking. He was tall and fair with high, sharp cheekbones. 'Dashing', one could call him and he dressed up really well too. He was quite a feast for all those women in the coffee shop. I then noticed he was drawing a lot of female attention. It amused me that he was wasting his time sitting with me and discussing things that probably didn't matter now. He could make better use of those looks, said the naughty girl in me.

We finished our coffee while it was already getting dark. Rahul offered to drop me but I told him that I'd rather take a cab. I usually drove to my office but that day my car was out for servicing at the service station. So I took a cab home.

He did try to insist but, since that day, I didn't want to be with him in the car alone, especially when it was getting dark. I didn't want to face any situation which would have all my emotions coming flooding back after all these years.

After all, he had a family and he had not exactly said that he was planning on giving them up. It did seem like he was fond of his wife and they were just away from each other for a few months, so that they could settle their differences. I didn't want to interfere and this was very clear in my head.

I was relieved that I could manage to keep the friendly meeting simple, or rather, 'less complicated'.

The entire week at work was busy. A delegation had flown in from Japan to meet our creative team for an Indo-Japanese project. Gagan expected me to take care of all their concerns with regards to the creative technicalities. It kept me occupied till late hours for the next four-five days.

The following Monday I was at my office when my phone beeped. It was a message from Rahul: 'Hey Sweetie. How are you doing today?'

I didn't know why he was checking up on me, especially on a Monday morning full of deadlines and fuss.

'I am good, Rahul. Have heaps of stuff to do. Everything ok with you?' I replied.

He replied with an SMS saying 'Yeah...I am cool. Was just thinking about you.'

I replied, 'What exactly were you thinking about...me?'

My phone beeped a third time, 'Don't know. You are still the same, Maaya. So transparent, so beautiful and so yourself,' he said.

'Thanks for the compliments, Rahul but this isn't exactly the time. My boss will not like it if I am not transparent on how I spend my office time,' I replied.

'Meet me in the evening over coffee? I am coming near your office for a meeting,' he replied.

Dev looked at me with suspicion when my phone beeped continuously after every two minutes.

'Ok done. Meet me at 6 at CCD. Now let me get back to work. See you,' I wrote and put the phone over my desk.

One last time, it beeped and it said, 'See you soon. Looking forward to it, Maaya.'

I found myself wondering what was wrong with him.

Dev finally thought this could go on forever, so he ignored. He was cute and sweet. He knew when not to ask the wrong question. I loved this about him.

This had almost become a regular practice now. Rahul would send me loads of messages about everything and whenever he was around my office, we would catch up for coffee and have a good time just chatting away. I was enjoying the new definition of our relationship and somehow it was even helping me. I had pretty much stopped talking to a lot of people after I moved away from Kunal.

One evening I was sitting at a couple's place, both of whom were my friends, when Rahul called up around 10:00 p.m. They lived in the same building as I did. We usually spent Friday evenings together while our children played with each other.

I picked up the call and he said, 'Maaya, please come out to your gate, I have to show you something.'

'I can't, Rahul, and what is it that is so important right now?'

'I've got a new haircut and you have to see it,' he said.

I made an excuse to walk to the balcony and talk to him. 'I am half drunk and it's like 10:00 p.m. and you want me to come out and meet you to see a haircut? What's wrong with you Rahul.'

'Oh, please, please, please, Maaya! I so badly want your opinion on it. Please come, it'll take only five minutes. I promise.'

I just didn't get the whole fuss about the haircut. He wouldn't budge.

'Ok...will be there in ten minutes,' I said and put the phone down.

I made a silly excuse to my friends again, of doing something at home which I would take me fifteen minutes and walked up to the gate. Rahul was already there in his Honda, waiting for me to step in. As soon as I sat in the car, he showed me his new hairstyle like this little child, fishing for compliments.

'Yeah, it looks nice, Rahul.' I smiled.

Initially, I found this whole exercise silly but soon it seemed rather innocent and cute. Then when he was happy that I approved, he started telling me about his day and the hair stylist and blah blah blah. I looked at my watch and realised twenty minutes had already passed so I told him that I needed to go.

As I was about to walk out of the car, he suddenly held my hand and said, 'No Maaya. You forgot that it's my birthday today.'

I didn't realise it really was 18th December and it was his birthday. I was wondering how I could forget the day that I had remembered for years together.

'I am so sorry, Rahul. Happy birthday! I am so sorry I missed it. I shouldn't have. I don't know what to say.' I was obviously very ashamed.

I looked at his cute innocent face. It was clear that he felt a bit hurt. I bent forward and give him a hug. It felt so nice. This was when I realised my body responded differently to his touch.

It was more of an embrace. Rahul then held me tight, as if he wouldn't let me go.

Before I realised, I felt his warm breath on the back of neck. Soon my whole body was defying my mind. I didn't want to let go of him as he softly kissed me on the back of my neck. Ripples went down my throat. The sweet smell of gel in his hair was so erotic.

I didn't know what I was doing, but automatically, my hands started brushing his hair and he started kissing me all over my neck, first on the back and slowly towards the front. Then his lips slowly moved up from my neck to my ears and then slowly up to my lips.

My lips parted as if it was the most natural thing to do. He kissed me long and soft and I felt my body melting into his arms. He was then kissing me passionately all over my face. It was so awesome that had a car behind us not blown it's horn really hard, we wouldn't have come back to the real world just as quick.

Suddenly, I broke away from him when I heard the horn and realised what had just happened. I didn't say a word to him but just composed myself, opened the door and walked away.

I'd only walked a few steps, when Rahul held my hand from behind. 'Don't run away from me, Maaya. I've waited for this moment long enough. Can we please go to your apartment and talk about this?'

I was still lost from what had happened. I just shook my head and we moved into my apartment which was very close to the main gate. Thankfully I had the keys in my hand since Aryan was still at my friends' place. I didn't know what I was doing but the impact of Rahul's presence with me was so overwhelming that I had lost the ability to think. As we entered the apartment and closed the door behind us, Rahul held me by the waist and looked into my eyes. His eyes seemed watery and full of so many emotions. I felt my heartbeat getting stronger as he looked at me, as if trying to find something in my eyes. He then bend forward and kissed me again. This time, it was much deeper. I felt as if something inside me was getting sucked into him. Our bodies were now touching each other. The feel of his body made me melt. It felt like we didn't have separate existences. The beauty was that neither of us were expecting this to go any further and we were comfortable in just being close, knowing that we were there for each other. He said to me, 'I may not have said it in so many words, but you are my goddess.' Having said that, he gave me a kiss on my forehead and left. I didn't understand what he said but it seemed like he touched my being somewhere deep.

I then realised I had to apologize to my friends for ruining the evening and also get Aryan from their place. We finished our dinner and soon Aryan and I were back to our apartment. That night, I went to sleep with a smile on my face and lightness in my heart.

When I woke up the next morning, there was a sense of fear. Whatever happened the previous evening put me at peace, and yet, I rose as if with this fear of being miserable all over again in my need for love from him again. It was a very painful feeling.

Just then, my phone beeped and it was Rahul's SMS. 'How are you doing this morning sweetheart?' he said.

'I am scared, Rahul. I can't allow myself to be hurt again. I just can't,' I wrote back.

'I love you, Maaya. I've loved you ever since I saw you for the first time, years ago. I let go of you because I wanted you to take your own decisions in your life. I didn't want you to break bonds because of me. This time, I won't let that happen, Maaya. You and I are meant to be,' he wrote back.

I read and reread the 'I love you Maaya' part of it in disbelief. There was a whole gush of emotions which were buried far deep inside me. Whatever I was trying so hard to avoid had just happened.

Tears started rolling down my cheeks for in my heart I felt that familiar pain which I endured for maybe years together. It probably never went away completely. I could hear the echo of when Rahul told me 'There is no 'US' Maaya'. I was so blank and so lost. I didn't know what to say or what to do. Here was this man whom I loved in ten days what I couldn't love my husband in ten years. Now when life was giving me yet another chance to love him and belong to him, I was so confused. I didn't quite know if that was what God's plan for me.

'Rahul, I don't know if we were meant to be. You are still married and I am not sure if we have anything to look forward to. Had it been all those years ago, I would have given anything for you to say this to me but things are different now. Life has taken us on separate journeys. Maybe we should just cherish the memory of what happened last night and move on our own separate paths. That's our destiny, Rahul,' I wrote back to him.

He didn't respond to that message. I kept the phone on my side the whole day, constantly checking if he had written back but there was no reply. I didn't even know what was I expecting him to write but there was so much anxiety inside me. I had a disturbed sleep the entire next night too.

Gagan had arranged for a lot of flex vendors to come and show us samples of the artwork they could do for a new client of ours the next day. It was a working Saturday. I was supposed to sit with him in the presentations and give my inputs on the quality and theme chosen by them. It was a whole list of ten vendors in one day and each presentation took at least 20-30 minutes. So it was a day packed with back-to-back meetings. In spite of the busy schedule, I would return to my desk after every meeting and check my mobile expecting a word from Rahul, but there was none.

I just went on with the day mechanically and that evening I got late at office. Aryan had called twice to check-up on me, telling me that he was having fun at my mom's place but missing me too. I constantly thanked God for giving me a child that I was never sure I deserved. Whenever there was something going on with me, he sensed it somehow and his energies gave me the strength to deal with it. I knew he had come to help me and ground me and he did that job pretty well.

By the time I was ready to leave, it was already 8:00 and since I again didn't have my car that day, Gagan offered to drop me on his way. I didn't know if I should take a lift from my handsome boss but since it was raining and dark, I decided I might as well. We had an almost quiet drive with Gagan just telling me to make a mental note of things we needed to do the next week in order to freeze the campaign.

As soon as I got down from his car, Gagan rolled down his window to tell me one last thing he wanted me to do the following Monday. Just then I saw Rahul standing on the other side of the road. I said good night to Gagan and walked up to Rahul. He seemed to be in bad shape. He held my hand and pulled me to sit in his car.

'We are going for a drive!' he announced.

'Wait Rahul. I have had a very long day. I am damn tired and I am hungry.'

'Just sit in the car, Maaya. We will eat somewhere, but just sit.' His voice carried some command coupled with some sadness and I couldn't argue with him right in front of my gate so I decided to sit in the car.

'Aryan is waiting for me Rahul. I need to call him and maybe go pick him up.'

He ignored my concern and started the engine. We didn't speak for a few minutes. When I looked at him, he seemed very low and upset to me. Looked like he hadn't shaved as well.

'Where are we going Rahul?'

He pulled over the car very near a CCD and then he looked at me. At first I thought it was my imagination but I saw tears in his eyes. He held me in his arms and said, 'I love you Maaya. I really love you. I don't know what is happening to me but I just know I don't want to lose you again. If you walk out of my life, I don't know what I will do. Please don't do this, Maaya. Don't ask me so many questions. Trust me Maaya, I wouldn't hurt you ever. You mean a lot to me.'

I could see it in his eyes that he really meant it.

I instantly hugged him because I couldn't see him in that state and definitely not because of me. He hugged me back but a real tight one.

'Please don't leave me and go, Maaya. I can't do without you. I love you a lot. Please be mine forever. I know I hurt you once but that was not intentional. I somewhere believed if you loved me enough you would leave Kunal and come but you didn't. I then convinced myself that maybe it wasn't love after all. I can't let you go again. I just can't,' he said, kissing me in my hair.

That moment, something inside me made a promise to him that I wouldn't leave him ever. I loved him too, always did but I had a lot of fears and insecurities with regards to our future. At that moment, all of that seemed irrelevant.

It seemed like all that mattered to me was to know that Rahul loved me. I then surrendered us to the one above and told him to make way for us. I let go of all my questions and insecurities at that point and said, 'I love you too Rahul. I wouldn't leave you, my baby. If this is what is God's plan then so be it. I love you too.' We stayed that way for what seemed like hours.

It was the beginning of a whole new phase in my life. I had never been loved so much. He was unconditional and unreasonable in every way, when it came to loving and pampering me.

We met at least once a day, if not more.

Very soon he discovered this perfect way to be with me at least once a day. He joined my gym. It took him a good 15-20 minutes of drive to get there but he said it was worth it. Sometimes I almost felt like a teenager and yet I realised that love makes people behave in unpredictable ways. That's the beauty of it.

He was adorable and I couldn't have asked for more. My life was magical and he made it so. We shared everything that went on in our lives and he was completely unabashed about how he felt for me.

A few months passed by and it didn't feel like that at all till I started noticing changes in him. He started getting lost while talking to me. Sometimes, he would want to say something but would stop. I didn't understand. His messages also started reducing. Sometimes, I could see the same old Rahul in him and sometimes, it felt I didn't know this person at all. He attributed it to work stress but I sensed something was wrong.

One day, he casually called me and said, 'Neha and Anushkha have come to stay with me.' I froze in that position over the phone. Over the past few months, I had completely forgotten about his wife and child. I had forgotten that Rahul was still married and this was also a possibility. We were so involved and so in love that we just lived in the moment each day and each night. With all the love and affection he showered on me, I never really wanted to discuss a future, etc. because I thought all would fall into place whenever the time was right.

'Maaya, please don't worry,' he said when I went silent for a few seconds.

'Anushkha was missing me and Neha just decided to drop-in. They will be here only for a few days for her vacation and then back to Jaipur. I am sorry Maaya and I know how you feel but trust me, it's just temporary. I don't know what she has in her mind but I love you only,' he said.

'I have a lot of work to do today. You enjoy!' I said as I kept the phone down.

I felt this sudden pain in my stomach as if someone had just pulled some string in my naval.

I told myself to focus on work since there was too much to do and Gagan was getting anxious about the deadlines. I just told my mind to shut up and focused on my work till the evening. I didn't hear from Rahul until next evening.

It was Aryan's best friend's birthday that evening and so we had to buy a gift and go for the party. I didn't really feel like going, since the last few weeks I was very stressed at work and now Rahul's wife was constantly at the back of my mind. I knew I owed some quality time to Aryan and he wasn't getting too much so I decided to do it anyway. We bought a nice gift and went to the party. Aryan seemed to be having a nice time. There were a few mommies I knew from school, whose kids studied in the same class as Aryan, so it was just sitting there and patiently listening to them discussing dresses and jewellery and most of all, their mothers-in-law. Not that I enjoyed all of the conversation but I must admit, it proved to be a good distraction.

Next evening, when I was finishing office, Rahul called, 'Meet me at the gate baby, I will be waiting'.

Suddenly, I felt alive all over again. I was dying to hear his voice and him addressing me as 'baby' just as he did, somewhere helped me that believe nothing had changed between us.

I quickly packed my bag and left from office. As I parked my car near my gate, Rahul came and sat with me in my car. He hugged me. He had something in his hands I opened his fist and it was a shishido eye shadow. Rahul always told me he loved my makeup and he loved the eye shadow I wore.

'I sneaked into the ladies store while Neha was shopping for some stuff and bought this for you. I loved its shade and thought it will look perfect on you,' he said, handing it over to me.

I kissed him on his cheek and said, 'Thank you sweetheart. I love it.'

I was so happy to have my Rahul back. 'There is something I want to share. My parents are planning to move to Delhi, from Kolkata. They want Neha and me to stay together and try and sort out our differences while they are here,' he said, looking right into my eyes.

I looked away from him as a tear rolled from my eye. He wiped the tear away and said, 'Please don't lose heart baby. You know I love you. I will just let them have their last say and let them see how she and I can't live together under one roof and then we will get divorced. You know I don't love her, don't you?'

'I know you love me Rahul but I also know your family wants you two to stay together. I really never intended to spoil someone's family and now I am becoming responsible for your family breaking. Also, I am not sure they will let you leave her just like that. I am sure if she is willing to be a part of this exercise means she wants to restore your relationship with her,' I said with a lot of sadness settling in my chest.

'Maybe she does Maaya but we have a history remember? I have told you everything Maaya and I don't love her anymore. There was a time when I did give her every opportunity to make it up to me. I went to every extent to save us from this but then she was the one who didn't want it to happen. I am not falling for it, Maaya. I am just doing this for the sake of my parents because they would be happier if I gave it one last try in front of them, before calling it off,' he said.

I didn't know what to say. I just nodded and he hugged me as if wanting me to understand. I loved this man so much that I was willing to do whatever it took to be able to tell myself that I would be with him always and that it was not going to change.

It had been only a few months that we had been together but somehow, the bond felt so natural, so old, and so strong that even the thought of being without him created a lot of anxiety inside me.

One evening when he dropped me at the gate, Kunal was standing there. He looked at Rahul and came closer to us. I introduced them both and immediately Kunal said, 'Is he the same Rahul you met in Kolkata?'

A shiver went down my body. Somehow, even though Kunal and I were no more man and wife, there was this effect that Kunal had over me. He made me nervous. I felt some sort of fear in his presence or in other words, he had the ability to intimidate me.

'Yes. He is the same one but we lost touch and accidentally met after so many years,' I said looking at Rahul.

'Yes I am sure that is the case. I just came to see if Aryan is around. I was in town so just thought would give him a ride. Was trying your number but you didn't pick up. I guess you must have been busy,' he said looking at me and then Rahul. I knew he didn't believe me when I said that Rahul and I had lost touch. I saw some sort of disgust in his eyes for Rahul.

Rahul left and Kunal left, too after picking Aryan up and it took me a while to digest the incident.

Rahul called asking, 'Are you ok, Maaya? I know how you must be feeling,' he said.

'Yes I am fine. Just that Kunal still manages to have some weird impact on me. He gets me stressed.'

'Yes I saw that. Can I say something sweetie, if you don't mind?' Rahul said.

'Yes sure. You can say anything, Rahul.'

'I don't know but I felt he still loves you. He thinks it was because of me that you guys couldn't have a successful marriage. I don't like the guy but I think he is not doing great without you,' he said. Rahul's statement sort of took me back to a ride of guilt trips over my marriage and that was something I always tried to avoid.

'Rahul, maybe you are right but the fact is, it is over and only I know how it made me feel to stay in that marriage so let's not discuss it any further. Additionally, aren't you happy that it didn't work and we met all over again and fell in love?'

'Of course, I am, sweetheart. That was just a thought. Anyway, chuck it. I guess something got triggered,' he replied. We exchanged our good night wishes and went to sleep.

Aryan was spending the night with Kunal so he was away. I had all the time in the world to relax and have a good night's sleep. I couldn't sleep too much anyway. Kunal's face and that look when he saw Rahul, were haunting me.

Finally, I must have managed to sleep sometime in the wee hours.

Those days, Rahul's behaviour was one big reason for my stress. I could see him changing everyday. He had started looking at things from a different perspective. He seemed sad many times and it looked like I was no more his priority in life. It was as if he was confused and yet in denial.

I did try and talk things out with him but he just kept ignoring this issue. He always tried to show me that everything was alright but somewhere within, I sensed all was not well. The gap between us only grew in the days that came.

Neha was trying her best to win him back and he had started falling into a guilt trap with regards to his child. Earlier, he used to discuss everything openly with me but slowly, all that started to change. He didn't pamper me as much, sometimes didn't return my calls in time and sometimes he even forgot he was meant to call me. I couldn't relate to him as the same Rahul I loved.

Things started getting worse and he avoided talking about them with me. I knew there was something brewing but he was not ready yet. The insecurity was killing me. I didn't know for sure if he really loved me anymore or the love was over by then. That is when I decided to take that step and move away from him. That is when I wrote that letter that changed everything.

□

Past Lives and The Karmic Cycle

Ever since that call to Rahul and hearing him say he didn't feel the same way anymore, I didn't know where my life was going. I missed him so much and all I could remember was the few months we spent together, loving and cherishing each other.

I didn't know what had gone wrong. Either I did not understand what had happened to him at all or I was in denial. I constantly asked myself that how could someone who loved me so much suddenly stop relating to it? But I didn't get a response.

The next few days, I decided to focus on my work. Rahul was constantly in my thoughts like a background process always running in the CPU. It was so painful, to walk around doing everything and yet feeling so incomplete.

'Hey Maaya. How are you doing my dear?' I heard a voice say while I was about to leave office one evening.

'I am ok Shirley. How about you?' I turned around greeting Shirley.

'Well, you certainly don't look ok, Maaya. What's wrong?' she said straightaway.

That is when I realised I must really look messed up that she could instantly notice. Suddenly, I found myself saying, 'Will you give me a past life regression session, Shirley? Please?'

'Oh yes, Maaya. I would love to. Do you want to talk about what's bothering you?' she said. I looked at Gagan's cabin and she said, 'Oh, it's ok. Gagan has some stuff to finish anyway, so you and I can spend some time chatting,' as she walked up to Gagan's door.

'Hey,' she said drawing Gagan's attention.

'Hey darling. Just give me a few minutes,' he said quickly looking back at his laptop screen after greeting Shirley.

Actually Gagan, Maaya and I have some stuff to discuss. So if you don't mind, while you wrap up, can I take her for a coffee? We can meet you at the Starbucks downstairs.'

Gagan was so busy that he barely managed to look up and say, 'Yeah. Please carry on dear. Will catch you guys in a while.'

We moved to the Starbucks in our office building.

'Sit Maaya. What shall I order for you?' Shirley asked me, pointing to the nearest comfortable sofa seat near us.

'A cappuccino please!' I replied almost instantly. It was my standard order which I would give without putting too much thought into.

'You have a seat dear. Let me go and fetch you one and then we can relax and talk. Is that ok with you?' she asked, placing her hand affectionately on my shoulder.

'Ah yes. Thank you Shirley,' I replied, slightly raising my head to look at her in appreciation of her gesture. We sat with our 'Venti' size cappuccinos to talk. That is how a big size cappuccino is addressed at Starbucks.

'So, tell me all about it, sweetheart.'

'I love this man, Shirley and he is still married. He loved me like crazy, at one point. I have seen my soul in his eyes and there is no denying that he is my soulmate. Now he seems to have changed. As if he has forgotten all those moments we spent with each other. His marriage isn't great but still for some reason he is in it. He recently told me that although he is trying, he can't seem to feel the same connection with me, the way he used to. It has broken me to the core, Shirley. I don't know what to do. I feel so lost. I can't imagine a life without Rahul,' and my tears started to roll.

I took a tissue, wiped my tears and tried to continue the conversation. Shirley was very calm and composed, listening to me with a lot of warmth.

'He is so much a part of me that no matter what he says, something inside me still keeps saying it's all temporary and he will get it one day. I need answers, Shirley. I need to know why all of this happening between us and what his role in my life is. Please help me get these answers, Shirley. I feel you can.'

'I know how it feels Maaya and life is not fair. We often get the biggest lessons in life from those who are closest to us and sometimes the pain is too much. The good news is that every suffering is an opportunity to evolve while the bad news is that it's so tough to find that opportunity and relate to it in the midst of the suffering that has such a strong hold on our mind, body and soul,' she said.

'We are starting our batch of Past Life Regression Diploma in three week time. I think you should do it. I sense this is the right time for you to open up to your inner self and really clear your baggage,' Shirley said.

'I am sorry Shirley, but I don't understand. What sort of baggage?'

'Ok let me explain. We all carry the baggage of emotions and relationships, both from our past in our current lives and our past lives. It's not a coincidence that some people get really angry in a situation and another person can be calm and serene in the same.

It's not a coincidence that one child gets more love than he needs from his parents and another one doesn't have any parents to experience love from. These are all *karmic* journeys. The first and the foremost thing to understand in all of this is that in the purest of forms, we are all gods in amnesia; we are pure beings of light. It's not about earthly beings having a spiritual experience but it's rather spirit beings having an earthly experience. There is nothing like punishment in the law of *karma*.

Sadly, while passing the information from generation to generation, it has started sounding as if we are being punished when life isn't really going smooth, but trust me, slowly you will understand that it's not about punishment, it's about learning lessons.

Just like we, at times, slap our children when they are not doing the right thing, we get emotional or physical blows, to shake us up and make us realise that a change in direction is required. I know all that I am saying might sound too bizarre and too abstract but slowly, you will begin to understand.

It has taken me a lot to get here and see life in this light, but trust me, it's so peaceful and calm where I stand. Make your journey Maaya. I see it in you. This relationship and this life situation are offering you a chance to identify with your spiritual mission,' she said.

I must admit, that entire she had just said sounded vague and I am not sure if I got a hang of a lot of things. Somehow, though, being in Shirley's presence did seem reassuring. I didn't get any answers to my questions and she didn't ask me anything more about me or Rahul. She did seem to open a new stream of thoughts in me, which said, maybe she was right.

Even being a Hindu, I didn't practice Hinduism to a great extent but did believe in the existence of God. As per me all religions are paths leading to the same supreme energy. Since childhood, I had always heard that everything happens for our ultimate good, so maybe this was the time to really believe it. Soon Gagan came and Shirley left me alone with my thoughts, to come back to me later when I had fully digested the information.

Suddenly, that moment onwards, something got initiated. I felt lighter and I felt this strong desire to explore parts within myself which I had never touched.

While I was on my way to the train station, I crossed Takashimaaya, a mall just next to the Orchard Road Station. Impulsively, I got drawn to the third floor to Kinokunia, I had been to earlier. I immediately moved up to the NewAge section and started looking around for something interesting to read on life and afterlife. The topic had intrigued me and ever since I had met Shirley, I felt more drawn to finding out for myself about what this whole *karma* thing was about.

I always knew Gita was the best place to start but somehow I found it heavy and a little overwhelming. I had a look at the shelf and came across a book about the journey of souls. This one looked interesting.

After spending a few minutes, I proudly carried the new additions to my book collection to the counter and paid for them.

As soon as those books were in my hand, I felt so excited to read them that temporarily, the thought of Rahul and all of our last conversation went into the background. I could do without it for a while.

Dev was out for drinks with a new friend he had made in town, who of course was gay, too. Dev didn't really fall in love with him, guessing from the expression he made when this guy entered our office but he did mind company. I was busy with work and was usually late at office. His job in the project was pretty manageable and he had time to kill. This guy was Chinese and I must say he had cute looks but Dev was taller and better looking than him.

I went through my routine of calling up Aryan in India and talking to him for as long as he wanted to, listening to his day's whereabouts, then taking a shower and then cooking.

That night, I decided to make some laksa. Laksa is one of the best Singaporean dishes. It's a noodle soup with rich coconut flavour and loads of sea-food. I imagined sitting beside my window, eating laksa, enjoying the view of the pool below and reading my new book. Even the thought was so exciting. I immediately put in all the ingredients and the laksa paste in a pan, cooked it and was ready to start reading my book.

Just as I was about to, I looked at my watch to see the time when I was reminded of Rahul since he had gifted me that expensive watch.

I immediately shifted my focus and started to read the book on the journey of souls.

Once I started reading this book, I couldn't lay it off. It was past 2 a.m. when I finally decided to go off to sleep.

This book was structured by the way of case studies, where it described the entire journey a soul needs to make from one death in one life to the next birth in another life. It went to the extent of even laying an almost physical structure to the spirit world. How a soul moves to the spirit world after their death, how they detach from the life they have just experienced, how they spend some time in gathering their energies, how they discuss the life with their spirit guides and understand their successes and failures. The most interesting was the last case study which was about 'signs of recognition'. Each soul is given signs of recognition before they reincarnate by way of which they identify their soulmates on earth. They are even made to practice the signs at times.

I remember when I saw Rahul for the very first time, something in his eyes told me I had known him before. When I first saw him sleeping on the couch was another moment I had felt as if I had experienced that before.

When we meet our soulmates on earth, we have these memories that get triggered and there is a subtle sense of 'knowing' that we shared a special connection. It resonated with me. I had experienced recognition of his soul, just that I wasn't aware of it.

I was slowly beginning to understand what Shirley had told me. Over the next few days, I read books after books on similar subjects and finally, one day I decided that it was my calling after all to study regression therapy. Maybe I could heal myself. I took Shirley's number from Gagan and called her.

'Hey Shirley. This is Maaya here.'

'Oh hey, Maaya. How are you my dear?' she answered in a soft polite tone.

'I am great Shirley. Firstly, thanks for sharing all that you did, with me, the last time we met over coffee. Secondly, I am interested in learning regression therapy. Can I take you out for a coffee, one of these days?' I asked.

Shirley and I decided to meet over coffee at Orchard road the next evening. She informed me that learning Past Life Regression Therapy was a three-step process where I could begin in two weeks but then it would require commitment, practice and self-healing to move further and really learn the whole thing.

It seemed like I was guided to this one. For the first time in my life, I knew it was something I wanted to do. I didn't want to think too much. I had no intentions of becoming a professional healer but I wanted to make this journey for myself. I was keen to understand the mysteries of the cosmos and this seemed like a good place to start.

I was given two books to read before my course started and I began by reading about hypnosis. Gagan agreed to give me a four-day leave in lieu of me working late hours and weekends to cover-up all the effort I was required to put in for the upcoming release.

Dev came home two days before the course was to begin. It was 9:00 p.m. and I had already had my dinner and was reading my book. Those days, I didn't see much of him since apparently, he was enjoying the company of his new friend and I also was busy with work plus my new found passion.

'So, now you are going to hypnotise people,' he said. 'I wonder if you could hypnotise Gagan so that he could give us a week off and not remember it,' he laughed.

'That's a myth. In clinical hypnosis, it's not possible to make the clients do anything that is against their basic belief system or does not agree with their subconscious mind. It only works when what the therapist is saying, resonates with their subconscious mind. It's almost like when we are watching an interesting movie and we get so lost that we eat our popcorn and don't even realise it or when we are driving and we reach home without noticing what's there on either side of the road. That is the level of trance that is required for Past Life Regression. We experience hypnosis so many times during each day,' I said with a smile.

'Maaya, I am not sure I understand much about Past Lives but sure when you are done, we can see what my soul chose to experience in this life,' he said with a smile. That made me smile too. I had read that usually souls develop a gender preference over a series of lifetimes and yet, sometimes, they have lessons that require them to be born in the opposite gender or at times, they decide to experience a challenging life by becoming a less acceptable part of the society. It's not that they want to prove something but mostly, it's about giving them a challenge by way of which they can identify their own inner strength and shine.

I had read many such case studies and it did seem like souls could make unusual choices in their physical being only to grow at a much faster level. In such lifetimes, they could have to struggle inwardly or outwardly. It's like when we know the exam will be tough, we are bound to learn our lessons more thoroughly.

I promised him that once I learnt the therapy, I would be regressing him. Dev was not unhappy with himself. To me, he was more lovable than any other friend who was straight. He was just curious to understand his lessons, which I am sure would only help him live a happier life.

The days passed quickly and surprisingly, though Rahul was always at the back of my head, I was already starting to understand a few things about our relationship at a higher level. This understanding was giving me a lot of peace.

I had this feeling that somehow I was on the path where I would eventually understand more about myself than I ever had. It all seemed very exciting and magical.

The workshop dates finally arrived. We were a group of fourteen people and Shirley was our trainer for the first workshop. We were supposed to be trained by Andy Tomlinson, who was a renowned author in Past Life Regression field, for the rest of the workshops. I was already looking forward to learning so much from him.

His books were awesome and there was so much clarity I had already gained from merely reading them. Shirley was great with the first workshop. Her style never failed to impress me. She had a knack of making difficult things seem simple and doable. I often wondered how she could be so innocent and so deep at the same time. It was a brilliant experience to be amongst such high energy people for those four days.

We had a group where each single individual had something about them that intrigued me. There was a couple from Australia who had come all the way from Brisbane to participate in the course. They were a lovely couple where Mark was Aussie and Sophie was German. They made a brilliant pair and looking at them, anyone could guess how much in love they were.

They were both past their 50s and had gone through their own share of pain and happiness in their lives. Ever since they had found a true soulmate in each other, life had been blissful. The bliss showed in Mark and Sophie and just by their presence in the room. There was a different energy in the room. Sophie and I got along very well and she would always call me 'my beautiful one', each time we met.

It was amazing how we all became family in just four days and how each of us had something to offer by way of our lives, experiences or skills, to make it special.

The workshop was about hypnotherapy. The first time Shirley taught us the art of hypnotising, we were told to go and practice it in pairs. Mark and I were partnered together and we chose the room on the top floor of Shirley's huge mansion.

'So, you want to go first?' I asked Mark.

'Well, I don't mind. Let me give it a go,' he said. Now I had this charming Australian man lying in front of me and all ready to be hypnotised. I was wondering, what if I couldn't say the script properly? What if I lost track of the pitch scales? What if he didn't get anywhere?

There were so many doubts crossing my mind and I was getting nervous. Just then, Shirley dropped into our room and said, 'You can do it Maaya. He is a charm. Just do it,' and went off.

I pulled myself together and started it just the way Shirley had told us. Mark went into a trance just in time. I was so happy I could do it and he was sweet enough to come out and tell me I was good at it. I was proud of myself.

Now it was my turn. 'Lie down and just take a few deep breaths, Maaya,' said Mark. His voice was seasoned and comforting. I knew it came from years of healing and life experience. For a few moments, Mark observed me patiently while I was getting ready for total relaxation.

'I am finding it hard to relax. Surprisingly, I have not enjoyed just being with myself in a very long time. Even the thought makes me anxious,' I told Mark.

'It's ok, Maaya. Just let go. Don't tell yourself you need to enjoy it. Don't force your mind to stop its thoughts. Just be. Just be and all will fall into place,' said Mark. This resonated with me. It took off the burden to perform and enjoy the experience and now I was more open to the process. Mark's voice and pitch were perfect to put me into a trance quickly.

Although my mind never stopped bothering me but even then, it was a relaxing experience. Mark included some bits of his own in the script to make it more effective and I could feel it was working. My entire body seemed heavy and restful.

Every single day that I spent in that environment, I became surer that I was guided and it was the right thing to do.

Most of the people who came for the class were more experienced than me in terms of healing and energy but that didn't bother me. I was there to learn and something told me I had been waiting for this experience. We went on to learn hypnotherapy and the amazing ways in which it could help in treating addictions.

The one important thing I learnt about hypnotherapy is that like any other therapy, unlike popular belief, it also works on the innermost desire of the client to heal. Just as I was thinking about this, Shirley asked the group, 'What if a client comes to you with a smoking addiction? How will you handle him?'

I raised my hand and on Shirley giving me permission, I said, 'I would first ask him what brings him to me. On getting smoking addiction as the answer, I would ask him for how long he has been smoking and does he think it's not good for him?'

Shirley looked at me with appreciation and said, 'Well, Maaya is right. You need to know if the addiction is actually considered an issue with the client and if they have the desire to get rid of it.'

Immediately, another student in the class raised his hand and said, 'What if a client comes to me and says, I have been smoking for the last twenty years. I think I don't have too much of a problem with it but it's my wife who wants me to quit. She forced me to you to see you,' he asked.

'Then I suggest you let the guy go and suggest the wife get hypnotherapy session to let go of her fears regarding her husband,' said Shirley and everyone started laughing.

'It's true. If the subconscious mind is ok with a belief and they think it's not bad for them, there is no way hypnotherapy will be able to help them. You would rather look at the emotional or other reasons that build that desire in them to smoke. However, if it's purely out of habit, the day they develop the desire to quit, they can be helped. Not otherwise,' Shirley said in a serious tone.

It was an interesting workshop and I learnt so much about other aspects of life that I had never considered existed. I could feel my knowledge and understanding expanding. I felt guided at all times. The positive energy in the workshop was so high that when I came home, I couldn't relate to my own home and the routine activities.

My perspective towards life was changing, since I was experiencing a whole new world. On the end of day two, I was just sitting on my sofa and looking down at the swimming pool from my window when I realised I had this familiar pain coming back to me. I was missing Rahul.

'Do you want to be with him?' said a voice to me. It didn't sound like my own voice, or one I had ever heard before.

I suddenly got a little alarmed and looked around but there was no one there. Just because I didn't want to lose this conversation, I said 'Yes.'

The voice responded, 'This is not the time child. Be patient.'

'When will it be the right time then?' I asked and the voice responded 'You will know.' 'What am I supposed to do till then?' I asked again. 'Walk on your path. You have a journey to make. Focus on that. You will know when the time is right,' it said.

'Does he love me?' I asked again.

'Trust your feelings my child. You know the answer,' it said.

'Who are you?' I asked again and this time there was no response.

I tried and tried but no more answers came. I was sitting on my sofa with this blank expression, trying to understand what had just happened. I didn't know who spoke to me but I wanted to trust the voice.

I felt an immense sense of peace in myself. I smiled to myself after a long time. This journey had begun to unfold mysteries of the universe for me.

Just a few minutes after this incident, Dev knocked. I stood up and opened the door. 'So, what's up Maaya? I considered you might be sleeping but still decided to check,' he said.

'Naaa. I was just introspecting a bit,' I replied.

'Of course!'

'You know what, Dev? Someone just spoke to me. It told me I need to have patience and Rahul will come back to me,' I told him with a hint of excitement in my voice.

'Maaya, it must be your own mind playing a trick on you. Relax! You are already doing this heavy stuff and I don't seem to understand why all of this is required. You have a great career in media and advertising so what draws you to learn this spiritual healing, etc.?' he said with an upset kind of a look.

'I am not doing this to make it my profession. I am just drawn to it and its doing wonders for me. You may not believe it but I certainly feel I am guided and I want to do this,' I said, getting up to keep my glass in the sink. My tone seemed to make it sound like the conversation should end here or the topic would need to change. Dev could gauge my mood.

'Gagan is giving me all your work to do as well and then when I do it, he doesn't like it. Seems like he's not too happy with the whole thing. Did he say anything to you?' he asked me.

'Nopes. I called him yesterday evening to ask if there was anything I can do at night. Surprisingly, he was quite sweet and told me to focus on my workshop and not stress about office. He said he is managing fine,' I replied with a grin.

We talked for another few minutes. He bid me goodbye at around 9:30 and then I made it straight to bed.

The next two days at the workshop were more intense and there was so much happening. I picked up a lot of knowledge about holistic healing, energy, charka system and other stuff that I had no clue of, from the others who had done some stuff before.

Hypnotherapy seemed to have a lot of potential. By the end of the fourth day, we were all set to go and release people from their lifelong addictions or give them confidence boosts. I had already booked in Dev to give-up his smoking, which he had wanted to do for a long time and another woman at office to give-up her nail biting. I had two case studies ready. I was pretty excited to see the magic begin.

Since that Wednesday, life got back to the same old track but I was overwhelmed with my experience at the workshop. I had already decided that the next progressive step was to learn past life regression.

The Regression Workshop was another four weeks from then and it was eight days long. I was yet to ask Gagan for leave and didn't know if he would approve. Our first phase of the launch was happening in ten days so I hoped it wouldn't be that bad but I was not sure it was a good idea to ask just then.

I spent Wednesday to Friday, working hard and doing late nights to cover-up the work for the days I was on an off. Dev asked me to accompany him to a disco on Fridays but I was clear that I had to do whatever it took to get do the PLR course. He understood and didn't insist too much.

I finished work late on a Friday since there was some stuff to go to the printers to get printed the following Monday. Once I finished, I walked up to Gagan's cabin and asked him if he could sit and talk. He offered to go for drinks to a pub. I needed a break anyway. We went to Orchard Road where there was a pub we both liked.

'What will you drink?' he asked me.

'I will have white wine, if they would have some,' I answered. He ordered some red wine for himself and white wine for me.

'So, how was the workshop? Did you like it?' he asked casually.

'It was awesome. I learnt so much. Shirley is such an amazing woman. I didn't know a lot about this sort of stuff but she made it pretty easy for me. It was a profound experience.'

I was genuinely keeping very happy ever since the workshop. Somehow, my energies had uplifted. I didn't find myself sad or thinking too much ever since that voice spoke to me.

'Sounds good! So what exactly did you learn?' he asked me curiously.

'Hypnotherapy. The science of using hypnotic suggestions to impact one's subconscious mind. Ideally to aid one to be able to do things they have wanted to do but can't gather enough motivation or strength to do them.'

'So, can you make someone do something against their wishes by hypnotising them? They show people making fools of themselves on stage or on TV.' Gagan delved further.

'No. Stage hypnosis is different and the purpose is also different. Clinical hypnosis is done with the intention of therapy. If someone is given a suggestion which is against their basic moral values or belief system, their subconscious mind has the ability to reject them,' I replied.

'Oh I see!' he said, raising his wine glass up to his lips.

We talked more about my experience. Then Gagan had some work to discuss with regards to getting some creatives sourced from another company in Singapore which I was meant to liaison with. He explained to me the business scenario and the expectations of the board.

All of a sudden, there was a silence that fell between us when this whole conversation was over. It was getting uncomfortable. He sensed it and immediately called the waiter for the menu and asked me to order something for us to eat. I chose two things and we ordered. Silence made its way again.

Just then, I started a conversation. 'Gagan, if you don't mind me asking, what is your interest in spirituality?' in an attempt to making a conversation.

'I had a difficult childhood Maaya. My father passed away when I was 13 years old. I didn't understand why it happened to me since I was really attached to him. My mother also passed away when I was 19 and though I belonged to a rich family, my relatives took away all the money and left me with nothing. I paid for my own education by doing part time jobs. There was this time when I just became disillusioned and I asked God, why he gave me a life so tough.'

I was listening quietly. While sipping my wine, I just nodded to let him know that he had my attention.

'I had so many questions and I needed my answers. That is when I went in search of them. I used to study and do part time jobs to sustain. I still made time to visit ashrams and seek answers from whomever I felt could give me some wisdom.'

I was not sure how to handle this. This was the first time that Gagan was sharing something so personal with me. Looking at him, no one could have believed that he had so much depth to him. I was looking at him intently, waiting for him to continue.

'I learnt so much from the wise ones. I came to understand the cycle of life and death. I saw things before they were coming. I could sense when something was about to go wrong. I started to understand the lessons of my life. I started to understand that God was not punishing me but this was some sort of a test. It was a lesson I was meant to learn. The anger that had grown inside me from so many years of disappointment and fear slowly started dissolving,' he carried on.

'I wouldn't have believed it if someone else told me this about you. Your looks are so deceptive.'

'I agree. I maintain a different personality while working but that is only to get the best out of people at work.'

'Please continue.'

'When I finished my media studies, I was placed with T&M for a job but it was to start after three months. I took the opportunity and went to live in an ashram in Coimbatore where I was meant to learn the sacred art of healing one's soul. By this time, I was really deep into this stuff. While I was living in the ashram, I met a woman.'

I then had a smile on my face. So finally, we had the mention of a woman in his life.

He still continued without much change in his expression. 'She was a German and had come all the way from Berlin to get *diksha*. She was an amazing woman. We got along well. I was astonished to see how well she had imbibed the customs and values of our country. She absolutely loved India. The more time I spent with her, the more I was drawn to her. She knew a bit of English and a bit of Hindi but she tried her best to make a conversation. She was at least seven years older than me and yet, I was attracted to her like a magnet. I just enjoyed listening to her broken words. Many times I wasn't even listening to her but beyond it, to the purity she carried in her soul. We did meditations, learnt new things and each day I felt my being become purer with her energy.

I didn't register it for a long time that what I was developing for her was a romantic inclination. It just seemed so natural to spend time with her, do all that we were to do at the ashram and in general, talk about life, soul, *karma* and all the things that mattered. She had a difficult childhood too and she would have tears in her eyes when she talked about her family. The pain she carried gave her that depth I could see in her eyes.

Slowly, two months had passed and I started to become aware that my job was waiting for me in a month's time and I would not meet Sara again, maybe never. The thought disturbed me. This was when I started to notice my feelings towards her were not that of just a friend. I was falling in love with her. Knowing that I would need to leave her and go bothered me.

One day, while we had just finished our evening meditation which we usually did in my room, I sat quietly, a little lost.

Sara came and sat closer to me and held my hand very affectionately asking me, "What's wrong? You are suppressing something. I could feel it in the meditation too. You want to say something? All ok?" she asked. I had never realised she could sense my energies and read my thoughts while we were meditating too.

Impulsively, I just brought my other hand on top of hers and kissed her hand. She looked at me with a very deep affectionate look. I looked at her, into her eyes.

"It's not meant to be Gagan. Let go of whatever is going on in your heart," she said with a little sad expression in her eyes and left the room.

I couldn't understand her behaviour. I would have understood if she felt offended, angry or upset but I didn't understand this. I was hurt and yet I craved for her even more.

From that day, she would just be like a partner to me in the meditations and rise up and leave whenever whatever we were doing was done. She started avoiding me though I often found her stealing a gaze at me when I was busy doing something. I was confused. I tried to make several attempts to talk to her but she was stubborn. My day of leaving the ashram was getting closer and I didn't want to leave like that. She had been a friend and a guide to me. I was guilty for destroying whatever we had. The least I wanted was to restore the friendship but she didn't give me a chance.

One day, when I woke up, I was told that she had flown back to Germany. I still had two weeks to go. I had this terrible sinking feeling in me when I realised that I probably would never see her again.

I silently suffered the whole night. Her thoughts, her smile, her affection, her care, her entire being was haunting me. I cursed myself for losing her. I was angry at her for not giving me a chance to make it up to her. The pain only grew each moment.

The next morning, I went to my guruji who was a silent observer of the whole thing. I had tears in my eyes. He knew all I was going through. I just lay my head at his feet and let the pain flow. He affectionately put his hand on my head and let me weep. I didn't know why I had grown so weak in the knees. I was experiencing this terrible loss but at the same time, I had questions: Why did she leave?, Why didn't she even say goodbye?, What wrong had I done?, etc.

Once I finished sobbing, guruji looked at me and said, "Child, it was not meant to be. Your life is meant for a higher purpose and you will not have anything taking you off-track from your journey." I didn't understand whatever he had said just then.

"I don't understand guruji. Can't I get love in my life?" I asked.

"You will get love, loads of it, but that will be different. Here you are looking for attachment and that is not what you are here for. Your lesson is to detach and develop universal compassion and love. Her role in your life is over. It was only till here," he said. What he said made me even sadder. I was curious to understand why he thought Sara's role in my life was over.

"She is dying Gagan. She is at the last stage of cancer and she was living in this ashram only to spend her last days at the mercy of the Almighty. She didn't know the Creator had one more experience waiting to unfold for her here. She also loved you. She was your soulmate. You will meet her again, when you leave this planet and go back home," he said.'

I was utterly shocked when Gagan said this. I got so involved in the story that I had tears in my eyes when he told me about Sara. I immediately took a napkin, cleaned my tears and started listening to him for the rest of the story.

The intense look of loss and grief was evident in Gagan's eyes.

'That old sinking feeling reappeared. My shock was so grave that for a few seconds or maybe minutes, I didn't have any sense of time and space. My ears became numb. I just fell on ground from my squatting position. I didn't have a clue of what was happening to my head. It seemed like my world was spinning.

After a while when I regained sense, I asked, "Why didn't she tell me guruji? Why didn't she let me take care of her? Why didn't she let me say goodbye to her," I asked with a slow, stammering voice.

"She wanted you to be the least affected. As soon as she realised your feelings for her, she decided to leave. She didn't want to die in your arms for you to carry her grief for the rest of your life. She wanted you not to know but I thought it wiser for you to know and understand the bigger plan," he said.

It was all so bizarre. Nothing made sense to me. Guruji handed over a letter from Sara to me in which she had written "*Make your journey Gagan. You are meant for so much more. We shall meet again and I promise, the next time, I will come to stay. Bless you!*" I don't have words to express the pain and misery I went through for the next one week.

One morning, at 4.00 a.m., just as I sat to meditate, I saw Sara in front of my eyes. She looked so pure, dressed in white. "I am going my dear. Will help you and love you from the other side. Live your life well and always remember you have a spiritual mission. I will always be proud of you. Goodbye, till we meet again," she said.

"Goodbye Sara," I said and she vanished. I had tears in my eyes and in the next moment, I sensed something pulling out of my heart and leaving. I knew she was no more and she had given me a chance to say goodbye before she left.'

Gagan's story was intense. I felt a deep grief. I wondered if one had to experience such a journey to realise the difference that loves makes in their lives. It touched me deep within. It was so pure, so serene and so divine.

An awkward silence came between us and then he said, 'Ever since that day Maaya, I do my work, go home and meditate. I use all my extra time in working for a *gurukul* I run for children in Coimbatore. We teach children how to live life guided by their inner instincts and inherent powers. They learn to stay in awareness of their emotions and learn to deal with them from a higher perspective. I need this job to survive and keep me attached to this world otherwise I will need to come back and balance.

She comes to me in my dreams whenever I need help or guidance. She tells me the right thing to do. Slowly, the *gurukul* is growing and now we have 167 children there. I have a dream to see 1,000 children getting their education from a spiritual bent of mind at *gurukul,* without compromising the learning required by them to make it in the material world. I have been blessed with this mission and that is my also a part of my journey within,' he said.

That day I realised how blessed I was for all that I had been given in life. My respect for Gagan as a person multiplied. I thanked him for sharing this part of his life with me. It meant so much.

The next day, it was decided that I was attending the next workshop. I had an arrangement in place with Gagan to work the following weekend to wrap-up whatever we might be left with before our first preview of the magazine. I was so excited because this was about learning Past Life Regression and that too from Andy.

I had never experienced a past life as yet and even the idea was very fascinating. Initially, I thought maybe I should get a regression done first but then I decided against it. The mystery of the process and the experience was worth the wait. I had a lot to do before I left for the workshop and the next few days got very busy.

It was nervousness and excitement that I felt together, when I stepped into Shirley's huge mansion for my first class. That was where we were to spend most of the next eight days and make the most fascinating and meaningful journey of our lives. It was a very high energy room in the basement of her house and the very ambience in her room made one feel spiritual and connected to the divine. I found it easy to settle down on one of the fourteen chairs laid down for us in the room while I waited for the others to arrive. Slowly, eight people, a few of whom were from my Hypnotherapy group including Mark and Sophie, arrived. It was so lovely to see them back. Sophie gave me a long warm hug.

We spent eight lovely days learning the most amazing healing technique. It later became the stepping stone of my spiritual journey and I was ever so grateful to Andy, Shirley and all who became a part of this experience with me.

□

Eternal Love

Now it was time for some regression practice. All through my regression course, I was waiting to be able to get ready and equipped to take someone to their past life. We had enough practice sessions at the workshop. Shirley said I was a natural at regression which was certainly motivating.

I met a woman on a social networking site who was going through a tough phase in life. She asked me if I could give her a regression and I instantly agreed.

Soon, it was time for my first professional PLR session. She was a young woman who was getting divorced. Her husband was a wealthy man and they had two kids together. She suffered from an abusive marriage, financial blocks and lack of support in life. She had to give up her children to her husband for she couldn't afford to give them a decent life. She missed them and felt helpless for being unable to keep them with her, especially her daughter.

Traditionally, I had devised a form that my clients were supposed to fill up and return to me prior to the session for me to understand them better. I sent her that form but she sent it only fifteen minutes before our session so I didn't get enough time to go through it.

She was a good looking woman of Asian origin with a polite warm voice. We discussed her concerns and agreed to allow her sub-conscious to take us to the most relevant past life which could resolve the most for her.

She was an easy subject for a hypnotic trance as she quickly entered a past life in which she was tied naked on a slab kind of structure and there was some guy who sort of played around with her. She felt that they were near a train station and that there were other girls who were being transported as sex workers to some foreign land. She was emotionally in a lot of pain in that scene. I sensed she was somewhere in the middle of that life. I guided her to visit the first significant event in that life and we unfolded the story of her life. It was a life in which she was a girl living in an orphanage. She was into drugs, didn't pay attention to studies, was rude and mean. She had only one friend who was nice and sober. Her friend warned her several times to mend her ways for she could land up in trouble but she didn't and hence landed up in that miserable place.

I worked on releasing her body memories and releasing the charge of the negative emotions she carried from that life experience using the technique I was taught.

When she died in that past life, I guided her to meet her spirit guide. We asked the guide about the lesson that she was expected to learn in that life.

He said she was meant to take right decisions independently and trust the guidance when it came to her but she didn't listen and she didn't trust. Her soul had decided to experience inner strength and independence in that life. She had failed that lesson.

Suddenly, she told me that her spirit guide wanted to take her somewhere. She felt they were spinning.

Finally, they stopped and I saw this very intense expression on her face.

Upon asking she told me that she had a miscarriage the first time she conceived in this life. They had come to meet the soul of that baby.

I saw tears roll down her eyes as that soul said to her, 'You don't have to blame yourself for me. I was not meant to be born. It was just an experience planned for you to start experiencing human emotions which you denied to yourself before that. I was not meant to be. I am there again, in another body and I am happy. Let go off the guilt.'

I was so amazed at the power of the experience. I could sense her relief after the release. She had been holding back that guilt for the baby for ten years by then. Then we went on to resolve her past life with rest of the characters and events.

When she met that friend of hers whom she didn't listen to in that past life, she identified her as an older male friend of hers in her current life.

That soul told her at that moment that it would come back to her again but having chosen to be much older to her, so that she would take it soul seriously.

In that life, she had another person who was close to her, whom she identified as her daughter in her current life. The whole experience became overwhelming for her and maybe me too.

We were then guided into another past life which was where she went through the life of a monk. She couldn't trust herself completely for her guidance in that life, in spite of being given enough divine support.

Both her past lives carried a pattern similar to her current life. Her guide mentioned that her struggle in her current life was also about reclaiming her inner strength, trusting herself and being independent and uninfluenced in spirit. That is when I realised the reason she was so lonely and deprived of all support system in her current life.

She was also told that she would reunite with her daughter when she learnt the lesson she had chosen to learn by being alone.

When she was about to end her journey in that session in the spirit world, she told me that her spirit guide had a message for me. I was both thrilled and scared upon hearing this. She said, 'He says, be patient. You are on the right path.'

At that point, I didn't know what this meant but this word 'patience' was coming too often for me to ignore it.

She hugged me and said, 'Thank you. Thank you for being my guide and friend and making this journey with me. It meant a lot for me. I will never forget you.'

That day I realised I was being blessed with this knowledge and skill. It gave so much inner peace and satisfaction. I was actually impacting people's lives to the core of their beings. I could touch their souls.

This experience also gave me another understanding at a personal level. It's not necessary that if we are going through suffering, it's because we are paying back for some bad karma. Our souls choose to experience certain difficult emotions like pain, loneliness, sadness, grief for inner strength as well. It is difficult to look at such life experiences from the context of the soul journey while we are still in it. When the experience is over; we often realise the good it did to us in terms of our growth inward.

I started doing healing sessions on weekends, as and when I could squeeze in an appointment and with every passing day, I realised how our past lives could impact our current lives and that there isn't too much we can do about it, till we acknowledge this connection.

I was given this opportunity to surrender myself to the divine as a channel for people to be able to experience and resolve their past. In this process, I triggered transformation in their current lives as well as in mine. This work gave a whole new meaning to my existence. I felt I had finally found the purpose of my life...maybe I was meant to heal souls.

I did seven-eight sessions while I was in Singapore and every past life experience of a client taught me about a new aspect of my own life.

Soon, it was time to leave Singapore. My project was almost over and Gagan had already arranged for a new assignment for both me and Dev in Delhi. It was hard since I had grown to love that city a lot. Singapore served to be a great milestone in my evolution as a person. At the same time, Aryan was waiting for me at home and I was also missing him dearly.

We said our goodbyes to our colleagues and friends and took our flight back home.

Everyone was excited to have me back at home. Pooja came over to receive me at the airport along with mum and Aryan. It felt nice to be back in Delhi. I loved the city and there was something in this city that drew me back from wherever I was in the world, with great force and intensity. It always felt right to be back.

I was on a different wavelength as compared to when I had left Delhi. It had been only seven months that I was away. The moment I landed, Rahul's thoughts started clouding my mind.

It was surprising because I thought I was getting over him. I could sense his energies. It was tough to keep myself from contacting him but somehow, I did. The initial few days went by in trying to settle down and catch-up with office work and Aryan.

Slowly, my work at office got time consuming and it was tough to take out too much time for my spiritual activities. While I was in Singapore, with the help of a friend, I had managed to write-up some content for my website. Luckily, I managed to get www.pastlifeconnection.com for my website, which was a pretty good domain name and I was excited about putting up my site soon.

I sat down for a few evenings in a flow and wrote about my understanding about past life regression for my website. Another therapist who had been practicing for longer than me helped me, to present a perspective on a variety of cases in which regression was a useful therapy. My website focused on a variety of issues people face and had some meaningful first-hand information, helpful to those who could see themselves exploring and resolving their past.

It took me a good two months and twenty-five odd cases to really get the kind of content that would form the basis of my website. I got involved in doing as many regressions as I could find time for. I had about two weeks of holiday due, which I took leave for. Apart from spending time with Aryan and taking him out to play and for movies, I tried to help people through my newly acquired skills. It was getting interesting each day.

Slowly, my website was launched. Thanks to Deeksha, because she helped me with optimising my site to reach the highest ranks in Google, Yahoo and other search engines. She had acquired these skills in her new job as a designer-cum-search engine optimiser.

She worked day and night on my website and in just a few days, it was coming up on search engines at a fairly decent position.

Initially, I started getting many calls from all over NCR and then slowly, from other cities too. People were getting more and more aware of regression therapy, owing to a reality show on TV that launched a platform for regression therapy in India.

It had been four months since I had returned to Delhi. I had spoken to Rahul just once. I had called him two weeks after coming back from Singapore. The conversation was still vivid in my memory.

'Hey Rahul.'

'Maaya, is that you?' he said.

'Hmmmm.'

'I could sense that you are back. Somehow I knew,' he responded.

'Do you still love me Rahul?'

'I think of you many times Maaya,' he said.

'What does that mean?'

'I guess I don't have those same emotions anymore. I am trying to save my family. My focus, right now, is not really on myself,' he said.

'Will you be fine without me?'

The line went quiet for a few microseconds maybe.

'I am sorry Maaya. You have had a very special place in my heart. These days I can't make sense of so many things in my life but I am trying. I know I have hurt you deeply. It's not that I can ever forget you completely. Maybe I never will but I have taken a stand to make my marriage work. I have my own reasons for doing so. I don't want you to wait for me Maaya. Move on. Live your life. You'll always stay in my prayers and good wishes.'

I couldn't believe I was hearing this from Rahul. I could die that moment. I saw no reason to live except for my Aryan. It was a terrible night. I was so lost. It was like my whole world came crashing down on me, all over again. All the misery, the suffering, the pain was back. I couldn't think of a life without Rahul. He was the very essence of my existence. I could feel a piercing pain in the middle of my chest. It was as if someone had taken away a part of my soul.

This time, I also felt anger and resentment. I didn't know how he would just get so insensitive to me. I almost hated him for a few moments. The pain was so intense that I lay on my stomach on the bed and screamed in my pillow, just to vent. I had to empty myself of all that I had left of Rahul. I couldn't believe I was so naive. Here I was trying to resolve with him at the soul level and here his physical existence had nothing for me, not even compassion. I wanted to ask God why this was happening to me. I wanted to know, forgetting all of the knowledge and wisdom I had gained that, why I was suffering so much. I just wanted to cry, scream and get over the whole damn thing.

The most atrocious thing about my emotions was that in spite of all that had happened, I sometimes still hoped he'd love me, he'd come back to me. I hated myself for being so pathetically hooked to him.

I just couldn't surrender. Yet again, I allowed the misery inside me to take control. Neither could I accept that it was not completely over, nor could I trust that I have the power to resolve it. I kept shuttling between the two for so many days. I couldn't let go!

I grieved for so many days to come. It took me so long to put that last conversation in the background and move forward in my life. It truly happened after I met Tessy a few days later. Through my experience with her, I learnt that whatever appeared outwardly was usually another story inwardly. I realised that much of what we did in our daily lives was driven more by emotions of guilt, responsibility and need than love.

Rahul wanted to make his marriage work not because of love but since he felt responsible to himself, to his wife and his child. In other words, he had a need to be right. We often get entangled in the 'rights' and 'wrongs' in our lives. In absolute reality, there is no right or wrong. Right and wrong are relative concepts. If something is right as per one criterion, it may be wrong as per another. Many times, our need to be right stems from something we feel guilty about. A better way to resolve a guilt-based situation is to accept the truth about ourselves. Mostly when we feel guilty for others, there is something about ourselves that is unacceptable to us. We judge ourselves. Once we start from accepting and loving ourselves unconditionally, usually the situation dissolves for good.

Rahul was covering up his need to love me, his need to be happy, by suppressing his emotions for me. His guilt for his family was because he was guilty for his happiness. He judged himself to be selfish. That is exactly what I had done the first time round when I chose Kunal, knowing my happiness didn't lie with him. When relationships are based on guilt, seldom do they last very long. Usually, in due course of time, they bring us suffering and in the end, we just prolong our misery and suffering. It takes a lot to release guilt. I always felt that we also get used to living in our misery. It becomes our companion. It's easier to stay in it than to face it and get out of it.

While I was going through this tug of war within myself where I was angry and upset with him, with myself, all this wisdom was pouring in and yet that need to be with him, to be loved by him was constantly in the background. One day, I received a message from my spirit guide during my meditation.

Love so deep in my heart
The pain hurts my very soul
Every breath touches the core
Beneath which lies the hope
The hope of being held again
Of being caressed and cared for
The purity of that transparent light
That bonds us and our very beings
Whispers in my ears each day
We shall be together again
When there will only be the love
The pain will go away forever!

I wrote it on a piece of paper and kept it in my bag as a reminder of the divine beauty of love. It was yet another message to surrender my need to be with him, to allow all to happen in divine order.

A few days later I met Daniel through a friend. He was an intuitive and a powerful healer. He used a modality that he also didn't know what to name. Somehow, only by being in the presence of his energy field, I felt so relaxed and energised. He was a short, dark guy with a very strong aura. There was this firmness in his personality. Initially, his looks told me he would be a little high headed and insensitive but slowly, I discovered that wasn't the case.

Daniel and I became good friends. Once, we decided to do swap healing sessions. He promised to give me a healing session with the modality that he created and in return, I was to help him find a solution to his current life situation.

Dan had an amazing ability to connect with his core. I could put him into a trance just by holding his hands for two minutes even in a busy restaurant. When he came out, his eyes were red and he said, "Why did you get me back, I wanted to stay there." He was very connected to the other side. His power was his problem. He wanted to become a healer professionally and give-up the job he was doing. He was not honouring the gift he had because of his insecurities. His biggest insecurity was that of not being able to financially sustain himself as a healer. Also, he realised that sometimes his powers got overwhelming for people to handle.

I intuitively felt that his journey was much more than that of a healer. He had to let go of his job and move in that direction but he was stuck. This was a problem I often saw with the most powerful healers. They could transform lives but when it came to them, they had issues with trusting themselves.

We decided to do Dan's session at his place, since he had a nice quiet room dedicated for his energy work. It took me only about five-seven minutes to put him in a trance. We hadn't exactly planned an objective for the session. I knew he probably would not find his answers in a past life. I just decided to follow the guidance of his higher self to see where we would be taken.

I made the intent for his higher self to take us to the place where he would get his answers regarding his current life situation. He immediately experienced an entry into a place.

'I see tall buildings. They seem magical,' he said.

'What's so magical about them, Dan?'

'They are suspended in...the air maybe...above the ground. Seems like they are based on vibrations of some sort.'

'Hmmmm. Interesting. Is there anyone else with you? What else can you see?'

'There are loads of balls of light roaming about. They seem to be made of some energy. White in colour. I think I am one of them. It's a huge place. Feels like some sort of a library. Everyone is quietly doing something. They're busy.'

'Is there anyone in particular whom you know?'

'Yes, there's a lady. She is standing close to me. She's dressed in white too. She isn't like us. She is more human.'

'Can you communicate with her? Ask her who she is? She'll give you an answer,' I encouraged him to have a conversation with the lady.

'She's my guardian angel. I am in the spirit world, in the hall of learning. It's where all souls introspect on their past lives and plan for their next lives. She says I've been here. I have some faint recognition of this place. She wants me to recall what I planned for this life.'

Almost the next second he said, 'She is transferring some white light beam from her head to my head. My head is getting heavy.'

He fell silent for a few seconds. It took me a lot of effort to get him to speak again. Seemed like he was too involved in that world.

'She wants me to visit another place.'

'Go with her then. It's ok,' I said.

In a few moments, I asked him, 'Where have you reached now?'

He seemed a little uneasy in that place.

'It is a weird place with so many colours. Many of these colours I have never seen before. Looks beautiful though.'

'What is weird about this place, Dan?'

'Every few seconds, the colours of the whole place change. Although it's a beautiful place, I can sense so much uncertainty in here. It even shakes when it changes its colour. It's making me very uncomfortable.'

'Is your guardian angel there with you?'

'Yes. She's got someone with her. An old man with a white beard. She says his name is Zadkiel and he's my spirit guide.'

'Ask your guide, what place is this? Why are you visiting it?'

'It's the place in my mind where the inception of my thoughts happens.'

That was a very surprising response. No wonder he felt the energy of the place very unstable and uncertain.

He says 'this is the place where the root of my problem lies. I have the knowledge and understanding of my life purpose but I get trapped in my own negative thoughts. I must learn to create more positive thoughts and stop negative thinking by addressing my fears and bringing my thoughts to my conscious awareness,' he reckons.

'How does he suggest you do that?'

He says 'I need to meditate regularly and learn to trust signs given to me for guidance. He also suggests I resolve my past life beliefs that stop me from trusting my healing abilities.'

His guide then asked him to follow them somewhere. After a few seconds, he said they had reached this beautiful place where there was a huge water like body. He was then asked to take a dip. As he did that, physically, his body had a huge jitter. It was some sort of an energy pool which evidently relaxed and energised him. He felt very relaxed and energised after having taken a dip in it.

He thanked his guide and guardian angel and we came out of the experience.

This was a huge step for Daniel and I could feel his energies were so much more positive and settled. As agreed with him, I then had to progress him into his future.

I requested his higher mind to take us one year ahead in the future in his current life. He saw himself in a peaceful, quiet place, writing something. When I asked him what was he writing, he said it was his first book. He could spell the title too. Then I asked him how it felt like to be in that time and space and how has his life evolved. He said he was more at peace. He saw that he had given up his job a few months back and taken up healing as his mainstream work. He didn't face any financial concerns and he was getting more and more aware of how vibrations could be used for healing.

I then progressed Dan to five years in the future. He realised that by then he was travelling around the world to different countries and teaching energy work. He was at peace within himself and he felt he was living the purpose of his life.

Further still, I took him ten years ahead in time and he found himself standing on a podium, somewhere in New York, addressing a crowd of over 200 people. Upon enquiring about it, he said they were celebrating the grand success of his third book. It was about vibrational medicine. He was happy to be making a considerable contribution to the planet.

I then guided him back to the here and now.

'That was quite a journey sweety!' he said with a smile and hugged me. I saw gratitude in his eyes for putting some sense to his otherwise confused state of mind.

Dan's session was a learning experience for me too. I learnt to trust my intuitive ability and allow the session to be completely guided. There was no way we could have accomplished so much, had I tried to consciously plan his session. Both of us were quite happy with what he experienced. He then needed time to settle down with the whole thing.

We decided to shift my session to another day so that he could get some rest and ground himself.

We met again in two days time and he seemed to be visibly more relaxed and at peace with himself. We again decided to use his special room for my session.

'Do you have any areas of your life that you would like to heal?' he asked me. I got tempted to quickly fill him in about Rahul and whatever had happened between us.

'I have got it Maaya and I will try and heal this aspect of your life. I can't say what will come up. I will present this as an area of concern for the healing,' he said.

'Thanks Dan. Really appreciate it. Though I'm not sure I can get anywhere, I am a tough nut,' I told him.

He placed his finger on my lips and said, 'Just let go, Maaya. Trust me and let go. We shall go wherever we are meant to. If I have a role to play in your life, it will happen today. Don't worry. Trust me. Trust yourself to deserve it,' he said with a smile.

He asked me to lie down, close my eyes and relax. I was to focus inwardly as he did something with his hands, about two inches above my body. In a few minutes I started feeling lightness in my body. Sometimes, he would just touch my feet and his hands felt like divine touch.

I was quickly transported to this world where I felt something moving within my body and at the same time, I saw some visuals. I saw two people standing facing each other in this amazing place that didn't seem like anything I knew. I can't really put words to it but seemed like everything was golden in colour and charismatic.

I sensed it was me and Rahul. I could feel his presence very strongly around me. There was a big ladder like thing in golden colour which appeared between us. Slowly, there were these thread-like things attaching him to me, passing through each step of the ladder from one side to the other. There were about 18-19 steps. Both of us then started growing taller, as tall as the ladder. In that vision, Rahul and I didn't seem to be in the bodies we are now. We seemed to be pure energies, formless. The experience started getting intense. I could see and feel those threads actually going through my body. It was so vivid.

Then something happened. Suddenly, each thread at each step started getting cut. As each step was free of threads, that step vanished and the ladder reduced in size. I was observing this process from the outside, while I was in it as well. Slowly, all threads from all steps got broken and the ladder disappeared. I felt a sense of release in my body, as if some burden had just been lifted off me.

Then I was facing Rahul and he was facing me. I felt a sense of very strong love between us, as if everything was okay, everything was fine. Rahul moved from his place and snuggled me from behind. It seemed like our energies became one and vanished into nothingness. Both of our forms started to merge. I almost felt a jerk in my heart and a sense of calm and peace overwhelmed me.

After this, Dan brought me out. I was not sure whether whatever I saw was my imagination or was real. I let Dan share his experience with me.

This was when I got another divine sign. Dan said he cut my chords with Rahul that we had developed over so many past lives. It struck me that those thread-like things must be those chords, so I asked him how many lives were they and he said 19. This is when something inside me told me that what I had seen was shown to me and was not my imagination. I was in complete awe. I thanked Dan profusely for the gift he had given me and returned home.

It took me the next few days to really, truly understand what I had experienced. It was an amazing way to experience how past life *karma* could be so intense amongst our energies.

This was my initiation to healing myself. I knew it was coming because one can't heal others till you go through the journey yourself. This healing played a very vital role in my understanding about *karma,* past lives and my own journey.

I gave myself a few days to settle down and learn from the experience.

Gagan and I were working late hours for a few weeks because of a new product launch. He was the best person to talk to about this new experience that life had given me. He knew nothing about Rahul but I did intend to tell him when the time was right. He had been following spiritual practices over the last few years and he understood me. He managed to capture the right side of each story and gave me insights to help others. Slowly, I started taking advice from him on various cases, without disclosing their identity of course, but really analysing them from another point of view.

Gagan had been researching for a few years on how to scientifically and logically establish the link between energy and diseases. He had gone a long way in his research and past lives had been a part of his work too. He had a good understanding of the underlying emotion a person might be experiencing at the time of an experiencing issue and he was working on reverse engineering the emotional root causes of various physical diseases. Maybe Sara's death through cancer still played heavy on him.

What I had concluded from my understanding and the various experiences I was having was that whenever a person has emotions that are unresolved or cluttered in them, those emotions start depositing in our energy body (it's a subtle body outside our physical body), just like fat deposits in our physical body. When they are present in a substantial amount in the energy body, they start to form imbalances in the various *charkas* in the energy field. If they are not resolved at that time, they attract diseases in the areas where those emotions are stored.

For example, if someone feels they are alone in the world, they have a lot of responsibilities, they don't have any support and if they carry this emotion for a long time, they will develop back problems. Back/Spine is where we store responsibility and support as emotions and if someone feels burdened with responsibility or experiences inability to deal with it, they will often land up hurting their back.

Gagan helped me a lot in my understanding of thoughts and emotions coming from past lives and how they affected the person's energy system.

I slowly started helping more and more people with their past life issues. This work came naturally to me. I just had it in me is what I thought until later I discovered more about my own past.

While I was getting more and more involved in my work, there was a feeling I had as if I was doing more than just healing. I was touching people's souls. One day I got a call from this woman called Tessy. She said she was desperate for a past life session. I told her I only did sessions over weekends and I was pretty much booked for five-six weekends so it could only happen later. She requested and pleaded that I give her an early appointment because she was desperate. She wouldn't tell me what her issue was. Somehow, I felt guided to go out of my way for her. I promised to get back to her in two days' time and see if I could shuffle something.

While I was still struggling to make a space in my calendar for Tessy, I received a cancellation call from another client. He was supposed to come that Saturday. He had to leave for an urgent business trip and wanted to postpone his appointment to a few weeks later. I adjusted Tessy's session in that slot. The vibes and signs I was getting from her meant we had more to our connection than what we could see.

It was still Monday and for about a week I had been feeling very anxious with regards to me and Rahul but couldn't really share it with anyone. I felt this very strong feeling that he wouldn't be able to manage without me, as if something would happen to him if I was not with him. It was silly since I had never felt that way even for Aryan. It was surprising and strange, yet too strong to ignore. I decided to call Rahul and check on him.

'Hello,' he said. 'Hey. It's me,' I said. 'How are you Maaya?' he asked politely. 'I am ok. How about you?' I asked him. 'Hmmm, I am good. Quite busy actually. Have started my own company and am busy setting it up now. What's up with you?' he said. 'I am doing fine. Doing my job as well as regressions. It's interesting. You and I have had quite a few lives together,' I rattled out just because I was so desperate to share it with him.

'Look Maaya. I am sorry if it hurts you but I don't really believe in past lives,' he said, sounding a little upset.

'It's ok Rahul. You are the one who said we are soulmates, didn't you?' I replied. 'Maybe I did but now things are different. I can't feel all of those things again. It was special but somehow I have tried and failed in feeling those feelings for you again. I am sorry, I know I am hurting you but if I lie, it will hurt you even more,' he said.

I was already in tears by then so I just said 'Bye' and slammed the phone down. I didn't know how that pain that I thought was gone, came all over again and still hurt as much.

I left office early and on the way, parked my car on the roadside. The thought that Rahul wouldn't be able to manage without me was overwhelming me. It was bizarre. He had just confessed that he didn't feel anything for me. And I still had this weird feeling that he was unsafe without me.

I called Pooja and told her about all that had happened. She asked me to wait there. This place I didn't realise was very close to her house and she came to me in another twenty minutes. I had no sense of time. All I was doing was crying and asking myself, why I was even feeling so much for Rahul who didn't even care. All those scenes kept flashing in front of my eyes about how he loved and cared for me.

In such situations, the first thing that always came to my mind was when Rahul said that his role in my life was to make sure that I wouldn't cry ever again. It was such an irony that I cried the most because of him in this life.

Pooja kept saying 'Maaya, let him be. He will get it one day. He will not get someone who loves him as much. Trust me; he will regret it one day. Don't be like this. No more crying for this man.'

It took me a while to have a decent conversation with her.

'I don't know why Pooja, it might sound stupid but I have this overwhelming feeling that he can't do without me. That something might happen to him if I am not with him. It's so frustrating because I honestly don't intend to think about him or have any illusions that he needs me anymore now,' I told her.

'He is a grown man Maaya. He is not your child that you need to protect him,' she said.

'Protection! That's it. This word resonates. I suddenly have a sense of understanding of what is happening to me. It's a past life Pooja. Trust me, I know this stuff. It's a past life that is causing this intense feeling. I need to see a therapist,' I told Pooja with a sparkle in my eyes. I felt like a child who had just scored a 10 on 10 in a math test.

I had an old friend, Yani who had recently re-connected with me and mentioned that he was also a PLR therapist. I called him that night and booked an appointment for the next morning. I called up Gagan and told him I would come after lunch on account of some personal work in the first half of the day. That night I slept better after a few days. I was so sure that the intensity of that emotion would go away once the past life came up.

The next day, I reached at exactly 9:00 a.m., ready for my session. I told him about the situation. He agreed that it was a past life. He worked on me for hours but I couldn't enter into any past life. The intensity of the energy was increasing. I could feel an intense fear and need to protect Rahul. Yani said I had a very strong conscious mind and that I was blocking the experience with my expectations. I was desperate and that was my block. He tried working on me for four days in a row but nothing happened.

I realised I had major surrender issues. He tried to heal me but the moment he would send me energy, I could sense a blockage in my system. It disappointed me. The emotion was still quite strong and there was no other way I could have resolved this one. I just knew it was a past life.

The fourth day, I gave up. I told Yani that maybe it wasn't meant to be and thanked him for his efforts. I was feeling very low that day. I had spent four days of work, time and effort and there were no results. I knew the problem was with me. Before sleeping, I did a little prayer and asked for divine help.

Suddenly, I woke up drenched in sweat and really scared at around 4 a.m., the next morning. It took me about ten minutes to realise that I had just experienced a past life in my dream. It was the most amazing and vivid experience of my life. Yani and I couldn't do it in therapy for four days but now suddenly this past life popped in the dream and it was exactly the answer to my problem.

I saw a past life in which I was a young girl about 14 years old. I was poor but I lived in a big house – probably as a maid or something. I had been living in that house since I was a child. I then saw I had two friends who had come to pack my stuff and take me away from there. I had decided to leave that house for good. As the story unfolded, I realised that the house used to belong to a very kind family but the owners died in an accident. Their only son was alive, who was about 11-12 years old.

I felt I was very close to the son but he didn't live in that house. He lived in some hostel. The house was managed by his uncle who was wicked. I was sure his uncle got his parents killed. I had a feeling that this boy would be killed by the uncle if he came there. I felt if I lived there, the boy would certainly come back to meet me. I didn't want that to happen.

I saw this elaborate scene of me and my friends packed every little thing I owned in that house into a big bag. As I was ready to leave, the uncle walked in and put his feet over my stuff and crushed it. Behind him, I saw the boy. I got worried for him and decided not to leave. My friends returned and I stayed back.

When I looked at the boy closely, I recognised him to be Rahul. The same eyes with the same purity in them. He and I were childhood friends. I was two years older to him. I had lived in that house since I was very young. His parents never treated me as an orphan. I was always treated as a part of the family. He hugged me tight when he came close to me. I was all that was left of his family. I felt the strength of the bond between me and the boy. He was a little scared. Probably by then, he knew he was unsafe with his uncle.

In the next scene, I saw myself washing dishes in the kitchen which is in the basement.

While I was busy with my chores, the uncle came to me from behind and I turned around. I saw the boy hiding behind the staircase and looking at what was happening. The uncle then said to me, 'I hope you know that if you don't do as I tell you to do, I will kill him,' and with that he moved my hair from my shoulder and kissed me on the neck. The boy was watching me being manipulated and abused. The last I felt was my fear and intense pain and saw guilt in his eyes.

The kiss seemed so real that I woke up sweating and scared because of my dream. Being a Past Life Therapist, I had listened to such experiences so many times. Yet it took me a while to register it was a past life.

I got my answer. The protectiveness I was feeling for him was coming from that life. I was responsible for him and I sacrificed myself to protect him. It gave me another answer. I had seen that same expression in Rahul's eyes during those days when he didn't tell me about his wife arriving. It was a mixed expression of guilt and shame. I didn't understand it then but this past life explained it all. He couldn't stand-up for me in this life too and it mirrored that emotion in him which he carried while being that boy.

The next morning, I felt fresh and released and I thanked God for it. The need to protect Rahul was gone. In fact, quite to my astonishment, a lot of my intensity of the background process of wanting to be with him was also missing.

I called Yani and told him about my dream. He was amazed that we couldn't get it out in the sessions and I got it in a dream. The energy was on the surface to be released. It just found the best possible outlet. The whole thing made perfect sense. If our energies want to release an emotion which is coming from a past life, either we will attract a life situation which will trigger that release or dreams will become a channel to release them. When our heads are too strong, dreams are the best way for our sub-conscious to release, since our head is busy sleeping.

Once this process was over, almost instantly a new one had begun. That entire day, I had a strong feeling of wanting something. I felt a space had got created in me which needed to be filled. I couldn't understand what that was. I finally found myself wondering about the purpose of my life. I asked myself, over and over, that day whether I was a healer, a mother, a professional...or more? Any explanation felt incomplete. It wasn't bothering me as much but I could feel this question hanging in my head.

It was Saturday and upon checking my blackberry calendar for the current appointment, I realised it was Tessy who was due for a regression that day. I prepared my room, did my meditation and was waiting for her to appear.

I somehow found myself in anticipation of meeting her. It was rare for me to feel the energies of a client much before meeting them. I knew this was something special. Saturdays were off for Aryan so he had gone to my mom's house to play with her and neighbourhood friends he had around that house.

Finally, Tessy dropped in at sharp 11 a.m. She was a good looking woman. Her slender legs were showing even below the long skirt she was wearing. She had a milky white complexion and short brown hair. I got her to fill my customary form so I knew she was 38 and unmarried, though she looked a lot younger than that. She and I clicked instantly. It was as if we had known each other before.

After she arrived I came to know that she was an energy worker and she was very connected to higher planes. I had never had any experience or read any stuff about the Master Spirits or Angels so this was new to me. Going by the way things were evolving and the way my life was taking a new direction, I was open to the universe to show me all the magic there was. I wondered what was in store for me next.

Not only was she polite and beautiful but she also had an angelic feel in herself. She had a relationship issue with a soulmate. She was sure there was a past life connection because she was guided that way. We decided to regress her on the intent to visit the past life from which she carried the source of her issues with this guy.

It was an amazing regression. Tessy had an enormous amount of surrender. She quickly went into a very relevant past life in which she and this guy were lovers. They got separated from each other but this guy still pursued her for a few years till they were together again. It was intense. All of her emotions from her current life came rolling in. She had been separated from him in this life too. It was overwhelming for her to handle the energies but it made so much sense to me as a therapist. We had tapped into the right past life. It gave us most of the answers about why her life was unfolding the way it was.

Once the past life was over, I guided her to the spirit world to meet her guide. She found herself face to face with her spirit guide. She received a lot of guidance about her current life. Just as we were about to end her session, Tessy said there was a message coming through for me. I got excited. She said, 'You are deeply connected to the spirit world. You have been a sage. You are an open spirit. We thank you for being one.' At the time, I didn't understand what an open spirit meant but I had more pressing questions in mind. I waited for more. She mentioned she was conversing with some master spirits. I had read in books that master spirits were certain wise spirits who help and guide humans through various ways with their wisdom. Upon asking for what they meant by an 'open spirit', they said these were souls who were open to receive from the universe and their ability to trust makes them capable of getting many in sync with the divinity within them.

I asked for help regarding the purpose of my life. She immediately said, 'They are saying you are a way-shower,' and she stopped. I didn't know what that meant so I asked her to ask them.

She said, 'There are so many people on that planet who are wandering about without knowing the purpose of their life. You will show them the way.'

It resonated somehow. I was happy. I got what they meant. Usually, in my sessions also, more than healing, my focus was on how to make the clients learn to take responsibility of their journey. I often guided them to initiate their journey inward, where past lives will only play a role but there was much more that they had to discover themselves. Many of them became good friends. Mostly, I was able to give some direction to each, as intuitively guided.

I thanked Tessy from the bottom of my heart for she served as a channel to give another sign to me that I was being watched over. Tessy and I helped each other in untying some knots of our respective lives that day. It was the beginning of a beautiful friendship.

She and I talked over the phone for the next few weeks. It was like I had found a long lost sister. Her ability to laugh and rejoice in a tough life situation gave me strength and motivation to go on. One day, I shared my life with her and told her all about my marriage and then about Rahul.

'I can heal you. Do you want to get some divine guidance about your journey with Rahul from the master spirits? I was guided to come to you for I was told there is something that you will help me unlock in my current life, Maaya. I am sure you could use some help too.'

It was tempting, yet scary. I didn't want to travel that road again. I had pretty much given up on him. I was focusing on my life, career and not really thinking too much about Rahul, ever since the last time we spoke.

Yet, something told me to trust the guidance would only lessen my misery. As if, they would only show me the way to whatever will only be good for me, ultimately. There was no reason to escape the truth, however harsh it might be. I was scared they might say yes it was just a *karmic* relationship and that I must move on. This was exactly what I needed to hear but I was still in denial of it. It was difficult to accept that Rahul and I didn't have something special, something that could last forever.

When all these thoughts were bothering me, I realised Rahul was still very much present in my system. I had to get over him once and for all. I had to face the truth. I agreed for Tessy to take guidance for me. I prepared myself, mentally, to be open in every way and release the hidden misery in me forever. I was hopeful she'd let me know how I would soon be out of my chase for Rahul and have a happy life ahead and I also hoped for some help with the process.

The next day Tessy called and she said she had received a long channelled message for me.

'Upon connecting and asking the wise ones about you and Rahul, I was told that you and Rahul can have a destiny together in this life. Right now the relationship has become more of a burden on you rather than love. You need to let go of the negativity in the form of sadness, fear, regret and anger you are carrying. In divine timing, everything will fall into place.'

I wasn't so sure this was a good thing to have happened. I had been miserable for longer than I should have been. I had got myself insulted enough and finally I had given up on Rahul. I was just expecting them to confirm that we were done. At least that is what I told myself. I was not expecting them to tell me we actually had a destiny.

'Why is he behaving the way he is now? Has he lost the love for me? I can feel it's missing in his energy so how can we ever have a future?'

Tessy said, 'He has unresolved *karma* with his wife too. You also have emotions in the sub-conscious that you are carrying against him and they need to go. You have healed some of your past lives but you still have more to go.

With all close relationships, we develop chords which transfer negative energy from one person to another. All this burden and negativity you are feeling with him is getting transferred to him. You need to disconnect with him for a while and let him make his journey back to you. It will take a lot of patience and courage but it's important for both of you to learn your own life lessons. Just trust the universe and start healing yourself to release whatever is bothering you and build your faith in your ultimate good.'

'He is trying to work out his marriage. I don't want to become the reason for his wife to get hurt. I don't want to do that.'

She said, 'I voiced this concern and I was told that everything happens as per the divine plan and no one will be hurt. It's already a part of your journey so let it happen in the highest and best way.' I didn't quite understand what that meant then, although I accepted that answer since it sounded right.

That night I couldn't sleep properly. Tessy made me realise how our own fears, insecurities or other negative emotions can create a block for our own relationships on a sub-conscious level. I did understand it from my work but when this was presented to me in my life, it gave me a whole new perspective. She also taught me simple ways of connecting with my spirit guide and some of the master spirits.

On one side, the guidance gave me hope but on another side, I sensed a fear of getting hurt all over again. The way Tessy and I had met was not a coincidence and it had become apparent to me that she and I had a role to play in each other's lives. I decided to trust the message and start working on myself. The least I could achieve was releasing my *karmic* blocks to deserve love and then if Rahul allowed himself to cross his own hurdles, maybe we could be together. By now, I wasn't even sure I loved him as much. Internally, I had started fearing and resenting him. They were right. I had a lot of negativity against him which wasn't helping me in anyway.

Over the next few days, I read more and more about the arch angels, ascended masters and master spirits and their abilities to help people. I was getting convinced that this was the right way to go.

I discovered that the best way to bring awareness about one's sub-conscious was to start writing a journal.

Tessy told me that the best way to start working on my negative thoughts and emotions in the sub-conscious was to start writing a journal. I also started calling my spirit guide in my prayers and requesting him to help me and guide me. Each time I had a negative thought, I asked the universe to take it away and convert it into a beautiful thought.

The journaling was brilliant. I slowly felt lighter. I made it a regular practice to express my emotions and state of mind through my journal. In just a few days, I realised that my thoughts were changing. I had greater acceptance of my insecurities and it was easier for me to resolve them too. My gratitude for the universe and people around me also grew. I was building a better relationship with myself.

Tessy removed the chords between me and Rahul through her healing. This was so that we didn't transfer any negative energy between the two of us and we could keep going as individuals.

I lived in a new reality from then on. Even though I was not very sure on how to really talk to various divine beings or get messages from them, yet I certainly felt their presence around me.

My life those days was damn busy. Weekdays I was doing my job and weekends I was doing healing sessions and taking care of Aryan. I had to go out to malls, parks, etc. with him as well. Surprisingly, I didn't feel very tired. I made time for everything that interested me and took care of my child's needs as well. I had never been that active in my life and it was amazing how things were just falling into place.

I was writing my journal, focussing on releasing any fears I felt towards my future, my relationship with Rahul and I was doing it without too many expectations.

Tessy called me in about three weeks' time and said, 'I am participating in a three-day workshop on how to connect with the creator to access a higher perspective on my life and how to heal my *karmic* past including past lives to transform my current life. It's through this therapy technique called "Serenity Surrender" or SS. It allows one to heal themselves for their own past lives and deep *karmic* patterns too. SS does not involve hypnosis and is pretty simple to practice to heal self and others. This way one can learn to be guided at all times and also help oneself while helping others. I think you should join me. What say?'

'Sure. I would love that.'

It resonated with me and I immediately signed up. So many divine beings were already helping me in my life so there was no doubt that this workshop was a channel to enhance that connection.

The day the workshop was to start, I reached thirty minutes before time and there was no one there. It was a quiet beautiful place and I just sat there and closed my eyes.

The moment I was focused inwardly a little, I heard someone saying 'Welcome my child'. I looked around but there was no one. For me this was a sign that I was about to do the right thing.

The venue was an old Parsi mansion with huge sprawling lawns and loads of greenery around. It was a cosy and high energy place.

In about twenty minutes, people started coming in. All of them were participants and I knew none of them except Tessy. We just sat quietly observing each person coming in and waiting for the trainer, Claire, to arrive.

Just as Claire entered the hall, my phone beeped and it was Rahul's call. I was amazed at the synchronicity of the two things. I excused myself to step out and talk to him.

'Hello,' I said. 'Hey. How are you doing?' he asked me. 'I am good. How are you?' I answered with perfect calm and balance.

'Just thought of saying hello to you. Hope things are working out well for you,' he said.

Something in my head was saying 'Oh so he actually called just like that. Not bad. That's interesting.'

We got talking and as per Rahul's old habit of telling me every little thing that happens with him, he started telling me about his whereabouts. It was as if it was a perfectly normal call and nothing had gone wrong between the two of us. I had to interrupt him in-between and tell him that I was busy and would give him a call later.

It took me a few minutes to get out of the disbelief that he had actually called me for no apparent reason. I went and hugged Tessy and told her, 'I can't believe Rahul called. He wanted to talk, just like that'.

'That's great, Maaya. Now you will start seeing this happening more and more. It's already working. Just keep faith and you are on the right track. He won't just forget you like that. I am happy for you,' she said.

The other participants were busy chatting amongst themselves till Claire started speaking and everyone went quiet. She introduced us to SS and told us how "Shivi Dua" conceptualised it while she made her own personal journey of healing herself. Each participant gave their introduction and then the day's agenda was initiated with firstly understanding more about the creator. A participant asked 'who's the creator?'. I was also curious to know what she meant by the word "creator".

The creator here refers to "pure unconditional love". We believe all of us were created from unconditional love and so were all out gods, goddesses, angels and other divine beings. SS allows us to unwrap the various distorted understandings about self that our souls have accumulated over eternity through various experiences. As we keep peeling off each layer of the sub-conscious and dissolving it as a distortion, we slowly start being the spark of unconditional love that we always were. Currently, we can only experience what we have accumulated. This is the reason we suffer at times in our human experience since what we accumulated was not all divine. We made mistakes, judged ourselves and then accumulated darkness too. It slowly became a part of us and we allowed it to become a part of our lives through negative life situations, unwanted relationships, fear of loss and so much more.

What she said touched me deeply. It made so much sense. I realised that healing ourselves is nothing but unwrapping the creator to realise the goodness in all that happened and brought us misery. It is the ability to forgive ourselves for allowing it to happen to us.

It was three days of pure bliss. Each day, Claire introduced us to new concepts that I was unaware of till then. She talked about *karma,* the cycle of evolution, sub-conscious, a soul's journey, manifestation and so much more. She also explained concepts of duality in the form of masculine/feminine and many other ways that were new to me. We did self-healing sessions on each day and partner healing sessions with each other, too, to help resolve our issues in that moment. It was a lot of new information and extremely interesting.

On the first day, during lunch time, we got the opportunity to walk through a stall of books and crystals which was laid out by the organizer. One particular crystal drew me towards it. I picked it up and had a closer look. It was a huge pyramid shaped clear quartz. It was extremely beautiful. I saw the price and it seemed too expensive. I didn't know if I should really be spending so much money on crystals so I kept it back and went down for lunch.

As we climbed down the stairs, upon stepping down the last stair, a beautiful butterfly crossed me from left to right. The butterfly seemed a little unusual and it circled me once for me to notice it. Then as I stood still observing it, it went around me in circles three times. Then it came and sat on my shoulder. I felt compassion and love in its presence. It was as if it was being reiterated that I was on the right path and was being watched. It was heartening to know that someone cared.

By evening, I couldn't get my mind off that crystal so in our next tea break, I finally decided to spend the money and buy it.

It seemed so pure. Everyone in my class wanted to feel its energies. I had not known till then that crystals can carry a lot of energy in the form of thoughts and memories.

It was an awesome day and I had learnt so much. The presence of divine beings could be felt all around us in the workshop. The effect didn't quite wear off even when I got home.

There were eight participants in my class and each of them seemed to be special in some way. It was nice to share our experiences and also realise how so many of us on this planet were going through a similar journey of finding our connection within. I kept thinking about the workshop even after getting home.

I showed my crystal to Aryan and he was so excited. We kept looking at it closely with the infinite amount of lines that showed inside it. At once I saw a small little cut right at the tip of the crystal and I got worried. It was very tiny but seemed like the tip was not really whole. I remembered the crystal guy saying that tips can tap in negative energy if they are not kept whole and safe. I wrapped it in a thick piece of cotton and decided to take it the next day to see what could be done.

By then, I had somehow got very attached to the crystal. I didn't quite like the idea of getting it replaced. I decided to ask Claire the next day and went to sleep.

The next day, when I entered the room, there was only Sophie standing by the window and looking out. She seemed to know more about healing than us and I hadn't really got a chance to communicate too much with her the previous day.

She seemed lost somewhere so I decided not to disturb her since there were still around twenty minutes for everyone to start pouring in. I silently took my place, unwrapped my crystal and sat down. In another five minutes, Sophie moved from the window and turned towards me.

'Oh hello Maaya! I am sorry I didn't notice you were here. How was yesterday and how is the sweety crystal doing?' she said lifting my crystal up.

'Sophie, it has a little damage on its tip. I don't want to return it since I have somehow got attached to it. What do I do?' I said to her with a sloppy face.

'Ok. Let me see,' she said, taking the crystal with her to her seat. As she sat, she closed her eyes and stayed in that state for about two-three minutes.

'Maaya, I will heal its tip. Don't worry, but remove that thought from within you that it's damaged. It needs to be loved and appreciated is what it tells me,' she said to me.

'What? Crystals talk? It needs love? I don't understand,' I said looking at her in astonishment.

'Yes my dear. We are all energy and so are they. It is possible to communicate with all forms of energy. One just needs to trust and surrender. Crystals need a lot of love. This one is special. It has been waiting to be loved for a long time. See all those memories it stores. It has come to you for a special purpose. You need to give it a lot of love and appreciation. Crystals are immensely powerful and when they resonate with you, they can draw favourable situations, energetically, towards you. Trust me. This is a divine one,' she said and she started working on it by closing her eyes and doing something.

This conversation was new to me. If it was me, one year ago, I would have discarded all this information. By this time, I had reached that stage where I could appreciate this new knowledge about stones and crystals and use it in my life.

'How do you know all of this Sophie?' I asked.

'Claire will teach you too. I am repeating this workshop. I have done it before. I am repeating it since every time I feel I need to stay focused inwardly and am ready to move to the next level of awareness, the group energies of the workshop and the partner sessions make it easier to make that inner transition,' she said.

Crystals were also supposed to be cleansed and charged before one would start using them. Charging meant once they had been cleaned, they were linked up to the energy of the one they belonged to. I had this very sweet and divine surdy guy in my class who knew how to charge crystals. He helped me charge mine.

Sophie worked on my crystal almost the entire day, as and when she could take time out from the workshop agenda. During tea time late afternoon, she came to return it to me.

'Maaya, something amazing just happened. When I was done healing it, it showed me a visual. I saw two souls, standing facing each other, on either side of the crystal and then one of them moved and came behind the other one and they merged. Then it said, 'I am here to attract your other half. It was a message for you. You are lucky sweetheart. Enjoy this one!'

That was sweet. I was overwhelmed.

A sudden spurt of happiness and amazement went through my heart when I heard what Sophie said. I kissed my crystal over and over for I had fallen in love with it.

The next few days, I worked with the creator to heal negative thought patterns and fears. I received many validations for me to trust it's all for real. When I bought more crystals for myself, Aryan insisted to buy a few for him too. I saw him talking to his crystals at times, as if they could talk to him. I wasn't surprised though because kids have the kind of surrender where they can experience subtle energies much faster than adults. This was when I realised that it was all about surrender. Once you trust and surrender, the path itself reveals so much light that it feels illuminated and safe.

As adults, we need to unlearn so much to be able to develop faith. We have highly developed minds and egos and they stop us from trusting anything that doesn't have a scientific phenomenon going with it.

Energy is subtle and yet it plays so much more critical a role in our lives. We often fail to recognise it since we grew up only to resonate with science. I was glad I was transforming and when I looked around me, I realised there were a lot of people like me who were initiating their journey of faith and surrender.

'What are you looking for?' my maid asked me when she saw me frantically looking for something in the bookshelf. I was looking for this book that I bought about year back. I remember it had a red cover and said 'International bestseller' but I didn't remember its name. I felt like reading it but couldn't find it anywhere. I was hoping I didn't give it to Kunal when he came to pick up Aryan last year. I did give him a few books but I didn't think I gave him that one.

'Ok, let me look for it,' she said. We looked everywhere but couldn't find it. Aryan and I were meant to go to the mall that day as he wanted to get a fish spa done. It was a special type of spa in which hundreds of tiny fishes called "doctor fish" were left to peel off the dead skin on one's feet. They ate the dead skin and it gave one a ticklish feeling on their feet. He used to find the fish foot spa very amusing. I allowed him the luxury since it was fun plus cleansing. I decided to do some shopping for myself.

However evolved I might get, when it came to shopping, my inner child rose and it was an uplifting and enjoyable experience all the time. It was a Saturday and I had decided to take a break that weekend to spend more time with Aryan. I didn't schedule any healing sessions.

We reached Select Citywalk in Saket. It was a very refreshing experience. I realised that in my need for more and more wisdom and mystic experiences, I was missing out on normal life of food, drinks and shopping. I gave myself permission to enjoy to the fullest that day and spend quality time with Aryan. My energies needed some indulgence.

We ate pastries, pop-corns, watched a movie, shopped, he had a fish spa and at last we ended up at a bookstore. While looking for book, I just realised I could actually try to see if I could find that book I was looking for at home, at the bookshop.

I started looking for it and I called upon the divine for help. I looked and looked for an hour but it was of no use. The book wasn't there and since I didn't know the name of the book or author, there was no way I could locate it. I gave up on it eventually and bought a few new ones and we decided to go for dinner.

There was this restaurant by the fountain where we decided to eat pizza and pasta. Aryan had fun with a few other kids on the ramp, in the fountain.

By the time we reached home, it was 9:00 and both of us crashed on the bed. Next morning, I unwrapped all our shopping and tried the new dresses I had bought for myself.

It had been a while that I had paid any attention to how I looked in a full length mirror. I closed the door and tried on a bright blue coloured dress. I noticed how beautifully the dress draped on my back and waist. I actually loved how it revealed my curves in a graceful manner. I liked my figure and beautiful fair skin. My hair looked pretty neat too.

When I saw my curves in the mirror, I remembered the day when I tried a black evening gown which Rahul had bought for me. When I wore it and came towards him, he said 'Wow'. I was standing right in front of a full length mirror. He went behind me, moved my hair off my right shoulder and kissed me passionately on the neck, still maintaining his gaze on me in the mirror. It was extremely seductive and then we made love.

It had been a few days ever since that random call he made to check-up on me. Since then, neither he nor I had connected with each other. I was hoping he would call again but he didn't. I had now slowly started taking it lightly and started telling myself that if it's meant to be, it will be.

I was just thinking about all of this when my phone beeped and it was him. 'Hey. I am in Mumbai. How you are doing?' it said.

I smiled and wrote back, 'I am good. What's up with you? What are you doing in Mumbai?' I wrote to him.

'Office work. Went to marine drive for a walk in the morning and thought about you,' he said. We had spent some awesome days in Mumbai and indeed that reminded me of those fantastic memories.

'Do you miss me?' I asked in a jiffy. 'Sometimes, on special occasions,' he wrote back. It sort of made me sad.

'Hmmmm,' I wrote back and the conversation was over.

I sat beside my bed for a few minutes and absorbed that he didn't really miss me except on special occasions. Something nudged me inside and said, 'It's all right. Take it easy.'

I then distracted myself with some chores. While tidying my room, I decided to line up all my new clothes in the closet and the books on the bookself.

As I reached my bookshelf, to my surprise, that book that I was frantically looking for the previous day, was lying right in my face on the bookshelf. It was so surprising since we had looked for it thoroughly the previous day but couldn't find it then. I realized I had received some divine help. It gave me an amazing sense of empowerment.

I then decided to read the new book while Aryan was catching up on his cartoons for Sunday morning. It was a blissful day. We rested, we watched cartoons together, ate and enjoyed. I realised I should have been doing this more often with Aryan. It was great to bond with him and know how he likes to spend his weekends and Mommy time.

After about three weeks, I took an off from work for a week. I and Deeksha decided to go to Benares. It was a spontaneous decision and we decided to take Aryan along.

I had been drawn to that place for a while now but never really thought of actually making a visit. Somehow I mentioned it to Deeksha that I want to go to Benaras and she said she also felt like visiting that place so we decided to do it together.

Aryan was excited because he loved travelling and also eating loads of junk food. It was so surprising that I was a non-vegetarian and so was Kunal but for some reason, Aryan was a vegetarian. He had watched a movie when he was 3-4 years old, in which, a little girl makes friends with a chicken and the same chicken is served for dinner. She refuses to eat chicken again goes on strike along with her friends in that orphanage saying we don't eat our friends. Aryan got so touched by that movie that he stopped eating meat all together.

Many times, I would be concerned about this since somewhere I felt guilty that he had less choices of eating especially when we went abroad. As my spiritual journey took shape, I realised it wasn't a coincidence that he was a vegetarian. He motivated me to be one almost every time I ate non-veg.

Slowly, I started noticing the impact of the food I ate, on my mind while meditating. It was huge. Many times, I could only get time to meditate in the evening. Whenever I did and if I had eaten meat before that, I felt the presence of a lot of cluttered negative thoughts and emotions in my mind. I found it hard to stay focused and my experience diluted. Slowly, I experimented with various types of meat and finally I decided to turn into a vegetarian. Also, the same food that I used to love at one point, now, didn't taste as good. It stopped giving me the satisfaction it used to. It was then only about making a conscious decision for the shift. Aryan's being vegetarian helped.

If one looked at Benaras as a tourist destination, well, it was like any other small city in India. It had loads of people, small gullies and unorganised traffic with loads of rickshaw pullers. Energetically, since it was a very old spiritual destination, there was a lot of divine presence to be experienced in there. I felt connected with the city almost instantly.

Even before reaching Benaras, through my research on Google, I had found that it was one of the oldest Hindu cities and was believed to be where Ganges moved out of the tresses of Shiva to become the huge river that it was. It also included the famous Sarnath, where Gautam Buddha delivered his first sermon about 2,500 years ago upon attaining enlightenment. Sarnath signified the moment when Buddha was mesmerizing, glowing and ready to address his disciples – the moment called *Dharamachakra Pravartan*.

We were to stay at the Radisson. They had arranged for a cabbie to pick us up from the airport. It was around 3 p.m. when we reached the hotel. We had signed up for two adjacent bedrooms which they called twins. The rooms were interconnected from the inside.

The cab driver served as our tourist guide, all along the way from the airport to the hotel and explained us about each place that fell on the way. I was amazed to see the number of temples that Benaras had. Aryan once said, 'Mummy, how come this place has so many temples. Delhi wouldn't have those many stationery shops also.' We shared a good laugh at the comparison he made. For him, a stationery shop was the most common thing to be found in Delhi. It was probably true for his age. The cab driver told us about all we could potentially do in Benaras. We had already done our research on the Internet so we knew exactly what all we would be doing. We had to attend the evening *ganga aarti* at the *ghat*, the *mangala aarti* which happened at 2 a.m. in the Shiv temple and the next day, we had to visit Sarnath.

We were informed that to get a good view of the *ganga aarti*, it was important that we reached there around 5.00 p.m. We were to then wait for the *aarti* to commence till around 6:30 p.m. The seats usually were filled if one reached there nearing *aarti* time. We decided to check-in, quickly freshen up and immediately leave for the *ghat*.

The *ghat* was getting all ready for the *aarti*. We got a brilliant seat on the deck nearby from which we could watch the whole event nicely, without getting disturbed by the crowd. We first did a small prayer at the *ghat* with our feet in the Ganges and then took our seats at the deck. Slowly, it started getting dark and we could see the pundits all dressed in robes of white and pink satin. They were getting their seats ready to be able to perform the *aarti*. Soon there were many people who hired boats and they sat in the boats to be a part of the elaborate show.

Aryan got all excited seeing this and said, 'Mummy, we should also have taken a boat. It would be so much more fun to watch it from there.' He said pointing at a boat next to us. I agreed. It sounded very tempting to move off to a boat but most of the good ones were taken and we couldn't risk leaving our seat for them. I managed to convince Aryan by saying would take a boat ride later.

Soon, the *aarti* began first in the Ganga temple next to the *ghat* and slowly moved to the *ghat*. Suddenly, it started raining very heavily. I loved rain and as a friend had once said, whenever I am up to something good, if it rains, it serves as a divine confirmation that I am on track. All those on the boats had to be offloaded and the *ghat* looked like a mess.

Aryan was happy to discover that we were actually better placed. Soon the sky cleared up and the *aarti* continued. It was a very synchronistic event and all the pundits together took their huge shells and blew them.

It was a divine experience. As I looked up at the sky, I felt the gods and goddesses were witnessing the event. Benaras sure was a magical place.

We soon got to the hotel and ordered some food. We decided to sleep early so that we could get up at 1:30 a.m. and attend the *aarti* at the Shiv temple.

The morning *aarti* was another unusual experience. In this one, they first washed and cleaned lord Shiva's symbol, the Shiv lingam with water and milk. Then slowly they decorated it with flowers, cloth and many other things. At one point, it looked so amazingly beautiful and almost alive. It was not about what they used to decorate it, but the whole atmosphere. There was loud chanting of *mantras* and it seemed to be decorated with so much love and compassion.

Aryan was fast asleep in my lap while Deeksha and I were involved in watching the whole sequence. This whole activity was happening inside a small room which had doors on all four sides for the view. They even had huge LCD screens on either side for those people to watch the aarti, who couldn't get a direct view.

At one point, when I was admiring the view, something on the top of the door through which we were looking in, distracted me. As I looked at the top of the door, I could see the carving of Lord Shiva on it. As I kept looking at it, it seemed to start moving. Lord Shiva was dancing with all his might and grace.

As I kept looking at him doing that, I felt like I was physically transported right in front of him. There was no expression on his face. He looked neither sad nor happy. It was as if he was just dancing in sync with the chanting that seemed to get louder and louder. I was mesmerised with this experience and I had completely lost the sense of time and space. It was so enchanting.

The chants stopped and I felt a hand on my back. It was Deeksha and when I gathered sense of my surroundings, I realised I had tears in my eyes. It was the most amazing experience and I couldn't thank Lord Shiva and Benaras enough for making me a part of this divine journey.

As we rose up to take *prashadam* from the pundit, he looked at me and said, 'You are blessed my child. You shall find what you seek. Just stay in faith.' and I thanked him while we left.

The next day, we woke up late and visited Sarnath and the Benaras Hindu university. The whole trip was more than what I had hoped for and both Deeksha and I were ever so thankful for the blessing of visiting that place. It was a memorable experience. I was so full of gratitude. There seemed to be so much peace within.

□

Welcoming The New

One of the happiest days of my life was when I decided to buy a new car. My mom and dad were so happy to hear that finally, I had decided to give-up my old car which had become an antique piece anyway. I had taken the decision a few weeks back but one day I arranged for the bank loan and was in the Tata Showroom to buy my new Safari.

I always loved the Safari and I had waited long to be able to afford it. I had already checked with the showroom for a black colour in the model I had chosen and I could walk out with the keys in a matter of four hours. Aryan went with me and both of us were so excited to drive it back.

We decided to take it to the temple first. While we were enjoying the music on the FM channels and driving down to the temple near our place, a song played up which Rahul and I used to hear together. It was a lovely Punjabi number and I had goose bumps on my skin the moment it started playing. It reminded me of Rahul's crazy ways of loving me.

It was an anchor to my relationship and beautiful times with Rahul. I suddenly started missing him. He would have been so happy to see I had finally bought my favourite car. He used to ask me so many times, 'When will you let go of this useless car Maaya?' and I would always say, 'Only when I can buy a black Safari,' and both of us would smile. I then distracted myself and started singing the next song which Aryan loved too.

We did a small prayer expressing gratitude for the car at the temple. Post that, we drove to my parents' house. Aryan ran up to the house to call my parents out while I was still looking for a parking space outside the apartments.

I was about to get off the car when my phone rang. It was Rahul. I saw his number flashing on my screen and for a few milli seconds I was not whether sure I was reading correctly. It was happening too often now that he was calling. Not that I was complaining. I took the call.

'Hello,' I said. 'Hi. How are you?' he said.

'I am good. How about you? Back from Mumbai?'

'Yes. Came back yesterday. Maaya, did something nice just happen to you?' he suddenly asked me. I was a little blank since I didn't understand what he meant by that.

'Something nice? What do you mean Rahul?'

'Nothing. I just had a feeling you were really happy.'

'Yes Rahul. I was just thinking I would call and tell you. I just drove home my new Safari,' I said.

'Wow! So we still have our telepathic link going. Good. What colour did you buy?' he asked me.

'You know it!'

'Yeah. I do. Black,' he said and laughed.

'Congrats Maaya! I am happy for you. Maybe you should come and give me a ride in your new car one of these days,' he said.

I was not sure I had heard him correctly. He was asking me to come and give him a ride. Well, this was too much to take in at a go but I gracefully replied,

'Yes sure. Will see you tomorrow then.'

It was such an amazing feeling to know that Rahul was still connected with me on another plane. This had come as a validation to me that things were indeed going to be all right, as I was always told.

My parents reflected pride on their faces the moment they saw this huge car. My dad hugged me and kissed me on the cheek. It was special for them to see how well their daughter was settling on her own feet and manifesting what she wanted. That day, I couldn't stop thanking God and the universe for having blessed me with so much.

When we reached home, Aryan told me, 'Mumma, don't you think you have forgotten something?'

'What?'

'Don't you want to ask your spirit guide to protect our car?'

Aryan was developing so much trust and faith in the life force. I was overwhelmed to hear him say this. Many times I felt he was a more evolved soul than me. As if he had come to this planet to ground me, to show me direction which he did without fail on so many occasions. I kissed him on his forehead and together we called upon our spirit guides to keep us and our car safe.

That was one beautiful night where manifestation, blessings and peace all came in one go. It gave me the message that 'ALL IS WELL'.

It was bright and lovely next day when I drove my new car to work. I was happy for two reasons that day. Firstly, for my car and secondly I was going to meet Rahul in the evening after work. It had been just a few minutes that I had been working on my design when Dev said, 'I haven't heard you humming in a very long time Maaya. What's up?'

'I got my new car yesterday, didn't I tell you?'

'Oh yes, Congratulations. I need a treat at lunch today. There is something more, Maaya. A car is not the only reason. Come-on! Tell me,' he said.

'Nothing Dev. Just feeling good today,' was all I could say when my intercom rang and Gagan summoned me to his office.

'So, how's the new car treating you Maaya?' said Gagan.

'It's good. I like that car and it's like a dream come true. I am really happy for I could finally buy it,' I said to him with a smile.

'Good. So now getting back to work, I have these designs we need to finalise today and send to the client. You may have to stay back late today evening. I hope you don't mind?' he said.

I certainly did because I was meant to meet Rahul that day.

'Gagan, I have to meet someone in the evening. Do you mind if I carry them home and get them done up tomorrow morning?'

'Yes sure. That will work. By the way Maaya, who are you meeting? Is it someone special? You seem to be happy today,' he said.

'Well, an old friend you can say Gagan. Will tell you someday,' I said and without looking at him in the eye, I just rushed out of the room.

I was admittedly a little lost that day. I didn't know what to expect. It was a mix of emotions. On one side, I was hoping Rahul was missing me and wanted to come back to my life. On the other, my mind said, 'Beware and don't get hurt again.'

I wanted to be cautious. With a lot of difficulty, I had been able to get to the stage where I had struck a balance between my emotions and my life and I was happy with it. I was not sure what was going on with Rahul. Somehow I still felt he was not going all out with it so he was surely holding back some bit. I didn't want to give it that much thought and build expectations.

I immediately went to the prayer room in our office. It was meant to be used for the daily prayers some people did in the day. I sat down and closed my eyes. I called upon my guide and asked him to help me and guide me for I did feel anxiety coming up. I heard him in my inner ears saying, 'It is a part of the process. All will be well. Just go with the flow and just be. It is all sorting out in divine timing. I am here to protect you. You'll be safe.'

I then asked him to shield me and I felt a sense of peace and relaxation dawn on me as I came out of prayer room.

The whole day I didn't think about Rahul again till it was time to leave and meet him at his building.

I reached his building and gave him a call. He took 10 minutes to come and sit in the car. He was visibly impressed.

'Wow. This looks cool babes. I am so proud of you,' he said.

'Thanks Rahul. So where do I take you for a ride?' I asked him. 'Well, let's go pick a coffee from a CCD.'

'Okay.'

We were silent while driving to the nearest coffee shop. Rahul was busy exploring the car and its interiors. He was very fond of cars and it was not surprising that he was looking at every little thing in detail.

Finally, he looked at the CD case, took out a nice CD and put it in the player. 'I absolutely love this car and I am glad you finally got it. It's quite cool,' he said, settling down in his seat and breaking the silence.

We reached the coffee shop and sat there. We were talking about my work, his work and all the normal stuff just as if no time had passed by. Both of us didn't touch the topic about whatever had been going on in our relationship lately. We discussed absolutely nothing about love, commitment, suffering, etc.

'I saw past lives between you and me Rahul,' I suddenly decided to mention.

'Hmmmmmm. So, how were they? I am not sure I believe in them but it will be interesting to hear them like stories,' he said.

'Nopes! I wouldn't like to treat them as stories Rahul. It's fine.'

'Maaya, I am sorry but I don't really believe in past lives in that case,' he said.

'That's ok Rahul. When it's time for you to discover that connection with your past, you will start believing and till then, you are good. Weren't you the one who introduced me to the concept of soulmates? I also remember your intuition is far stronger than mine. We used to do everything based on our feelings and the moment we didn't feel like going somewhere or doing something, we just followed the feeling rather than logically analysing it. You have powerful energy Rahul and I just want you to always remember that. Past Lives or no Past Lives, you will be guided,' I said in a flow where I was not sure what I was saying.

I guess there were a few messages which I wanted to convey all at the same time which got mixed. We finished our coffee and moved to the car for a ride back.

Out of the blue he said, 'Funny that you mention my energies. These days, I have to just think about someone and they either call or appear. Sometimes, I surprise myself with the precision,' he said enthusiastically.

'So those are vibrations you are able to pick. You are a natural Rahul. Just keep following your inner guidance and you will never go wrong.'

'Can I ask you something?' I finally mustered the courage to talk some sense with him.

'Yes Maaya.'

'Were you missing me?'

He was quiet for a good two minutes.

'Maaya, let's not discuss this right now. I do think of you often,' he said.

'What happened Rahul? Did I do something?'

'No. You can never do anything to hurt me. You didn't. You were right, in those days I was confused and somehow, I still am. I still am married, Maaya and when I look at Anushkha, I feel she deserves a daddy. I don't know. I know I hurt you and I have not forgiven myself for it,' he said.

I sensed heaviness in his voice so I stopped my car on one side of the highway. When I looked at him, he had tears in his eyes. I don't know what went into me but I could not help it. I drew him closer to me to embrace him. All of a sudden, he kissed me passionately on my lips. It was this hungry kiss where I could feel all his hurt, pain and so much more. I wanted to tell him how much I had gone through when he said he doesn't feel for me anymore but I couldn't. He was already broken, I didn't want to give him more guilt. We kissed and kissed for a few minutes which seemed like ages.

'I love you Rahul,' I told him in a meek voice.

'I love you too baby. Always have but I don't know what I am doing. I am lost Maaya. I have responsibilities. I can't be there for you,' he said and suddenly got off the car.

'I am sorry Maaya,' he said after he got off the car and touched my cheeks.

I was so lost. I didn't know how to react. I just sat there looking at him while he quickly waved to a cabbie and went off in the cab. It took me a while to come back to my senses and really understand what had just happened.

After all, I had just thought Rahul was back with me but the next minute he just walked off again. This was what I was afraid of. He had done it again. He had shaken up my life and my emotions all over again and walked away and now I was to deal with them all over again.

This time it was bad because now I also knew he loved me but he was stopping himself from being with me. I felt helpless. For some reason, I never developed anger or blamed Rahul but this time, there was so much anger. I hated myself for allowing this to happen to me. I felt like a doormat.

I drove home to Pooja and told her all that had happened. She didn't know how to respond. I didn't know what was I expecting from her but I just needed to talk to someone and get it all out of my system. Pooja seemed to be a little angry at Rahul too but she chose not to express herself and infuriate me any further. She just said one thing.

'Just let go and surrender Maaya. Let him make his own journey to self-realization. If he loves you and his happiness lies with you, let him find that out in his own way. Maybe he has unfinished business with his family. It will all happen just the way that's best for you. Just give it some space. Let go!'

Having said that, she at least pushed me to the awareness that I was losing my balance. I was being obsessive about him. It was not easy for me to lose Rahul all over again. Yet, maybe he was never mine anyway. I had to work on this obsession. It was hampering my life.

It had been two days since I had met Rahul and I was not sure I was completely out of that experience. I decided to talk to Tessy about it and ask for help. Tessy's phone kept ringing without an answer. After a few tries, I recalled that she was meant to travel to Hong Kong for a workshop during those dates and maybe she had left her phone behind. This was disappointing because then I was left to myself to discover what to do.

I put Aryan to sleep and just before I was about to hit the bed myself, I remembered something. Tessy once suggested that if I found my mind interfering while receiving a message, I could just put the intent on a piece of paper under the pillow before I sleep.

I took a piece of paper and wrote 'My dear guide, please help me understand my future with Rahul. I need your help and guidance. I request you to come in my dreams to help me.' I put the paper under my pillow and slept. That night, I don't know if I dreamt anything but I was a lot more peaceful when I woke up in the morning. I passed the day with routine work, somehow ignoring my internal clutter. I repeated the same exercise the next night as well.

This time, I saw a weird dream.

I saw Rahul, standing on one side of a kind of seesaw, facing me. When he was naturally left free, he fell towards me and looked happy. Suddenly, something pulled him back while he was positioned upright and then he got sad. I wanted to raise up my hands and help him to get to me but just then a man in a white cloak appeared. He said 'That step is his to take. You can't interfere my child. You can only be.'

I woke up in the middle of the night. I knew I had a seen a dream but I couldn't recall it completely until morning. I wrote bits of it in my journal as it came to me and till morning, I finally understood the whole sequence. It was sort of funny the way he was swinging but I understood the message. The message conveyed that although Rahul was naturally inclined to be by my side, he had resistance to taking that stand. Since I couldn't see the source of the resistance, I assumed it could be external or internal. While he was coming to me, he was happy but every time he was pulled back, he got sad. He was in some conflict, inwardly, that needed to be resolved.

The journey from the head to the heart is a particularly difficult one. I could imagine what he was going through, yet I blamed him for not being there for me. I was left to only witness it but not participate directly. It wasn't so much about standing up for me as it was about standing up for himself and his own happiness. Deep in my heart, I knew that if he left everything and came to me, only because of my love, he might regret his decision at some point. I wanted it to be his call for his own peace and happiness. He had to be brave. It wasn't easy but it was important for him to know what he wanted and then have the courage to get it.

I felt much better the next morning. The dream sort of gave me a release to the anger. Those days, I was reading a wonderful book and the author's way of looking at life particularly intrigued me. I had read this book years back too, but couldn't relate to it that much then, but I picked it up again and now it made so much more sense.

The two important messages that I understood from that book coupled with experience of life were firstly that 'at any given point in time, we deserve what we are getting'. It was certainly a very bold statement to make because so many of us might think well, I don't think I deserve the shit that I am getting nor did I do anything to deserve it.

Let me explain. Here, my understanding and experience with healing past lives and my own journey helped me. The ideas that we do actually get what we need/deserve at every point, but it's just that we don't have a memory of why it is the way it is. The deserving is at a sub-conscious level and we may or may not be able to understand it with our conscious mind. The sub-conscious mind carries memories and thought patterns from the numerous past lives that we have lived. These understandings have negativity in them from when we suffered or were helpless. We tend to attract similar life situations and relationship patterns in our current life only to remove those negativities and to build higher understanding of our past experiences. On the outer level, we might say we want happiness and yet on the sub-conscious level, we might have believed that 'happiness comes only by way of suffering first', which was created when in some past experience one had to suffer before being happy. In such a case, one will attract a lot of suffering to build deservingness for the happiness to arrive. Such experiences leave incompletion in souls for they can't then relate to being the creators of their own destiny.

It took me a while to understand this aspect of our energies. I went back to it again and again in my own life to relate my experiences to my sub-conscious mind and it made sense.

The second thing I understood was even deeper. At any given point in time, the creator never wanted us to suffer. We, ourselves, in our subtle being, have built beliefs that suffering is the only way to pay back for a bad *karma*. We have what are called 'hooks' in our energies that attract negativity/suffering/pain our way.

I recalled an example here to enhance my own understanding of this concept. I had a client in those days, who had a boyfriend who was initially the most loving, kind, compassionate person she had ever met. He treated her like a queen and she felt blessed to have him in her life.

Slowly, when she observed his conduct with other people, she at times found him rude, rough and maybe not classy. Slowly, she started having doubts as to whether he was the right guy for her.

This guy was extremely sensitive to their relationship and he sensed she was a little lost, with regards to their relationship. He confronted her and she admitted she felt they were not compatible enough, didn't have similar likings, etc. The guy was extremely possessive about this woman and he couldn't take it. He tried to talk her into changing her opinion but she wouldn't budge.

Slowly, the distances between them kept increasing. He couldn't really let her go. He belonged to a rich, political family. This woman got scared of his ability to ensure he gets what he wants by whatever means. He started using his power to force her to stay in the relationship because he had this intense need to have her in his life. She was scared of his power and the fact that he could stoop to any level to get her and slowly that is what happened.

He started threatening her. He said he didn't care if she did or didn't love him but she would marry him and that was it. He would call her parents and warn them of kidnapping her or killing her on account of them marrying her off to someone else.

In this situation, this lady came to me and she was very stressed, frustrated and scared. She wanted me to help her and release past life *karmas*. The little problem was that she was expecting magic to happen. Somewhere this situation was intense and her parents were also involved.

When I did her SS healing session, we found two past lives. In both past lives, there was pattern. They got into a victim-victimiser type of conflicting scenario in a close relationship and in the end, in both lives, when this woman left him or got separated from him, he died.

This revelation was surprising but it made so much more sense now. When I resolved those lives and she came out of the session, I asked her if this guy associated her with his dying. She confirmed my analysis that he did mention a few times that he was sure to die if she abandoned him. So, what I gathered was that he was using all his might and being what he didn't really want to be to her, not because he wanted to torture her but because he had a very deep fear that the moment she left his life, he would die.

Also, when we were resolving the emotions from these two lives, this woman carried a lot of guilt for him because she held herself responsible for him dying. So, in this life, she had 'a need to suffer' because there was this belief that 'only by suffering through him can I pay him back for the hurt I caused him'. She also had a need to be punished for hurting him by hurting herself.

It took me a few more sessions to release all the energies but finally, their *karmic* contracts were resolved. As and when I removed her beliefs to suffer, to deserve suffering, etc., this guy started distancing from her automatically. *Karmas* are like threads, if they are between two people and they are released from one, the other end has no choice but to let them go. It's just important to use the right technique to completely remove the stuck energies and deal with mutual forgiveness.

When the interest level in her had significantly reduced from the man's side, she even talked him into having a session with me. This gave me the opportunity to release his fears and his side of whatever more emotions he might be carrying. Finally, both realised they were not meant for each other and decided to go on their own individual journeys.

From this case, I concluded that 'We transform and so do our realities'.

Our future, our realities are variable. We have the ability to transform our future by making the intent to be guided. If we have enough faith and surrender, it happens in divine strength. We are able to manifest whatever we want.

Slowly, the cobweb of my life was also getting resolved. I had deeper and clearer understanding of my *karmic* patterns and what had happened with me. My chase for Rahul settled and though the desire to be with him stayed, I was at peace with it in the background. I that understood he is driven by his *karmas,* just as I am driven by mine. There was surrender and serenity building in me. I was able to be at peace with myself and just be in the moment.

Interestingly, I met such people very often who came to me not because they wanted to release the past, but wanted to live in the past because it projected a more glamorous proposition. Initially, I took out a lot of time and effort to make them understand that it's not the right thing to do but slowly, I realised that lesson also comes to them in divine timing.

I was enjoying this new journey inward. The best thing about making this journey was that everything was about surrender and being with oneself. The only ego that was to be dealt with was self. Slowly, I built my routine in such a way that I would find thirty minutes in the morning and thirty minutes in the evening to just enjoy the stillness in my mind through meditation. I didn't practise any chanting, focusing on pictures or things. I knew each practice had a good reason to exist but I just followed the simple way, by watching my thoughts and not engaging with them.

Slowly, my thoughts were slowing down. I saw a kind of settling of energies, this was bringing in my daily life. It had been a few weeks since Rahul and I had not kept in touch and slowly I was getting used to it. I hardly cared. Just that at times, there was this wave of emotion which left me ungrounded. In spite of everything, I kept doing my meditations and I was constantly reminded that surrender is the key. Additionally, I was guided.

Gradually, Claire and I became very good friends. She helped me in believing that we are truly the sparks of the creator and we didn't need to look for love outside till we recognized it within. Claire had been able to imbibe SS as her way of life. She incorporated a lot of what she'd learnt into transforming her relationships, thoughts and even physical body. She shared several experiences with me where, by the way of SS, she was able to bring about a change in her own or someone else's situation. Her trust in SS inspired me to go further in manifesting a magical life.

Every time I healed myself, I felt the shift instantly. Slowly, I could identify the deep beliefs of my sub-conscious that made me do whatever I did in my current life. My conscious mind found its answers for why things happened the way they did. Every moment I could feel my energies getting lighter and a general happiness sinking in.

I always had this concern that I couldn't regress myself and yet I needed to help myself in my evolution. Claire's guidance and the knowledge of SS were very powerful in my being able to get past this block. Claire had given me a gift. Ever since I had found my connection with the creator, I realised so many truths about my eternal being.

I thought my dad didn't really believe in all of this stuff I did with regards to past lives, *karmas*, etc. Whenever I went to mom's place, my mom was ever so inquisitive to hear about my latest experiences and insights. My dad was always least interested.

I knew my dad was very spiritual and used to meditate for hours during his college years. He had slowly fallen into the routine of just doing the daily *pooja* but really had let go of the awareness of his connection with his divine. At one point, my dad's intuition was very powerful and he used to trust it for his life decisions but slowly, he had moved away from it.

One day when I was at mom's place, my mom and Aryan were busy watching *My Friend Ganesha*. It was Aryan's favourite movie and it seemed like my mom was enjoying it too. I was sitting with dad, while he was watching some stock news on the TV.

I just saw his pack of medicines next to him and randomly asked him 'Papa, don't you feel you want that connection you had with yourself in your younger days? You were happier then. Weren't you? Now look, how many medicines those are. You don't need any of those. You just need to find time for yourself and sort your emotions out. All those diseases will go away.'

He was quietly listening to me. He let me finish what I was saying but was still facing the TV.

When I was done, he looked at me and said, 'Honey, do you think I enjoy taking these medicines? I want to be happy again. Tell me what should I do? I don't know how to get back that self that I used to be. I have come a long way.'

I was surprised at his reaction and sort of ashamed too. Here I was healing the world and for my own dad, I couldn't see the need for healing in his eyes. Maybe till then I didn't trust myself enough to be able to help him. Actually, I had assumed he wouldn't take what I say seriously so I didn't bother.

I always thought if he believed I could heal him, he would tell me so. That day I realised, sometimes, some people find it difficult to reach you but that doesn't mean they don't have the intent to. I was touched by his expression. I told him I would help him rediscover his old self and get rid of all his medication. He said, 'Ok,' and smiled.

This incident reminded me of a dear friend whom I met after years almost immediately when I came back from Singapore. He lived in the US and had come for his check-up for a nodule he had developed in his throat. The doctors had scared him that it could be malignant. He somehow trusted the Indian medical system more so he combined his tests with an official trip and flew to Delhi.

He called just to catch-up with me when he happened to tell me about his throat. I told him to come and see me for a PLR session. He had read books about PLR so he was open to giving it a chance. As a practice, I did a pre-session interview with each client to know their problem and do some trust building.

I asked him, 'So, how is your life? What's up?'

'Oh well Maaya, all is fine. I am doing well. Life is great.'

I obviously didn't manage to crack it with that so I decided to come straight to the point, 'So, Johnny, do you have a problem in expressing yourself?'

He went quite for a few seconds and then said, 'Maybe I do. I am not too comfortable with public speaking. At my position, I have to do it many times but it takes me a while to prepare myself and gather the motivation to do it. It doesn't come naturally to me.'

'What about expression in your personal life? Treat me as your therapist and be open. Are you expressive in your personal life?'

From this point on, Johnny opened up to me and it turned out that he was going through a bad marriage because his wife was the controlling, dominating types and he was allowing her to be so. He didn't express himself at all at home and slowly things had got messy. His lack of expression was suffocating him and at the same time his wife and child thought of him as a weak person because he couldn't voice his thoughts. He was suffering internally and even though professionally he was quite successful, he had started feeling that didn't help.

This gave me enough clues to the fact that he had a blockage in his expression and his nodule was a physical sign for him to recognise and release it. I then regressed him with the intent to visit the past life that was the 'source' of his expression problem.

He immediately went to a past life in which he was a little prince, 4-5 years old. His mother was running the kingdom and his father had passed away. His mother was very strict. While growing up the only friends he had were a brother and sister, who belonged to a poor family. When the queen found out how close he had got to some poor kids, she got them killed. He was about 16 then. He knew his mother got his friends murdered. Out of the boy and the girl, he had also started loving the girl. He was shocked, yet he didn't express his shock or grief to his mother. He grew up to be a mighty king. He fought many battles, took care of his people and was loved by all but in his personal life, he was a loner.

He never forgave his mother and neither did he confront her. He lived his life alone carrying the grief of his friends in his heart.

Later on, he identified his current wife as his mother in that past life. He also identified the woman he loved in that life as a common friend of ours. When I asked his spirit guide if there was more to be resolved, he redirected us to another past life. This time he saw himself as a tribal leader. He was again fighting a war and was a very brave, fierce warrior. When returned from a particular battle, he found out that his wife had been raped and killed by someone from his rival tribe.

The moment he discovered this, he sat on a pavement outside his house. He had people coming to him and grieving but he was in shock. In a few minutes, he just left his body and died in that life.

He again identified his wife from that life as the same woman who was our common friend in this life.

I asked his guide about the significance of each of the lives. I was told that the first one was the 'source' of his expression and the second was the 'intensity'. We resolved both the past lives.

He requested me to heal him further for whatever I thought was important for him to get rid of. I called him for three SS sessions in a row. SS was faster and therapeutically deeper, I thought. As I connected with his energies, I realised that he had choked his expression for several earth lives. I then asked the creator to guide me as to what was the lesson his soul was trying to learn by way of not expressing itself. I was revealed that expression to his soul was linked to his expression of love in his being. I worked on his soul's understanding of the concept of love and the expression of it. The healings allowed his soul to realise that it was indeed created from love and that expression of love was the most natural thing to do. There was profound guidance being given for him to realise that by choking himself, he was only punishing himself for nothing.

Johnny called me in another week's time and told me that his reports showed the size of his nodule had reduced significantly.

I never questioned him on his emotions for our common friend. I was sure when he was ready, he would let me know. Over the same call, he himself told me he loved her since school but he could never express it to her. He somehow mustered the courage and expressed all he had felt for her in the last twenty years over a dinner the previous night. He was so happy that he could throw off the burden and he thanked me profusely.

Slowly, things took off and that experience changed the face of so many lives for good.

It was a very profound experience to see someone's resolution coming through me. A perfect example of how our stuck up emotions can impact our physical body, relationships and sometimes our entire being. I was so thankful to the universe.

That night, Deeksha called me crying because she and Maanav had recently had a huge fight. It seemed to me that he wanted to control her life and she wasn't ready to give in anymore.

'Calm down Deeksha. I will help you. I know how this situation will resolve. From my new understanding about how our emotions work, you need to let go of some beliefs in your system and I know just the person who can help you.'

I fixed up an appointment for Deeksha with Claire. I was not confident that I would be able to help my best friend in her intense situation so I decided that it was best that Claire helps us. Claire made me heal Deeksha using SS, in her presence. She reckoned I could help her and since I was nervous, she guided me all along.

Deeksha was already feeling better after the first session.

She called me the next day and said, 'You know what Maaya, it works! Yesterday was the first night that we didn't fight and he even listened to what I had to say about my need to work. It's no less than a miracle for me. I think it will help me resolve a few things with him. Thanks Maaya. What would I do without you?'

'That's great. I am so happy it has started working instantly. I will let Claire know and we do our next session in 15 days.' And I kept the phone down.

This episode helped me develop trust in myself to be able to heal people for their deep *karmic* patterns almost instantly and motivated me to adopt SS as a way of life. I could make things happen my way or could remove my fears to evade a negative situation. I used the power of my intent and unconditional love even in small things like finding my lost ring, getting a good parking space or ensuring I get free flowing traffic. Life started becoming so much smoother and divinely guided.

Winters were near and I loved winters. It was raining heavily those days and every time I saw rain, I felt like dancing. It was so refreshing to look outside the window and see droplets of water falling through. For me rains were blessings from above and they felt so. Tessy and I decided to go winter shopping.

All the stores were ending their sales and the new winter collection was on the stands. We decided to do a trip of Gurgaon where we'd spend the whole day shopping and eating the coming weekend. Aryan was on a day out at a friend's place and I had kept the weekend free for a refreshing break.

Tessy and I met up at Gurgaon and the first expedition was at Ambience mall. It was the beginning of a whole day of adventure. I wanted to buy a black skirt and Tessy wanted a few things including tights, shoes and earrings.

I was a sucker for good costume jewellery. I could do anything to get my hands on a good pair of earrings. I offered to help Tessy with her jewellery shopping.

We went to almost each and every shop. This was probably the first time that I had dedicated an entire day to shopping ever since I had come back from Singapore. It felt so nice. I was hardly fond of shopping those days. Usually, I only went exactly where I needed to get something, picked it up and came back. That day, it was different. I chose on a bit of adventure. Probably, I wanted a break from my usual serious self and just be. We tried clothes, shoes, scarves and everything else we could. We even ended up getting a make-over done for each of us. It was so much fun. It was already 2:00 p.m. Tessy announced that she was hungry. The moment she said so, I realised I was also hungry. We decided to go and eat salad at the Potpourri along with soup and breads. I always found it a healthy and interesting food option.

It was a Sunday afternoon and the restaurant was jam packed. There was a waiting of at least 25 minutes. I found it very hard to wait for food when I was hungry. Just as we asked the manager about the waiting time and decided to step out, I heard someone said, 'Maaya'. I turned around and it was Gagan. He seemed to be sitting there alone enjoying a drink and some salad.

Tessy gave me a twitch at the elbow and said, 'Who's the dude?' and I said in a very low voice, 'Shut up, Tessy. He's my boss,' and we both moved towards his table with smiles on our faces.

'Have seat ladies,' he said courteously. He shook hands with Tessy and I introduced the two.

'I am assuming since there is no other table free, you guys wouldn't mind joining me for lunch,' he said with a smile.

'Yes sure. We would love to Gagan. Are you eating alone?' Tessy asked him.

'Yes. I like spending time alone and treating myself once in a while. I don't really mind company though so the pleasure is mine,' he swiftly called for a waiter.

We had a great meal with some of the ala cart menu items that Gagan insisted were quite nice. By the time we were done, our bellies were bloated. Tessy and Gagan clicked instantly. It was interesting to see Gagan laugh and talk that much because somehow, I had only seen him either in a serious professional mood or serious personal mood.

Tessy invited Gagan to join us for the movie we were about to watch. It was based on what could happen in the New Age, post 2012. I was so excited about watching this movie. I was curious to know what others thought about the planetary shift.

Gagan was game for it and we decided to meet him at the movie-hall entrance in another three hours. Tessy and I had to finish our shopping and Gagan was to meet a friend. We decided to part and meet again after our respective missions were over for the day. The movie was at 7:00 p.m. so we had ample time to catch-up on our stuff.

I got two beautiful pairs of earrings and a pair of shoes for myself. My skirt was a hassle but thank God, I had managed to get back in shape after gaining 5-6 kilos in Singapore so I could fit into my regular size 10. We bought some makeup too. I saw these really sweet yoyos at one of the shops out of which I picked one for Aryan.

Finally, we were ready for the movie. We met Gagan at the hall entrance. He had his friend along, who it seemed was also going to watch the movie with us.

'This is Tarun. I hope you guys don't mind him watching the movie with us,' said Gagan.

'Of course not. You are most welcome Tarun,' I said.

'Tarun is my cousin. He lives in Chicago. Just came here on a business trip for a few weeks. He was the one I was meant to meet so I asked him if he would like to watch the movie with us,' said Gagan explaining Tarun's presence.

'Oh that is nice Gagan. We sure don't mind and he looks like a fine young man. Come on, let's make a move. I don't want to miss the trailers,' said Tessy and quickly stepped towards the door.

Tarun was a good looking guy with a tall and fit body and gracious looks. Seems funny but I didn't notice by then that I had actually checked him out.

Tessy sat in the corner, followed by Gagan, followed by Tarun and then me. Somehow this odd combination was because Gagan and Tessy were so busy talking that they didn't realise we were left behind. The movie was interesting and intriguing.

'Do you really believe in the arrival of the New Age?' I heard Tarun ask me in a low voice. His accent was strong and it was sort of tough to get him in that low pitch in the middle of the movie.

'Yes I do, though my understanding of what will happen is not what is shown in this movie. This movie is focused on end of this world. My understanding says it's going to be a new beginning in this very world.'

'That sounds interesting. I would like to know more about this, Maaya.'

'Sure. After the movie Tarun,' and we both shifted our focus back to the movie.

During the interval, Gagan stood up and said, 'Popcorn guy coming...any takers?'

'Yes Gagan. Popcorn for me please!' said Tessy and so did Tarun and I.

Tessy decided to go to the ladies room and Tarun and I were left there in the hall so we got talking.

'So, what do you do professionally, Tarun? Or maybe otherwise too?' I asked him.

'Depends,' he answered.

'Depends on?'

'Depends on what profession you want to know about. I do a few things.'

'Ok, then let's hear the list. Shall we?' I replied with a smile.

'Ok. I run a Real Estate business in Chicago, which is my family business. I sing, for my passion and I travel the world for my work and I love exploring new places,' he said.

'Interesting. Real Estate, singing and travelling. Quite a variety of interests you have.'

'Oh by the way, I left reading. I am a voracious reader,' he added.

'What do you do Maaya?'

'I work for a media agency as the creative head and that happens to be the same as Gagan's company. So your cousin is my boss. Also, I am a past life therapist,' I said with a smile.

I saw this eye brows raise. 'Past Life Therapist! Wow! Does that stuff really work?' he asked in the same breath.

'Yes Rahul, it does.'

'Tarun, not Rahul. Who's Rahul?'

'Nobody. Forget it.' I said and turned around towards Gagan who had just entered our row of seats with a tray full of popcorns and coke in his hands.

Gagan handed over the popcorns to us and took his seat.

'So, you two have had your introductions, haven't you?' he said, looking at Tarun and me.

'Yes we have bro. I just came to know that she is a past life therapist. I didn't know these things are real. I always thought it's a sham,' he said, looking at me.

'They are very much real. In fact, if you ask me, they bring out the reality in us,' I said to him, with a smile.

'I would want to talk to you about it, if you don't mind. And about Rahul too,' he said, looking into my eyes, almost whispering.

Suddenly, Tessy came in and wanted to enter the row, to her seat. I avoided his gaze and stood up for Tessy could easily pass through. We watched the rest of the movie in silence.

'Really nice movie. Wasn't it Maaya?' asked Tessy.

'Yeah. I loved it. The 3D effects were mind-blowing,' I said acting as if I was very involved in the movie.

Somehow, ever since I had mistakenly mentioned Rahul and Tarun caught it and mentioned him again, I had been feeling uncomfortable. There was a deep sense of loss.

All those moments came back to me. The moments when Rahul and I shared everything with each other, when I was his lifeline and he had no shame in admitting it, when our hearts and lives were in sync. Honestly, I avoided coming to malls, outings, movies, etc. because I realised I didn't enjoy them as much without him. The tiny bit that I enjoyed also went away when something in my head would say, 'How can you be happy without Rahul? Maaya, you are forgetting him. Your happiness is only Rahul.'

It was weird but I was guilty for my own happiness. I couldn't imagine myself enjoying a day without the thought of being away from Rahul troubling me. He was present every single moment at the back of mind. It seemed pathetic and yet, every single breath of mine was like it was waiting for him to feel it. In spite of all that I was doing to clear my *karma* with him, this one thought that he and I are meant to be didn't go. It was, in fact, stronger, almost like a knowing. It was like a constant pain I was carrying in my heart. I was coming to accept that maybe this pain was meant to be. Maybe I was meant to carry it no matter what. Maybe this was a part of the path I chose for myself in this life.

I was lost in these thoughts when Gagan proposed we all go for dinner together.

'No, I can't. I have to go and pick Aryan from his friend's place,' I said, looking at the watch.

'Come on Maaya. I will send my driver and he will pick Aryan and get him here. Is that ok?' said Tessy.

'Sounds good!' said Gagan, looking at me.

All of them were looking at me as if I was the one who was a spoilt sport.

'Ok Tessy. Let me call him up and ask if he wants to go to his grandmother's place,' I said dialling his friend's mom already.

Aryan was more than happy to go to my mom's place because he had his PS2 there which I didn't let him keep at our place to avoid him playing with it all the time. Tessy sent her driver to get him picked up and dropped at my mom's place. I felt a bit relieved after the arrangement. I knew Aryan enjoyed at my parents' house.

'Excellent. We are in business now. Any preferences for food?' Gagan said looking at all of us.

'Thai?' said Tarun.

'I love Thai, too. I don't mind,' I said.

'Ok, I am good with Thai. Where then?' said Tessy. We decided on a restaurant in Vasant Vihar and drove down to it in Gagan's car.

All the way, soft music was playing and we were all busy in our own thoughts and nobody was really talking. Gagan had a Mercedes and a very comfortable one at that so I was just enjoying the ride.

Gagan had already called up and got a table reserved for us. It was a very nice restaurant with a great ambience. We made ourselves comfortable and ordered drinks first.

Tessy and Gagan got talking about meditation practices because Gagan seemed to be really keen to know more about them. Seemed like Tessy didn't mind Gagan's company either. I was playing with my fork and just noticing the people around.

'The crowd here is nice. What do you think?' Tarun said, looking at me.

'Yeah I guess so. This part of Delhi is slightly hep. I like the crowd here too.'

'Tell me about Past Life Regression. What drew you into it? From media to past lives? Sounds like quite a journey,' he said.

'I often get that question from my clients too. Life has ways of pushing us into discovering/identifying our life purpose. I had situations in my life that pushed me to a journey inward. I am glad I did because I have found myself now,' I said to Tarun who was looking at me with a rather intense gaze.

'Was it Rahul?'

'Why do you want to know?'

'I don't know. I just want to know more about you and your journey. I feel some connection. How old is Aryan?' he said.

'Aryan is 8 and my journey has been intense. I thank the universe for I have experienced depths of emotions that many people can't touch in their lives. I have learnt so much more about life and myself in the process.'

'Are you still married, Maaya?' he asked me yet another question.

'Nope. It's been a while we divorced. He lives in Canada.' I said looking at him and then moving away my gaze casually.

'I have a feeling you did the right thing. I am proud of you to be able to take a stand and make a life for yourself in a conservative society like it is here,' he told me.

'It's not that conservative anymore Tarun. Things are changing. Plus I believe because of the new age arriving, the planetary vibrations are rising and people are naturally driven to resolve their *karmic* issues and move towards inner peace. This implies they are getting enough conviction to move out of relationships that are not working for them,' I said to him.

'So you believe that there is a new age arriving?' he said.

'Yes, I look at it as a positive transition. A new light. A new hope for this planet,' I said.

Gagan and Tessy were done with their chatting and the food arrived. Between the four of us, on our table, we discussed a variety of topics as we ate. Overall, it was a good dinner and good evening.

Finally, Tessy dropped me home and left for hers. It was a day well spent.

The new age and what life will be on this planet with the new planetary energies was an interesting topic. After watching the movie, it was on my mind.

I had been researching on it for a while now. I had written a small note for an article on the so-called 'planetary shift for the beginning of the new age' which never went for publishing but I guess I wanted to write it then. After so many days, I took it out to read once again.

There is so much of diversity in opinions about how will life be post the 2012 energetic shift. I had clients asking me, 'Do you know what will happen in the New Age? Will all be the same?' Well I am no authority on the subject but I would like to share all that I have understood from my journey of faith. This planet has been preparing for a new beginning since long. I have come to understand that the 'New Age' energetically began from December 2012 and spanning through a transition time of around two decades, it's going to bring about many positive shifts on this planet. This shift signifies the end of negative energies and moving forward into more neutral energies.

The way our body temperature impacts our physical body and adjustment is needed if it goes high or low, similarly, our energy body responds to the vibrations of the earth. Referring to Astrology, consider if planets like Saturn, Venus and Jupiter can have so much impact on our lives, what sort of impact will this planet, where we live, be having on our beings. The impact is huge. It's just that it's treated as a constant.

We have spent so many lifetimes here and in each lifetime, inevitably, we have created karmic links with the earth. We have given and taken energy from this planet. As this planet moves into higher dimensions, it is causing a sort of chase within our energies to match up to those vibrations in order to survive. The need to catch-up with the rising vibrations can already be felt in most of us in the form of a sense of 'hurry' or 'there's not enough time' thought forms or emotions.

People have used various methodologies to measure the vibrational rise. It is believed that earth's vibrations are like 'heartbeat' to the earth. With higher vibrations, the normal 24 hours in a day could finally leave up to only 16 hours in effective earth time. This phenomenon will need our physical bodies to attune themselves to the newer vibrations. As one can look around to see, there is a steady rise in negative energies too in these times, which is because they are surfacing to get released. They will slowly find ways to get transmuted into light through us. More and more people on the other hand are moving towards 'self-realisation'. Holistic practices, meditations and chanting are signs that humans are naturally attracted to resolving their own negative emotions, thoughts, beliefs and relationships in order to raise their vibrations. This is the only way. The faster one is able to reach the awareness of the earth's energies and is in sync, the more at peace they will find themselves in the new age.

We are moving to an era of 'love thyself'. Everything that expands or enhances one's experience of 'being love' will stay and everything that shows them their 'lack of love' will want to leave, hence giving birth to suffering. It could be through losing relationships, feeling abandoned and lonely or by realizing the futility of their chase in so many ways.

It's not that those who are not working on their soul evolution are not adapting to the rising vibrations of the new age. We live our karma through every breath. We move into higher dimensions with each act of light or each darkness we become aware of. It is happening naturally as well. Some souls have chosen to experience an expedited pace of learning through healing their past completely while others have not.

This era brings with itself a promise. A promise of higher human consciousness, enhanced ability to connect and experience the divine and greater understanding of their soul by all humans.

Each one evolving here will experience great amount of shifts in his consciousness and connectivity with the lifeforce energy. While we live on this planet, evolution is inevitable. It's only how we perceive it. In these times, we have the opportunity to consciously increase the speed of our evolution by staying guided, knowing what we want and allowing trust to be the natural way of being. The more we allow the universe to mould our journey, the more effortless living will become.

There is a lot of guidance being sent our way. There are so many light beings and other divine forces working to ensure a smooth transition of this planet into the new age. There are special souls coming here to witness this transformation and to make their contribution to it. Many souls have reincarnated on earth, especially to participate in this shift and make their contribution to saving this great planet.

Many who have been on this planet for a while but have not been able to contribute positively to the planet or so is what they believe, will leave the planet and go elsewhere to complete their karmic journey. Many divine souls are here just to experience this shift and go. They have subconsciously placed themselves at sensitive energy centres where they will become a part of the energy moving out of this planet. Many souls have planned to be a part of the new world so they will stay on and grow. Every realised soul will be able to help others around them to raise their vibrations and survive the change.

The New Age is about moving directly into the 5th Dimension. Being in the 3rd Dimension, which is what this planet has always been, means for each manifestation, we need to create a thought, an emotion based on it, then do some action that is capable of manifesting what we wish to and then it will happen.

In 5th Dimension, the manifestation process will be shortened where thoughts will directly have the power to manifest in the physical reality. Obviously, we will still manifest only that which serves us in our highest good. We are slowly stepping into a new world exhibiting the power of our thought.

The process is for the good and is enveloped in love and light. I look at it as an 'awakening' of some sort where the planetary energies are helping us rise above our personal consciousness and be a part of the universal consciousness in a positive way.

ALL in ALL...I would say 'STAY IN LOVE AND LIGHT' and rest all is well.

I don't know if all of that was right but I had done some channelling and research on the subject so I thought I'd share my view. It was an interesting domain and I could certainly feel the whole thing coming.

I got a little lost while reading it though. I was wondering if Rahul and I were meant to aid each other's growth in the best way. I didn't know and something told me I couldn't know just yet. I must just take life as it comes and in the now.

Tarun had given me his e-mail address for he wanted me to send him this note. I mailed it to him and slept. It had been a long day so I fell asleep almost instantly. The next day was heavy at work so didn't get enough time to relax at all. By 5:30 next evening, it seemed like I had been working for ages. I had no more work for that day so requested Gagan and left early. Dev was busy with work those days so we didn't get to talk too much with each other. He was working on another assignment so only working all day seemed like the best option anyway.

Next evening, Aryan and I decided to do some oriental cooking. I had bought Thai red curry paste a few days back and we decided to eat Thai for dinner. We went to the grocery store to buy veggies and some coconut milk, came home, put up a nice movie on the DVD player and cooked dinner. It was *Mummy* and that movie always managed to hook both of us on, no matter how many times we had seen it before.

Around 9:00, Aryan seemed tired so I put him to bed. I couldn't help myself from watching the movie till it ended.

My phone rang and it was Tarun. 'Hello,' I said.

'Hi Maaya. I hope I am not disturbing you? Is it late?'

'Nope. It's fine. I was just relaxing and watching a movie.'

'Cool! Which movie?'

'*Mummy*.'

'Oh wow. I love that movie. I have seen both parts a few times. Which one are you watching?' he excitedly asked.

'Part 1. I like that more,' I said.

'Well, I would agree. I like that one more too. So, how have you been? Hang over?'

'Nopes. Just feeling tired. Came early from office today. Thought I could do with some relaxation.'

'Thanks for the note Maaya. It was amazing. I wonder why you never got it published. I never took this New Age consciousness shift seriously but I guess I need to now. Who knows I might have chosen to go,' he said in a witty tone.

'Good. So what do you plan to do then?' I asked him.

'I plan to take you out for dinner on Friday. What say?' he said in one breath. I wasn't expecting it and didn't know how to react.

'Why do you want to take me out for dinner Tarun?'

'Just like that Maaya. I don't belong here and after work I have a lot of time to kill. I thought what better than learning something from you by spending a little time. Is my company so boring?'

'No, actually...I don't know...' and before I could finish, he said, 'Oh come on Maaya. I'll pick you up at 8:00,' he said and put the phone down. I was wondering then, why was it that this man had a say in what I do and I couldn't even object to it.

Anyway, Aryan was planning a weekend at a cousin's place so I had time on Friday and admittedly, Tarun didn't seem like bad company.

I was still contemplating if it was any harm in going for dinner with Tarun when my phone beeped. It was a SMS from Deeksha.

'Thanks darling. Maanav and I are getting along so much better. My doctors think I might finally be able to conceive now. My reports are getting better. Thanks for changing my life. You are the best. Love you.'

It brought a smile to my face. I was glad she was finding peace and love in her marriage. It was a relief.

□

Flowering Consciousness

On Friday, Tarun was waiting for me sharp at 8:00 p.m. outside my gate. He was in an Audi. I thought that was pretty neat. He waved when he saw me and I sat in the car.

'So, what's up Maaya?'

'Not too much, Tarun. I just relaxed a bit today. Our media presentation happened last evening so today was easy.'

I was noticing and appreciating his attire from the corner of my eye when he caught me and said, 'You look beautiful.'

I just smiled and said thanks and was wondering why would I do a silly thing like that. He was sure an attractive guy.

'Where are we going Tarun?' I asked him. 'What do you prefer? Thai?' he asked. 'Yeah, Thai is always good with me.'

'Then I know a very good Thai joint, I had been to on my last visit so took some instructions from Gagan about the route. It's in Promegrade Mall,' he said.

'Cool!' I said and started looking out of the window. Soon, as the silence was becoming disturbing, Tarun put on some music.

The restaurant was quite chic. They had these private sections where one could sit and talk without having to bother about what the others were doing. It was elegant and when I saw the menu, it seemed pretty expensive, too. Tarun was the very courteous kinds, as in, opening the door to pulling the chair for me.

'What will you prefer to drink, Maaya?' he asked as I made myself comfortable. I ordered a white wine and he ordered a beer.

'Tell me more about yourself. Why do I see this sadness in your eyes? It keeps drawing me to you,' he said.

'Sadness? How can sadness draw you to me Tarun?' I asked him a bit surprised at his observation.

'I don't know. I feel I can help.'

'I am fine, Tarun. There is no sadness. It's just that I am tired. Have not been doing anything but work for a few weeks now. I think I need a vacation.'

'Look at me in the eye and talk, Maaya.'

I looked at him in the eye and said, 'What are you looking for, Tarun? Let's talk about you.'

'Well, I don't know. I have recently registered I may be looking for something. Never felt the kind of emptiness in myself the way I feel now,' he said unabashedly.

'Do you have a woman in your life?' I asked him looking in the eye.

'Never felt the need for one. I mean I have had relationships but couldn't give myself fully to anyone. I am kind of happy with myself. I find it difficult to make someone more important than myself. Yet, I feel that is how lovers should feel.'

'Well, if anyone feels they love someone more than themselves, they are lying. We love and give to others because at the least, we get happiness out of it. I don't say I don't believe in unconditional love but it's rare. Otherwise in most relationships, you can, at the most, place the needs of someone else as a priority but always remember you do that when you place the happiness you receive by loving them on top priority and that itself is also a part of self love,' I said to him with a smile.

'Right! I never thought about it that way. So, let's say I never felt the happiness of placing someone else on top priority in my life,' he responded with a wink.

The drinks came and so did the snacks. We toasted to the opportunity to sit and share.

'Tell me more about whatever you know about life in these new times,' he asked me.

'I believe we have blissful times ahead. The bliss is within and we are now getting aware of it. The focus will shift to our inner beings so it will be different for each one and yet we'll find convergence of thoughts/relationships/geographies.'

Tarun was listening to me intently and it also seemed like he was thinking something.

'What are you thinking, Tarun?' I asked him.

'Don't know. I wonder what my journey in this life is. I wonder what is the purpose of my life? Maaya, I have been questioning myself on these lines almost since I was in my teens but I grew up in a country where nobody would have understood. When I realised you were a past life therapist, something got triggered and all those questions I had stopped asking myself came rushing back. What is the purpose of my life? Why am I here?'

I could sense a depth hidden in his persona. I had never thought Tarun could carry that kind of depth in his thoughts. This side of him resonated with me and I suddenly found myself more comfortable in his presence.

'The way I look at it, Tarun, is that life is an experience. Purpose of life is also a belief that we have created for ourselves because somewhere there is a need to have a purpose. Life is about flowing and being. It's not about reaching somewhere but rather enjoying the journey itself. In any case, we are guided on the path that is in our highest good and which will lead us back to the source. Something may feel like one's purpose at one point and they may move on from it at another point when something else takes precedence. It's not that I don't believe that souls carry a purpose for each life but usually all journeys must end at rising above all of these limitations and at universal compassion. The individual purposes are more of our own ways to perceive what will take us closer to that ultimate goal we all wish to achieve. In fact, I would say, it's wiser to realise that the purpose of every life is to understand that we don't have a purpose. Our existence in this moment and the awareness of it is the highest our soul can achieve.'

'And where do past lives fit into all of this, Maaya?'

'I can explain as per what I have understood about past lives and their role in my current life. Every soul is a spark of the same light, the same lifeforce energy. The moment it gets separated from the source, it starts an almost magnetic journey back to it because that is where it finds its completion.

For this to happen, it must acknowledge and appreciate the knowledge that it is pure light – a spark of the creator. The soul is all knowing but what it needs is the wisdom of its own knowing through experiencing all there is.

This is where the journey of evolution begins. It's intense. Our energies reincarnate on many different planes and forms to be able to understand and deal with emotions, life forms, a body, a mind and many other aspects we may not be aware of.

The physical plane, or for us, the 'Earth' is the most difficult of the planes. This is the plane where we experience duality. There is a mind and soul, there is a body and emotions, there is light and dark, there is white and black, there is negative and positive, there is good and bad. Everything has another side to it. We come back here again and again, to experience the balance of our physical existence and our energetic existence.

The idea is to experience and appreciate all that there is and slowly learn to realise this is all an illusion. It is Maaya.

The idea is to relate to the Buddha within. The day our energies can relate with the absolute within, the relative ceases to matter and that is when we merge back with the source – we become the light. We live, henceforth, being the light.'

Tarun kept looking at me, with an intense gaze, for a few seconds before he sipped his beer and said, 'That was so beautiful Maaya. You not only understand it but explain it in a simple way. It answers a lot of my queries. I would like to ask you another thing. I have read that we as souls choose our lives and journeys whenever we reincarnate. Why would a soul choose to become a beggar or maybe a handicapped person?' he asked me.

'Ok, in response to that, let me ask you a question. Imagine you are a theatre actor and there is a big play being planned. You are been given these two choices of characters. Both are lead roles but in one the guy just needs to keep sitting on a chair throughout the play while the other one is a challenging role. It needs you to fight, love and talk too. Which one would you choose?'

'The second one I guess,' he said, realising he had the answer to his own question.

'Exactly! For souls, an earth life is like a role they will be performing in a play. All they are concerned about is evolving faster, about growth. It's like you as an actor would choose the challenging role to learn more and get recognition, similarly, the soul will choose a difficult life for it wants to grow and evolve sooner. It can see the bigger picture. It's only when we come to the planet with amnesia that we realise how difficult it can get.

I once healed a mentally challenged child on the request of his parents. They wanted to know why he had manifested such suffering in his life. I must admit when this case came to me, I was also curious to know what the perspective of his soul about itself was and why it chose this sort of a life of intense misery.

To my astonishment, when I connected with the creator, I was revealed that it was a much evolved soul who had chosen that life because his family members, especially his parents had contracted to learn the lesson of unconditional love and sacrifice through him. It was a choice to help them evolve by bringing that life situation to them. I also found out that he was willing to go through this experience for his family members because they were souls who had helped him in a big way in some other lifetime and he believed he owed them this experience which would bring a big leap to their soul consciousness.

This healing really made me understand the amazing way life works. You can never be sure that one who is rich and successful is an evolved soul. In such cases, the souls' choice is inevitable but by healing it, their experience can get lighter and they slowly develop inner strength to accept and deal with the choices they made about their physical body. I advised the parents to attend the three-day Serenity Surrender workshop with Claire for her to be able to guide them to unburden themselves of their guilt for their child and live a life of acceptance that he is also growing through his choice, whether or not it is physically evident to them. It helped them look at life from a new perspective.

On the contrary, I have realised that bigger the lessons, the more difficult the evolutionary journey. Sometimes, easy lifetimes may only be for a soul that is new to this planet and is yet in the initial lifetimes of adjustment here. As we come here, one lifetime after another, we create so much *karma* and hence the journey gets more and more difficult and challenging. The thing to remember is to stay focused on the learning from the hardships than on the struggle itself. Usually, there is a good reason why a soul will choose certain struggles in its life on earth. Unfortunately, we never come here to enjoy this planet, but to evolve. It takes a lot of wisdom to enjoy evolution and experience the magic in every breath we take.'

'You have such passion in your eyes when you talk about souls and past lives, Maaya. I can see you not only understand this whole thing but also truly believe in every word you say. I am glad I bumped into you. That gives me a lot of insights,' Tarun said raising his beer glass to finish all of it in one sip.

'So, what is your story, Tarun?'

'My story! I don't know if it's a story but I have been a simple guy all the way. Fell in love once while I was in grad school. She was a Swiss woman and both of us were much in love. It was like a dream but one fine day, she just left. I don't know what happened. I also don't know where she went. I just know she left the country and moved back to her home town. She left a letter for me saying she had the most amazing time with me but our role in each other's life was over.

She wanted to focus on her career and she saw no future between the two of us. I was shattered. I didn't understand why that happened. I did question it for a good few years and ever since, never felt the same with anyone. Somewhere inside, I think I am afraid of another relationship and failure of keeping it Maaya. I do wonder sometimes that maybe I don't need a relationship because I am really happy by myself. Other times, it does feel like I am running away from something,' he said looking at me.

'I can understand how that feels. I think neither are you running away nor are you self-sufficient. It's just that you are not ready yet. The life situation with this woman triggered fear of deserving love and acceptance. Life is such; it puts us in the most challenging situations, for us to realise the power of the most basic emotions like love. One day, you will meet someone whose mere presence will dissolve that fear to the extent that you will be willing to look at life from a fresh perspective. In the meantime, whenever you want, I can help you release those emotions from your energies,' I told him.

'Do you believe in soulmates, Maaya?' he asked me.

'Yes, I do believe in souls and soulmates are mates on the soul level. Simple! What exactly makes you question their existence?' I asked.

'No, I have been wondering if I will also have a soulmate.' he said.

'Ok, here is the way I would answer that question. The word 'soulmate' is usually very overrated. You will already have many soulmates around you in the form of your parents, siblings, close friends, etc. Souls also have soul families like we have earth families and all those souls who have spent a few lifetimes with us and are helping us evolve by playing different roles in our lives are our soulmates.

Out of these soulmates though, there are a few that we have very strong romantic links with and we come across them again and again to experience intense and romantic relationships. I guess that is whom you refer to as a soulmate.'

He nodded his head to express his agreement to what I had just said.

'You will most certainly have at least one soulmate of the kind waiting for you. When the time is right and you are ready to meet her, she will appear. You will recognise her. There is no failing in recognition of our soulmate. It's instant and natural. Just release the thought to the universe that, 'I am ready and now I want to meet my partner/soulmate for this life, and it shall happen.'

'I guess you are right. I wonder the entire universe is so logical and yet we can begin to understand it only when we just trust without asking for logic,' he said.

We both laughed for that was so true. The universe starts to reveal its secrets only to those who can connect with it through love and not question its beauty. It's about unconditional acceptance and that is where the magic begins.

'What about you Maaya? Have you found the other part of your soul yet?' he asked me while I was still amused at his last statement.

It suddenly reminded me of Rahul and I didn't realise but the expression on my face changed. I was not sure if I had found him or lost him after finding him. I felt a little sad.

'What happened? Hey, I am sorry if I am poking into your personal life. I didn't mean to do that. I was just a little curious.'

'I don't know what to say, Tarun. I found him and yet I lost him. I am not sure if we will be together again in this life. I have been guided to surrender my togetherness with him to the divine. Lately, I have started feeling that I am getting tired of chasing him. I guess I will just leave it at that, else I will start getting depressed.'

'Maaya, I may not be as wise as you but here is what I have to say. There is a fine line between "giving up" and "surrender". If you say you are getting tired of it, it means you were still expecting something and that in turn means you still didn't surrender. Surrender means trusting the unknown and dropping expectations. Surrender is a divine feeling and since you give the power to the divine to work for you, it elevates you.

Giving up is when you fail to match your expectations and then you escape what you want by believing it is not in the divine plan.

Surrender is coming from inner strength and giving up comes from inner weakness. I think you have more to work on surrender since you are not weak, Maaya. Truly surrender and see the magic happen,' Tarun said as he slipped back into the sofa with his beer in his hands.

That moment, something hit me hard. He was right. Although I thought I had surrendered, I was still hoping, still expecting, still anxious about how, where, when, etc. This meant I was still latching on to it. He was damn right. I failed to surrender. It was so funny that I could be so wise when it came to other people's lives but when it was about my own, it was difficult to step back and observe. We talked about so much stuff that day and it didn't feel like I was really talking to this guy for the second time. It felt like I had known him before.

Sometimes, life threw up such surprises that it made me wonder about the small mercies of the creator. It was an evening well spent and it gave me a lot of food for thought.

I could suddenly see my relationship with Rahul in a whole new light. There was probably no more that I could do to make him realise our connection but I could at least stop trying so hard.

By the time Tarun dropped me home, it was past midnight and I fell flat on the bed the moment I entered the house. I slept till late the next morning. It felt as if a big burden had lifted off my shoulders.

The next morning when I woke up, I was alone at home since Aryan was still at mom's place. While I was sitting by the balcony sipping my coffee, I was still thinking about the realisation that had dawned on me the previous night. After a while, I decided to sit in front of the small temple I had created in my house where all the deities' energies seemed to be present. Being in that place gave me a feeling of being closer to the divine and the higher energies. Tears started rolling down my cheeks as I realised that now I had to let go of the last thread with Rahul which was my hope that we would be together again.

Slowly, I recalled each memory I had with him starting, from the last to the first. Every time I observed one sequence of memories with him, I told myself, 'I now surrender this moment to the divine and place myself in pure unconditional love.' It was a hard task to do; as if I was just letting go of parts of myself, but they did relieve me as they went. By the time I finished, I felt free. I felt free from my own expectations of bringing him back, of getting that same love back and so much more.

I slept again, for a few hours, after lunch. Maybe it was the wine still affecting me or an impact of the release, but I just stayed in the bed for as long as I needed to be. I saw my Blackberry blinking from the corner of my eye and picked it up to check for calls and e-mails. One message drew my attention and I sat up straight in my bed in amazement.

It was Rahul. He had written 'Hey! Hope you are fine. I just felt this very strong need to check-up on you. Is everything ok sweety?'

I couldn't believe my eyes. I didn't know what was expected of me then. I didn't know if I was being tested. I felt alive again seeing Rahul's message but then I was also concerned of losing my surrender and getting miserable again. I didn't know what to respond to him so I just said 'I am ok Rahul. Was upset last night but I am better now. Thanks for checking up on me.'

I spent the evening all by myself for I needed sometime to just be. I went on Facebook and connected with some friends, read a book and watched a bit of TV.

At about 8:30, Tarun called, 'Hey, what's up?' he said as I picked the phone.

'Not too much. Have been sleeping all day.'

'Ok. That sounds like a lazy day. Hope you feel relaxed now.'

'Yes I do, Tarun. What about you. What have you been up to?'

'Well, I have been sorting out some pending work. Caught up with an old friend and now was thinking of dinner so wanted to check-up on you…have you had your dinner already?'

'Nopes, I haven't but I guess you have yours. I am not so hungry.'

'I can get some sandwiches packed and we can have them together. Is Aryan home? I can get a pizza for him too. I am getting bored…want to talk or do something.'

I thought about it and then told myself, what the heck! I ain't getting any peace by running away from the world too.

'Aryan isn't home. You get the sandwiches and I guess we'll go for a walk. There is this nice place near my house where we can walk. I haven't done my yoga today and will sort of feel guilty eating without exercising. Is that good with you?' I said to him.

'Perfect. I'll be there in thirty minutes. See you,' he hung-up the phone.

He gave me a call when he was out and I locked the house and joined him in his car. We drove to this Japanese park near my place. It was a beautiful park and very well maintained with proper lighting, fountains, etc. Many times Aryan and I would go there just to walk and Aryan could take a few rides on the swings there. It was one nice thing about our neighbourhood.

'Tell me about Rahul,' he said out of the blue.

'Why do you want to know about him?' I shot back.

'I want to know more about you, Maaya. I see mystery in you. I just feel like knowing more about where you get your depth from.'

'That was a nice way of putting it, Tarun. I am sorry but I wouldn't like to talk too much about Rahul right now. I just love him and right now, we are at a crossroad in life where I am not sure whether he will be with me in all the ways that I would like him to be. Only time will tell. I just know that the universe is guiding me and if it's in my ultimate good, it will happen.'

'I am sorry if I hurt you Maaya. That wasn't the intention. I just find myself wanting to know more and more about you. That's all. You can share it whenever you are comfortable,' he said when he noticed the apparent discomfort in me after our conversation about Rahul.

'Why do I find myself getting so attracted to you? It's like my heart only beats true when it's with you?' he said looking at me.

I couldn't help laughing while he said it on a serious note.

'Are you up for some poetry, Tarun?'

'Not really, Maaya. Don't get me wrong but we barely know each other. Yet there is something in you that pulls me to get to know you more, to understand you, to be there for you. I haven't felt this way in a very long time.

I am not saying all of this to make you uncomfortable but I have been wondering, there could be a connection that we also have from our past lives, couldn't there?' he looked at me with childish excitement in his eyes.

'I am sure we must have some past connection but let's just let it be. You are just missing love in your life sweetheart. It's not so much about me. It's just that you have not been paying much attention to yourself and your needs of having a partner. Maybe somewhere just because we can talk and laugh, I sort of become a prospective candidate for filling up the space.

Otherwise, we hardly have anything in common. Don't you think?' I asked him looking right in the eye.

Now suddenly, his eyes seemed deeper and attractive. It was already late and there were hardly any people in the park. Something caught my attention as I looked at him. Love...attraction...some crazy voice in my head asked me, 'What's wrong with him? How long do you plan to wait for Rahul anyway? He may never come...forget him, Maaya. Tarun is good looking, affectionate, he likes you and to top it all, you can see it in his eyes.'

He was gazing at me such that I couldn't take my eyes off him. Alongside, all these crazy thoughts were going on in my head. I was confused and couldn't decide whether or not I should have stopped that silly thing in my brain and taken my eyes off that look on his face. Surprisingly, I was doing neither.

He then took both my hands in his hands. It was weird, but I felt ripples through my entire body. I was just blankly noticing him and not reacting to anything. I was lost. The voice in my head also went silent, all of a sudden. He held my hands for a few seconds while maintaining his gaze at me. Then he bent slightly and coming closer to my face and whispered, 'I don't think so Maaya...it's not a coincidence that we met...there is so much that you also don't know...your angels sent me here and now, you shall never be alone.'

He then gave a very soft kiss on the side of my cheek, as if trying to break the spell and then he let go of my hands. I stood there dumbstruck. I couldn't believe what had just happened. I loved Rahul and there was no space in my life for anyone else. I couldn't allow Tarun to get so close to me.

I pulled back my hair in nervousness and embarrassment, both, and started walking ahead, straight up to the car. He dropped me home. Both of us didn't exchange a single word on the way. I was thankful for that. I needed time to reflect on whatever had just happened. I guess he understood.

'Good night, Maaya. Sleep well,' he said as I quickly rushed out of his car without even looking at him.

Unlocking the door of my house was a mechanical thing I have no recollection of. I just remember grabbing a bottle of water, putting out the lights and going to bed. Sleep of course was not invited in my bed that night. I felt so guilty. I felt guilty for Rahul. I felt as if I had betrayed him. What would I say to Rahul when he came? How would he feel if he knew about Tarun? How come I had let Tarun get so close to me? Had I really started feeling for Tarun? Was he right that the angels had sent him, after all? Was it a coincidence that he came after I decided to surrender my fate with Rahul? Was I being tested again? Was it true that Rahul and I were not meant to be? Hundreds of questions were doing their rounds in my head and I didn't know the answer to any of them.

I couldn't sleep all night. My thoughts went back to the scene where Tarun held my hands. I did realise there was something that clicked. There was a connection. I couldn't deny that there was some recognition and this bothered me. I needed answers and now I wanted to know why this man had entered my life at this point. I didn't want this and yet here I was. I decided to call-up Claire the next morning and seek her help.

Next day, I took an appointment with Claire and was at her place at sharp 4:00 in the evening. Her living room was simple and elegant. All the walls and the flooring were wooden. With two elaborate bookshelves and the fragrance of camphor, it felt like an old British library-cum-meditation room. It was one of the cosiest places I knew of.

The energy of her living room was very high. I was admiring the Buddha statue in the corner when she came in.

'How have you been, darling? What is bothering you so much that you urgently needed to see me?' she smilingly said holding my hands.

In Claire's presence I felt comforted, as if all would be ok, she would handle it and also show me the way. Over time, she had become a guide to me and whenever I found myself in a situation where I was confused, she was able to add perspective to it.

We hugged each other and she sat beside me.

'Claire, I met this man and somehow, I feel we have a connection. He likes me and I like him too but I still love Rahul. I am confused as to why this guy has come into my life,' I told her almost on the verge of tears.

'Did Rahul connect back, Maaya?'

The last time I took help from her was when I had this brief encounter with Rahul where he said he couldn't take our relationship forward. She had helped me get some guidance for my journey with him and she had got that it would happen when his transformation was complete. She told me to just stay focussed on my manifestation for my togetherness with him and all would fall into place slowly. She advised me to keep cleansing *karma* with him and the more I did that, the stronger my belief became that it would happen one day.

'Yes he did. He sent me an SMS the day before that he felt as if I was sad and hence, was checking on me. It was sort of weird because I was sad and it was surprising that he was concerned about me.'

I also filled in Claire on all that was happening in my life. We hadn't been able to talk for a few days then.

'Interesting! It's ok. Don't worry. Let me connect and ask the role of this new guy is. What is his name again?'

'Tarun. His name is Tarun.'

Claire excused herself and moved to her healing room. She always did that when she wanted to channel something.

While sitting there, somewhere this thought started coming back to me, as if I was being selfish by wanting Rahul, for I would become the reason for his marriage breaking. No matter how much I convinced myself of the fact that his marriage wasn't that great, anyway, it still affected me to know that I could potentially be breaking a home.

I decided to connect myself and ask the creator for how could I resolve this guilt. I don't know if it was the effect of her living room or my need, but almost instantly, I was shown a visual in which there was this form, which felt like it was me. It was appearing as a transparent form in which I started seeing some colours developing. Some shades of pink, it seemed.

The colours were light and only concentrated at one place in the form. I felt my entire body to be very light, as if I had become the form. I felt my heart beating hard.

Slowly, there was a piercing pain in my heart. That was exactly where the pink colour was in the visual - very sharp - and so many thoughts started rushing in. My thoughts said, 'Cut it away, it's not a part of me, it betrayed me, I will do without it.' The thoughts seemed to have become voices and they were growing in my head. The pink colour was turning grey and the pain grew. I then felt this rush of anger in me. The pink portion which was partially grey was moving away from me, as if it was going out of my form. The pain was intense and there was a very deep sense of loss as that part moved further away and detached from my form. I was numb for a while and in blankness. Slowly, the pain subsided and I found myself coming out of the experience. I was all sweaty. It was so surreal and yet I didn't understand any of it.

Just then, Claire came in. I shared my experience with her. I didn't quite have the right words to express what I had just gone through, but I knew if anyone could tell me what it meant, it was her.

She heard me out and then she held my hand. 'I had seen this long ago Maaya but I didn't share it with you because I was not sure if you were ready. Now since it has been given to you, I guess it's time for me to tell you a few things. What you have just experienced is the memory of your soul splitting,' she said.

'My soul splitting? I don't understand.'

'Yes. Rahul is the other half of your soul. Also note that there may be nothing romantic or fascinating about this. Hear me out carefully, Maaya. This information is only meant to help you release yourself and him from this trap.'

'On the journey of evolution, there comes a time when two souls who carry the same seed, spilt from each other to experience two different bodies. There is a higher purpose for why this split happens. Each of these souls is known as "twin-soul", "twin-flame", "other half" of the other. This experience leaves an incompletion in both these souls and they crave for each other lifetime after lifetime. They do meet each other in several earth lives but whenever they come closer, they tend to become the source of the most difficult *karmic* lessons for each other. They, in their understanding, can only become the reason for transformation in each other's journey. Their love for each other is deep since they can recognise each other from when they were one. At the same time, they are also deeply aware that holding on to each other only allows them to distract themselves from their journey of realising self. Hence, meeting and separating seems to be the phenomenon they have manifested for several lifetimes in which they experience the depth of their connection and when it's lost or they separate, they can shut themselves to the external world and get submerged in self and at some point realise self. It's not that the destiny of these twin souls is only to stay incomplete or only crave for each other, but that is what they believe till they realise self and realise that they never were incomplete. Once they start facing and healing their *karmic* past with each other, they tend to transform themselves into feeling complete within, with or without the other.

Once they rise above their need to suffer through each other and evolve through separation, they can possibly attract lifetimes in which they re-unite and live happily. Whatever the fate of the twins might be, going through a journey of transformation within is sure to happen.

In this era, as we have stepped into the new age energies, more and more twin souls are meeting each other. It may not mean a happy reunion for them. As they touch each other deep, their own internal deep conflicts surface to help them grow wiser. On a higher level, this is how they help each other and as they imbibe the learning through each experience, the universe takes them into the direction of their ultimate good and they can effortlessly flow,' she explained.

'Why was there so much pain Claire?' I asked her, still trying to completely understand what she had just revealed to me.

'Pain is because it's a part of your own soul going away. That pain plays an important role, Maaya. Whenever he will separate from you on this plane, that familiar pain will arise in both of you. That is how the original emotions of the split get surfaced in the sub-conscious for you to resolve. That is the memory to the seed, until transmuted to love,' Claire said.

'You feel this strong connection with him even while you guys are not in touch because, energetically, you carry the same seed. That connection cannot be severed. The important thing to remember here is that he came to give you an experience of transformation. You may not reunite with him on this plane, yet. You must allow the universe to decide in your highest good. You need to heal every aspect of you that feels incomplete without him and as you keep doing this; you will find your own completion within yourself. That is the key. Surrender the need to be with him physically. For now, just focus on filling that void you feel without him and allow yourself to move into a higher plane of consciousness.'

Tears rolled down my eyes as I heard her say this. The whole experience was so vivid, so fresh in my memory. I could even see it with my eyes open.

'Does that mean we cannot meet, Claire?'

'No dear. I can't say.

Maaya, re-uniting with your twin will happen when you have completed all your *karma* which you created with them or otherwise as an individual soul. You both have *karma* left that needs to be resolved. His fears of the society and his responsibility for his wife and child are also a part of his *karmic* journey. He can't escape that and be with you, for this way he will only bring incompletion between the two of you too. He will need to resolve it within himself. He will be able to give you true happiness only when he has realised himself enough and where anything else doesn't matter to him. Allow it to happen that way. Don't chase him, Maaya. You are in this because you have also got yourself stuck in your need to be with him. Open yourself, Maaya. Open yourself to the power of creating love within. Heal your need to only get love from him and instead, realise it in yourself. That way, you will truly free him and your future from your fears. What shall be created then, will be the most blissful.

We all can trust what we know, Maaya, but the real test is when you have to trust the unknown!'

I almost felt a burden lifting off my chest.

'What did you get when you connected with the creator, Claire?'

'I was told two things. First, that Rahul is going through transformation. He is being guided but he will have his own realisations about the truth of your connection with him. He is scared that he might not be able to take your relationship to its logical conclusion and is guilty for his wife and child. He will see a lot of inward movement in the coming few weeks and he will find his answers and then find you. You need to let all of it happen. It's his own way and you must not interfere. His free will plays a role too,' she said.

'Do you really believe that is the case?'

She rubbed my hands with her fingers while holding them and said, 'I don't doubt the guidance I get, dear.'

'What is the other message you got?'

'The second message was that when you heal yourself, you don't have to keep the intent of re-uniting with Rahul. You must keep the intent of moving towards your highest best. In your relationship with him, it's a choice of both souls to grow together. If he chooses to block his journey due to whatever reasons, you will not stop. In that case, you'll move on to find a more worthy partner who will not only love you more than him but also stand-up for you. In this state, even if Rahul is with you, he will not be able to give you anything more than misery because he's miserable himself. You must allow things to happen the way they will bring happiness to you. Tarun could be that person or maybe someone else. Be open to your happiness and heal your guilt for it!' she said.

We both talked for a bit. She was a very graceful woman with this presence which was not only calming, but reassuring too. When I walked out of her house that day, I didn't realise it then but it was with a new understanding about my own evolution.

Tarun went back to Chicago the very next day. He just sent me a message saying, 'I am flying back tonight, take care.' I have to admit it pinched a bit but now with my new found awareness about my truth with him, I was very sure I was ready to release whatever there was between me and him.

The next three weeks, I just went to work, came back, helped Aryan with his home work and played with him. Every night after putting him to sleep, I spent about an hour on self-healing. I just connected and asked what was it that I needed to work on that day and I kept releasing whatever I was told.

I had started enjoying the process. As I started removing energetic blocks in my work life, my relationships, my evolution, I noticed a lot of positive changes in my life. Even my relationship with my parents had started changing. My anger significantly reduced, I slept better, I felt an inner peace with regards to all aspects of my life, I felt more compassionate towards people, I could let go of negative thoughts as soon as they came and all of this was happening at an amazing speed.

This is when I realised how much clutter our sub-conscious minds carry and how we can actually transform so many things in our lives by getting rid of what's not serving us anymore.

It was Friday, 24th November when my phone beeped almost at 11:00 p.m. I was asleep but just because it was so late, I thought of checking my phone. It was Rahul. He asked me if I'd heard the song "Tujhe Bhula Diya..." which is a Hindi song that meant 'I have forgotten you...'

Listening to that line, I instantly got anxious. 'No Rahul. I haven't heard the song but have you really forgotten me?' I sent him a reply.

'Maaya…please…just listen to that song. It's exactly what I feel for you,' He wrote.

'I will listen to it but just answer my question. Have you been able to forget me?' and the anxiety level in me was rising. I couldn't take yes for an answer and that line of the song was haunting me.

'Naah…baby. I can't. Never!' I read and my breath started getting normal.

'I want to meet you Rahul.'

'Me too. Tomorrow evening, will pick you from office at 5:00. Please listen to the song first...I want you to understand what I want to say.' He insisted.

'I will. See you tomorrow.' I wrote back and kept the phone back on the table. I can't express what I felt at that moment. There were intense mixed emotions. I couldn't stop myself from opening my laptop and downloading the song. I listened to the whole song about five times in a row and every time I would hear it, tears began rolling down my eyes.

The song basically conveyed that forgetting me was unacceptable to his heart and no matter how hard he tried, he felt my presence in his breaths. It was hard to believe he actually shared that song as his expression to me. I went to sleep feeling peaceful that night.

The next day went in looking at the watch and waiting for 5 p.m. My excitement was evident and Dev had already asked me twice about the secret to me being so happy that day.

'I am meeting Rahul today.'

'Not again, Maaya. I thought it was over,' he said while he stood up from his seat and came towards me.

'You know it cannot get over. Don't you Dev?'

'Yes I know darling. I just want you to be happy. Come give me a hug. He will get it,' he said pulling me to a tight hug. I could feel the warmth of his affection for me.

The clock finally struck 5:00 and my phone beeped where it said he was waiting downstairs, in his car. I quickly picked up my sling and took the lift down. I saw him waiting in the car as I crossed the road. He was probably talking on the phone as I opened the door of his car and entered. He put the phone down and looked at me. It had been very long and at first I felt awkward.

He said, 'Hey,' and I said, 'Hey. How are you doing?' feeling the silliness of my question. 'I am good,' he said as he drove the car towards Café Coffee Day.

There was complete silence in the car. There was this distance and yet this craving in our energies. I wanted to say so much but more than that, I wanted to hear so much but none of us broke the silence. We soon reached the parking lot of the mall.

As he parked the car and put off the ignition, he looked at me properly for the first time that day. As I was about to unlock my door to step out, he held my hand and then used his other hand to hold my head from the back and pulled me towards him to give me a tight, passionate kiss. I had been waiting to be held by Rahul for ages now and it was so sudden that I didn't get any time to think.

My eyes closed and my lips parted. He sucked both my lips in hunger as I was running my hand through his hair and ears. He wouldn't leave my lips for what seemed like minutes. Our longing for each other was evident. Neither of us attempted to break away for a long time. He broke away once, hugged me tight and then started kissing me again starting from my neck, all the way back to my lips.

'I missed you,' I said as we finally broke away from the kiss.

'I missed you too sweety,' he said to me still holding my hand and looking into my eyes.

I wasn't sure all of this was happening. It was like a dream. I wanted to pinch myself and check and yet, I didn't want him to let go of my hands. It was him, the same old Rahul I fell in love with.

Finally, he left my hands and headed out of car and gestured for me to open the door and come out. It was the Café Coffee Day, right opposite Taj Palace hotel. It was set out in these green lush surroundings and was the best place to sit and chat without the disturbances of traffic and a lot of people.

'Did you hear the song?' he asked me as soon as we sat. 'Yes I did…a few times. Every time I heard it, I cried,' I said looking down.

He put his hand above my right hand which was placed on the table and said, 'I didn't want you to cry. I just wanted you to know how much you mean to me. It took me two years to understand and acknowledge that there is some connection between you and me that I can't get over with. I tried my best to forget you, Maaya, but every few days, I would remember you for something and then hold that thought for the entire day. I kept missing those beautiful moments we spent together. I admit I have been an escapist and I am not as brave as you, I admit I couldn't stand-up to commit to you because I was scared, I don't know if I can do it even now but I have realised that running away from you isn't helping anything,' he said as if lifting some burden off his chest.

'Did you miss me? Did you have another relationship?' he asked me.

'Naah. I didn't miss you because you never went away from my thoughts for any moment. Yes, I missed being with you but I was told you will realise the strength of our connection and I trusted my guidance,' I said, looking up to him.

'Who told you?'

'I know you don't believe in energy related talks and the work that I do. At the same time I know you understand there is divine intervention between us. I have this friend Claire, she and my another friend Tessy, both of them are very powerful healers and they have been helping me get guidance on my life and us.'

'Interesting! You know there is something I never shared with you, but I would like to now. When you first realised that I was changing, I was going through this guilt phase where my parents and Neha, both wanted me to give our marriage another chance. They held me responsible for Anushkha, for her future. I was still trying to resolve it internally when they suddenly decided to drop-in.

It was a very bad time for me because here I could see you crying, whom I loved so much, crying and there, I didn't know how to handle my guilt. The fact that my folks expected me to give the marriage another chance also didn't help. I didn't have a good enough reason to say no. While all of this was still happening, Neha and I had a spat one day and she popped a few pills down her throat, right in front of me.

I got really scared, Maaya. I couldn't have become responsible for anything happening to her. That was when I decided that I would let go of you thinking maybe we would meet in another life. I don't think I have been able to love her though, I don't think she loves me either. She just wants to stick with me for some reason best known to her. All this while, I have just been living in this fear and guilt that she might do something to herself if she ever finds out about us.

I know I gave you a lot of suffering. I know I hurt you and I am sorry for all of that. It took me a while to say all of this to you Maaya and now, I don't know what to say. I don't know what the future is for us. I don't know if I can ever get out of this marriage. I don't know if I can give you what you deserve,' he said looking evidently sad.

For a moment, I didn't know why he came back to me if he was so unsure. Just then something nudged me and said, 'He needs to be guided. He needs help. He needs your strength. Don't ask him for anything now. Just be there for him and he will find his way.'

'Rahul, I don't know if it's my prerogative to say anything here but just that, you need to stay in a relationship for the right reasons. If you can't see a solution right now, maybe you are trying to do too much in your own strength. Maybe we can just leave it to someone up there. Make the intent to the universe that this is what I want, kindly help me manifest it, with the least hurt to all involved. Trust me, it works. It will happen. I am with you in everything you decide. Just walk the path of faith. You will see how all will be resolved in divine order.'

'Ask yourself this one question. Can you see yourself growing old with her?'

'No, I don't. I don't see myself going anywhere with her,' he shot back.

It was now my turn to put my hand above his, rubbing lightly. He looked up at me and my eyes reassured him that all would be well.

That day, it seemed to me as if I had finally been given what I had prayed for but that was only the first step. It didn't take Rahul too long to fall back into his guilt trap. The only difference this time was that he didn't run away from me but he tried to internalise it and that was also not helping.

Our relationship had transformed. We had grown out of being silly, crazy lovers to mature adults. He replied to my messages whenever I sent any. He hardly ever initiated a conversation over a call, a message or even a meeting. I could evidently see his discomfort in getting intimate with me. His pain was evident in his eyes and yet he will try and be nice to me. Every time I expressed that I love him, if he was in a less guilty mood, he would reply otherwise he told me he needed time and space to sort himself out.

This was yet another test for me. Till now, I was handling my own mood swings and I could happily ignore his side assuming he will arrive when he has to. Now, I had to worry for him too and he wasn't so open in telling me whatever was going on with him.

One evening when we met, he said, 'I am very low these days.'

'Why sweety? What happened?' I said, rubbing my hand in his hair in a loving affectionate manner.

He was sitting on the car seat next to me, in my car, with his eyes closed as if he was utterly exhausted.

'Nothing. I just feel people use me emotionally and when they are fine, they desert me and go. For some reason, I feel used and abandoned.'

'Who did that to you?'

'No one in particular. Just that it's happened so many times in life,' and he quoted a few examples of his old friends whom I knew and how they chose to walk out on him.

He was feeling lonely. Most of his friends had also moved on in the recent period. He had no one to share his issues with.

This was a phenomenon which I had observed in myself as well as a few of my friends. Whenever our energies shift and we transform internally, we go through this phase of 'friendlessness' where the old people whom we used to be friends with, stop resonating with us and move on and the new ones are yet to arrive.

This phase is actually the time when we are forced to spend time with ourselves and focus inwards, hence speeding up the transformation. Everything said and done, it was a shitty place to be in and I could understand whatever he was going through.

'So, how's Tarun doing? When's he back?'

'Next week. He must be fine. Why did you bring Tarun into the conversation?' I was a bit surprised.

'Just like that.'

'Ok, we are having a small party with food and drinks next Friday and you are coming along with me,' I told him. 'No baby. I don't feel like partying at all. Some other time maybe,' he said.

'No. You have to meet all my friends. Please do it once for me. You will feel better and the change will help you,' I insisted and he agreed.

I met Claire over Rahul's state of mind and about my stand in the whole thing. She suggested I leave him to sort it out on his own until he sought help which was when we could help him. She helped me release my *karma* with Tarun since he was due to arrive. I couldn't really avoid him, but I wanted to be sure we had nothing left to deal with between the two of us, at least from my side. I worked on transmuting the energy from the past between me and Tarun intensely and I could feel I was getting detached from him day by day. It was all working.

Friday came and I dropped Aryan to my mom's place and moved up to meet Rahul at my gate. He was already there before I got ready and reached.

'You are looking hot!' he said and surprisingly looked like he was in a slightly better mood.

We reached the party. It was at a glitzy farm house of a common friend of ours. There was a huge mansion right in the middle of lush green lawns and right outside it, on the left hand side was what looked like the venue of the party. There was a small hut-like structure which looked like a Goan beach bars with cane furniture, dim lightings and small trees around. It looked like the perfect place one would like to spend an evening.

As we got closer, I could see Gagan, Tessy and Claire and a few others already there. There were old sultry numbers playing and I could see a small dance floor right in the middle. It all looked so perfect, especially with Rahul next to me.

I looked at Rahul and he looked pretty relaxed. He knew pretty much no one there though he had heard about all of them from me. As we entered, Claire rose up to hug me and gave me a kiss on the cheek. As she looked at Rahul she said, 'Well, let me guess. This is Rahul,' as if she hadn't known that already and we shared a laugh. She welcomed Rahul and soon Gagan and Tessy who were lost in their conversations as usual, noticed us and came to greet us. I introduced all of them to Rahul and we took our seats.

'So dude! What can I get you to drink?' Gagan asked Rahul. 'A beer please,' he said smiling back at Gagan and thanking him with a hand gesture.

Soon after, Gagan got me a white wine and then I saw Dev coming up with his new partner. 'Hmmmm,' he said clearing his throat when he saw Rahul with me.

'Hey Rahul. What's up man?' he said to Rahul, shaking his hands.

'I am good Dev. Hope you are good too,' he said winking back at Dev.

He teasingly looked at me from the corner of his eyes seeking approval for his tall and fair partner. Dev and I hadn't been updating each other too much lately because we were working on different projects so I was sure he was a little surprised seeing Rahul with me. I made a mental note to fill him in with the details the next day at work.

Rahul was busy chatting with Claire, Tessy and Gagan and was hardly paying attention to me. I couldn't complain because I was glad to see he was getting along with my friends. Suddenly, as I was lost in my thoughts and admiring the elaborate disco lights in the place, a hand came and landed on my shoulders. I looked back and it was Tarun.

I said, 'Hey,' and Rahul looked at me while Tarun's hand was still on my shoulder.

'I didn't know you were already in town,' I said to him.

'Yeah, came in this morning. How are you doing Maaya?'

I then turned around to Rahul and said, 'Tarun, this is Rahul and Rahul, this is Tarun.'

Both of them gave a good glance to each other and suddenly, Rahul got up from his chair and offered his seat to Tarun while he walked up to sit next to Claire. Everyone got busy and back to their conversations. Tarun was telling me all about his flight and the fiasco he had when his passport couldn't be found, etc.

I couldn't help noticing that Rahul was ignoring me. Occasionally, whenever I would look at him, he was busy talking to Claire and laughing his wits out. It was affecting me but I tried to behave as normally as I could.

'Ok guys. Let's shake ourselves a bit. Shall we?' said a husky voice which seemed to be the DJ.

'You might want to dance with Rahul,' Tarun said to me and as I looked at him, he was already heading to the floor with Claire.

Tarun noticed my apparent disappointment and he gave me his hand. At this point, something inside me popped. I had chased this man enough and the chase wasn't getting me anywhere. He doesn't stop playing games, does he? I just decided that I was going to enjoy myself and not get affected by whatever he was trying to do. I took Tarun's hand and we started dancing.

I have always been a good dancer and that day I discovered that Tarun was also not so bad. Both of us made a great pair and suddenly a salsa number was played. We took on to the beat and danced the whole sequence. I didn't realise that everyone including Rahul stepped aside from the floor to watch us dance as Tarun swayed me in the air and made me bend.

Rahul and I used to dance like that and I am sure he hated seeing me and Tarun dance together. I didn't know realise when he just left the party and went.

I wouldn't say it didn't bother me but I guess I was not up for the swing again. He left me a note at the party.

All it said was, '*Maaya, I will always love you but maybe I am not brave enough. I don't deserve you. I realise I am struggling with my own fears of facing myself and my reality. I need more time to sort myself out. I need more courage to face myself. I haven't done enough of it yet. I have nothing to offer you. This time, let sort myself out first, before showing you my face again. I am sorry for walking away like this...don't mean to hurt you and yet I know I have. Forgive me...forgive me for everything, Maaya!'*

It seemed like the chase had ended. I didn't, feel like crying anymore, I had gone numb.

The next few days, neither of us contacted each other and I lived in a vacuum. It was a weird feeling. These were the first two weeks in the last two years that I was not thinking of Rahul, I was not thinking of when he would come to me or whether he would come at all. I was just being in this space within myself and all seemed to be at peace. I don't know if I had lost the ability to feel emotions or I had shut myself inwardly but somehow, I felt I just needed to be.

I mechanically went around my work every day. Tarun and I met over dinner the following week. 'I am sorry Maaya. I don't know if I became a reason for your suffering,' he said.

'No Tarun. This isn't about you. You only became a reason for something to happen that had to happen anyway.'

He sensed the sadness in me. We had a quiet dinner. Near the end, Tarun said, 'I would like to be there for you, Maaya. In case you want someone to share your life with, I would like to be the one.'

'Thanks, Tarun. I am sorry for bringing you till this point. I am not sure I can make you understand but I am not capable of a relationship anymore. I fear I may never be able to let Rahul out of my energies. He is so much a part of me that I don't know where to start pushing him out.

At this point, I have lost the ability to feel love again. Maybe I will someday, but I don't want you to wait for me.'

He put his hand on mine. 'I can understand, Maaya. Take your time. If he is a part of you, accept yourself as whole. When that acceptance comes, your need to be with him will not hold any ground. If I love you, I shall accept you as you are. Maybe what attracts me to you is that depth in you. Your ability to give is amazing. I would still be there for you. Whenever you need me, I'll be just a thought away. This shall also pass, Maaya.'

His reassuring eyes said he understood.

Aryan was off with Kunal for his winter break and I was free to do some soul searching. I had this very strong urge to go and spend some time with myself in an ashram I had been to earlier in Rishikesh. I took an off for four days the following week and made my way to Rishikesh. Deeksha offered to come along but I told her that I needed some space and time with myself.

It was a blissful feeling to sit at the edge of a mountain, by sunset and just observe the sun setting, with no thoughts going around in my head. My head seemed to be pretty empty and I was enjoying every moment of being in that beautiful place all by myself. I couldn't help but remember this one card from a healing card deck that showed a sun. Whenever I saw that card in readings, it told me it meant 'manifestation' but today, when I saw it in my vision, it told me it was for new beginnings and a fresh start.

Maybe Rahul came to my life to bring me to this stage where I understood myself so much better. I had the strength to be able to deal with anything. I can't explain what I felt in those moments I spent alone. It was a sense of completion. As if I had been chasing completion where all this while, it was right within me. I seemed to carry no anger, no frustration, no regrets...nothing for Rahul. I blessed him for his own journey and prayed for him to be guided to whatever was in his ultimate good.

That is when I realised the meaning of complete surrender. So long as something is a concern for us, there is more to work towards surrender. Now, Rahul was not my need. I was not incomplete. I was able to leave him at a point of compassion. I didn't need him to leave everything and come to me. I didn't want to possess him. I just wanted to love him. I could love him with every breath. Love is meant to be effortless and so is surrender. They come from within.

It was the last evening before I was to leave for Delhi. After watching the sunset, I walked to the *ghat* for the Ganga *Aarti*. I loved the *aarti* on the *ghat*. The energies of the place were awesome. I sat just two stairs above the water was. During the *aarti*, I closed my eyes and focused inwards. Once the *aarti* was over, mostly everyone left. The *ghat* was empty. I decided to stay. Just sitting by the holy waters was the most amazing experience. I didn't want to leave. Something guided me to stay and enjoy the bliss even further.

Suddenly, as I sat there on the stairs, in *sadhana,* I felt enveloped by some divine energy. It felt as if I was encircled with two beams of light from behind. As the beams of light embraced me, I felt my entire being melting away and merging with the molecules of the universe. I heard someone whisper, 'You have a long way to go, Maaya. As you re-unite with your twin soul, you initiate the journey to re-alising it's not only him but the entire universe which is a part of you. You are a spark of the divine. It's time to walk the path to reunification with the source. We are with you.'

I then saw a heart-shaped light emerge in the sky. It was the most brilliant white light I had ever seen. The heart grew bigger and bigger in the night sky. Slowly, as it grew bigger, it started to dissolve in the sky. In just a few moments, it completely merged in the sky, closing into a pink ray of light that came straight into my heart. I felt a slight jerk in my body. Suddenly, there were moments of complete peace and bliss within. I felt whole and complete. I felt one with the universe.

As I slowly opened my eyes, I realised I had tears. I was in complete sync with the universe. Everything around me seemed to be connecting with me. The world suddenly seemed illuminated.

In that moment, I realised the inherent power of the entire existence, within me.

When I accomplished my journey within
I found I was always pure, always love
Nothing but serene to the core
As I rose above all that there is
The universe kneeled to me and said
Take my child, take what you please!

□□□